PREFACE	
1. THE BEGINNING	
2. THE JOURNEY.	33
3. A BRAVE NEW WORLD.	59
4. OBSERVATION.	72
5. RIDICULE.	94
6. TAKING STOCK.	99
7. OBTAINING THE PAST.	108
8. RECOVERY.	120
9. THE CATALOGUE.	131
10. REVELATION.	147
11. THE TRUTH WILL OUT.	161
12. CELEBRATION.	179
13. COMPLETION.	189
14. AND ON THE SEVENTH DAY.	198
15. REVULSION.	203

16. GHOSTS	**223**
17. THE FINAL DAYS.	**232**
18. DISASTER.	**252**
19. THE ROUNDUP.	**265**
20. FOND FAREWELLS.	**270**
21. THE POWER OF THE PRESS.	**283**
22. THE FINAL GOODBYE.	**292**

PREFACE

This book is not an attempt to discredit the established thinking, nor the world religions that have been in place for many thousands of years. Nor is it an attempt to persuade the reader to change their way of thinking, their lifestyles, or their present religious beliefs. It is not even a basis or the creation of a new type of worship. What the author intends to portray is his own personal view, a view that has been formulated over many years of reading, listening and evaluating all of the various information he has come into contact with, information that has allowed him to formulate his own opinions.

As a child I had the opportunity to spend an inordinate amount of time with my grandmother, she was what could be called a god-fearing woman, she would quote the bible to me on many occasions, and it must be said that I did become quite familiar with the stories. As I grew older and became more able to formulate my own interpretations to the stories, my perception of the past, and of evolution began to mould itself into the way in which I presently see things. A great influence on my thinking came from watching and developing a great interest in science fiction, from the appalling 'Plan 9 from outer space' to the highly technical productions of 'Star trek'. All of them held a fascination for me.

A vivid imagination is the building block for all good stories, but this book attempts to go beyond mere fiction. It aims to explore my own theories into evolution, religion, the past and the future. It is a possible account that may, or may not offer some answers to those people who feel, as do I, that the way in which we have been taught is not the only possible explanation.

1. The Beginning

Leaning back in his chair, David grasped the back of his neck. He could almost feel the tension. He gave a sigh of relief, leaned forward and switched off his computer. He spun round in his chair, rose to his feet and walked into the dining room where his wife Mary, and their two friends were already beginning the meal. Tonight was a very special occasion for David and Mary, it was their first wedding anniversary and they had asked Alan and Amanda over to celebrate the occasion with them."
I'm sorry that the baby sitter has let us down" said Amanda. Mary politely emptied her mouth and waved dismissively "don't be silly, we have plenty of room and besides, we love to have them here". Lucy and Gary were ten year old twins who had been constant visitors to David and Mary's since their birth. The frequent break from the children had been good for Alan and Amanda's relationship, and the twins had no qualms about being here. It was like their second home, they even had their own rooms. Mary got up from the table and proceeded to clear away the plates that had just been used for the starter,
"Hey you guys haven't finished"
The twins looked down into their laps dejectedly "It doesn't matter" said David and then whispered to the twins "I never used to like melon either"
At this they perked up, shuffled in their seats and readied themselves for the main course. David

smiled at them, and Alan shook his head, knowing that any further words on the matter would be lost, so he resigned himself to a submissive, good natured giggle. Mary reappeared at the doorway pushing a hostess trolley. She positioned it at the head of the table and proceeded to place several bowls of food onto the table. When she had retaken her seat she humorously announced "dinner is served". At this point everyone began to help themselves. As Mary was just about to take her first bite of dinner, the phone rang. "Isn't it typical, it always rings when you don't want it to"? She got up and placing her napkin neatly next to her plate, she went into the living room.

David was sitting with his back to the living room door, and although he, Alan, Amanda and the twins were engaged in general conversation, he was more intent on eavesdropping into the one sided conversation that was now taking place in the other room. Although he could not quite make out what was being said, he had worked out the gist of things.

It was about fifteen minutes later before Mary could return to the dining area, by which time the meal was almost over, and everyone was ready for coffee. Mary decided she would warm her dinner later in the microwave, and that now she would join the others in the living room.

As the party walked into the comfortable, spacious living room, Mary turned to the twins and suggested that they went into the outer living room to watch television. The children were pleased, as they were becoming increasingly bored with the adult company. Mary was also pleased as this would give her the opportunity to explain the phone call she had just taken. She sat in the large easy chair next to the fireplace and taking a sip of her coffee she turned to Amanda. "I'm so sorry Amanda, we can't take the kids to the mountains next week. They are going to be so disappointed". At this David stood up from the stereo, looked towards his wife and said "that was the commander on the phone wasn't it" Mary nodded. Everyone knew what this meant. Mary had been selected, once again, to be the navigator for the next shuttle flight.

David and Mary had met when David's company had won the contract to build the new reception area at the base where Mary was completing her shuttle training. He had always thought that one day she would give up space flight and concentrate on becoming a mother and wife of an architect. After all, they were comfortably off, and it would be no hardship for them to live on the substantial income that David enjoyed.

Mary confirmed that it was indeed the commander she had spoken to "they have found another planet and it will soon be in range. The exciting part about this one is that they think it may be able to support life. I have to leave tomorrow".

David crossed the room and sat on the arm of his wife's chair. He put his arm around her shoulder and sat silent for a moment. He hated it when she had to go way, not least for the fact that he held an intense dislike for her job. He did not trust space. He considered that orbiting the planet was one thing, but for his wife to travel to different planets was definitely another. He had always dreaded the thought of losing her, although he had never said so.

There was an awkward silence. Alan and Amanda were aware of David's feelings and could see from the look on his face that this was not the time to voice an opinion. Everyone looked at Mary, each with a different, yet similar look of puzzlement.

"I have handed in my notice" explained Mary "It becomes effective immediately after this mission".

To himself David was pleased, and at the same time relieved. He knew how much Mary's job meant to her, and so, not to give anything away he put on his concerned look, turned to face Mary and began to argue against the decision. "Sweetheart. Why? You love that job and you're damn good at it. You haven't been fired have you?" Mary let him continue until a smile broke over her face. She could contain herself no longer. David was confused. "I've thought long and hard about this, and I am sure that I am doing the right thing" she paused for a while so that she could achieve maximum effect from what she was about to tell everyone. "After all I don't think that it would be fair of me to be hopping from planet to planet and try to be...the mother of our child."

The awkward atmosphere that had filled the room minutes earlier was instantly replaced by a stunned, shocked silence. David leaped to his feet and somehow seemed to take Mary with him. Dancing in circles he was half crying half laughing, trying desperately to speak. "How? When?!" "Calm down, calm down" said Mary. After a few more minutes of jubilation they both sat down in their original places. This time David was closer to his wife and squeezing her shoulder much more tightly. "I've been for all of the tests, they were positive and you are going to be a father.

"Well" said David proudly, "I think that this is the time to open that special bottle of champagne that we have been saving for just such an occasion". By the time David had crossed to the drinks cabinet the children had entered the room to see what all of the commotion was about. Amanda proceeded to tell the youngsters the good news, which sparked another wave of excited dancing and cheering. David had poured drinks for everyone and was attempting to weave his way through dancing children to deliver one glass to each of his friends, and to his wife. "I think that on this occasion even you two can have a drop" He gave a small glass to each of the children and they all raised their glasses. David stood in the middle of the room facing everyone. He composed himself, and quietly said, "To life, to the future, to good friends and to my darling wife...Thank you". "Here here" said everyone in unison and began to drink. Lucy didn't like the champagne as was evident from the grimace that spread across her face. Gary however gulped down his drink and asked Lucy whether she was going to drink hers. When she said that she wasn't, he proceeded to dispatch her glass in much the same manner. Everyone laughed then the children returned to watch the rest of their program.

The rest of the evening was taken up with initial

planning for the forthcoming event and with the drinking of more celebratory champagne.

Many names for the new baby were discussed, and finally it was sort of agreed that if it were to be a girl it would be named Susan and if it was a boy, Jeremy. David secretly hoped it would be a Jeremy.

Before anyone had noticed the time, a second bottle of champagne had been consumed, and the children had all but been forgotten. "Oh well" Alan sighed, "we have an early start and a long journey tomorrow so I think, that it must be bedtime for us". Everyone agreed, and the usual all hands to the deck ensued to make tidy the living room. Turning out the lights they moved into the outer living room where the children had fallen asleep in front of the television. The video was still playing a program called 'The Art Of Magic' that the children had been watching earlier. David quipped to Alan that he was rapidly tiring of this particular tape as it was all that was played when Lucy and Gary were visiting. The two men then picked up a child each and put them to bed. As they quietly closed the door to the children's rooms Alan looked at David and said "your turn soon old man", David smiled, bade Alan good night and disappeared into his own room.

By the time that Alan, Amanda and the twins had come downstairs the next morning, Mary and David had finished their breakfast and had prepared the same meal for the others. They all sat and chatted until it was time for the Andersons to depart.

The party of friends slowly walked to the cruiser. As they walked, they made plans to spend time on the coast with Alan and Amanda as soon as Mary's mission was over.

At the cruiser handshakes, kisses and hugs were exchanged. Tears were wiped away as the Andersons got into their car and pulled silently out of the drive. As they drove away Amanda pressed herself against the window to wave a last farewell to David and Mary, an uneasy feeling came over her. Somehow, this time things felt different. For some reason she felt that this would be the last time that she would be saying goodbye to her friends. To her it almost felt like it was the end. She shrugged away a cold shiver, dismissed her thoughts and settled down to the journey.

Back in the house, the atmosphere was one of peace and quiet. David and Mary stood for a while and hugged each other. After a short time, their eyes met, they nodded and together they said "it's that time". They burst into giggles, kissed briefly, and began to busy themselves preparing for their respective day ahead. They had done everything possible to delay the inevitable. But now the time had come. Locking the front door, David followed Mary to the two cruisers that were parked at the top of the driveway. They stood between the two cars and embraced passionately. After a few minutes they leant back in each others arms "See you in three weeks" said David. "I'll be back before you know it". Mary replied. There was an obvious tear just about to run down her face. David raised a hand and caught the tear on his index finger, and then he drank the tear from his finger and placed his hand over Mary's mouth.

"You had better hurry home, and bring little Jeremy...", "Susan" interrupted Mary, "whoever, home with you". They kissed some more and then they finally agreed to part.

"I love you" said Mary. "I love you too" David swallowed hard as they each got into their own vehicles. After a final wave, and a blown kiss they left for work.

For David the journey to work on this particular morning had been a tedious one. It did however afford him time to reflect on the fact that once again he was losing his wife for three whole weeks. After seven missions, he thought to himself, this one was going to be the last. A horn sounded behind him. He had been daydreaming and for an instant he had forgotten that he was in the car. He shook himself back to reality and caught up with the car in front. He leaned across to switch on the radio, and as he did so he noticed a small note stuck to the dashboard above which simply read 'I LOVE YOU'. He smiled, settled back in his seat and listened to the radio. As he pulled into his parking space he spied his friend, Bob Majors. It was hard to miss Bob's car, even in the dark, as it was painted in a strange luminous green. Bob had always joked that when he had been out for the night, he was nearly always the worse for wear and that it was useful to be able to find the car. This was not the case; Bob was one of the most grounded people that David knew.

David waited for Bob and they walked into the building together. "Morning David, how's Mary?" "Pregnant" Bob was just about to say "oh, good", until he had realised what David had just said. "Well I'll be... that's brilliant news. This calls for a celebration, how about tonight at the 1066?" David sighed "I'm afraid that isn't possible. Mary has had to go to work". As he spoke he gestured with his hand in the fashion of a craft taking off.

"Oh well definitely when she gets back then". The two friends agreed as they walked across the foyer.

Everything that day had started slowly for David and the journey to the fifteenth floor was no different. During the lift ride he never spoke. Bob turned to him and enquired if everything was OK?. David assured him that it was. He shrugged off the question as the lift reached his floor. He said goodbye to his friend and promised to meet him in the bar during their lunch break. David had not wanted to burden anyone with his thoughts but he was obviously preoccupied with his wife. He had always felt these emotions every time that she had taken on another mission. He knew that his fears were irrational, as there had not been a space accident for countless generations. This fact, however, did little to calm his worries. He knew that the next three weeks would be an eternity.

As Mary approached the base, she could already see the nose cone of the shuttle rising from its underground hangar. She could imagine all of the ground crews feverishly working to ready everything for the take off later that day. The radio had been on during her journey, but she had not paid much attention to it until she heard a song which had stirred something inside of her. She turned up the volume as the song was ending "That was for a special lady, Mary. David loves you very much and can't wait to be together with you again, and he wishes you a safe journey. Stay tuned because next we have the news, and indeed the news that you have all been waiting for".

Mary already knew what the great important news was, however, hearing it on the radio made it somewhat official. "Today, the government announced that there will indeed be a three hundred and sixty hour public holiday as sunlight returns to our planet. The holiday will officially commence in twenty hours time from. . . Now! Volunteers are now being accepted at your local town hall and the rate of pay this time is a staggering four hundred credits per hour. So, if you are not going to be one of our volunteers, I suggest that you dig out your sunglasses. More news on the hour, now back to the studio".

Even as she listened, Mary could feel an intense rush of adrenaline surge through her body. She mused over the fact that she would be one of only a handful of people in her lifetime, which would have the opportunity to stand on an alien planet and maybe breathe without the aid of cumbersome apparatus.

She swiped her card through the reader and she could see through the glass doors all of the frenzied activity within. As she entered, she could hear snippets of various conversations that were being held. They were a mixture of excitement for the public holiday, excitement by a few people over the extra credits that their families would earn by becoming power volunteers, and not least, that the orbit of their planet would once again take them within reach of a planet, not visited for over twenty generations.

When she walked across the lobby she was greeted by a pleasant receptionist, "Good morning Mary, everyone else is already in the briefing room. Good luck, I wish I was coming with you".

Mary smiled and passed through a door marked B1. Immediately upon entry she was confronted by two security officers who demanded her handbag, her security pass, and all items of metal that she had about her person. She was only too happy to comply with their wishes but she did however feel reluctant to remove her wedding band. Having completed this first stage of entry she was directed towards a scanner beam, which not only checked for anything missed by the security guards, but also was designed to give her a preliminary medical check. She always passed through this machine with a little trepidation; a red light at this stage would almost certainly preclude her from the mission. As she passed through an almost inaudible beep was heard and a green light was displayed on the end column. Mary breathed a small sigh of relief and continued through the next door at the end of the corridor. As the door closed behind her she was met by two people dressed all in white. "Morning Mary, big day today" said a man's voice. She hated this room "I'm sorry Mary but you know the drill" he said. Mary then, somewhat embarrassingly began to take off her clothes. As she stood on the travelator she could not help but think to herself how totally degrading this part of the security procedure was. The way in which she coped with the embarrassment was to sing the song that had been playing on the radio earlier to herself. After passing through another doorway, she had reached the final room, she was pleased to leave the embarrassment zone as she called it, and passed into the final stage. There was no one in this last room. It was, except for a small pile of clothing, completely empty. She immediately recognised the clothing as being part of her uniform. While she was dressing she could feel the warmth of the uniform, it felt comfortable against her skin. Impatiently, she sat on the small white seat that was protruding from the wall. It would be approximately five minutes now, and there would be no further contact with the outside world, except for verbal communication, until the mission was over .She thought to herself as the room went into its final cycle. No sooner had she made this thought when a hum was heard, the lights dimmed to an iridescent purple. The lighting and the humming seemed to pulse in unison as the room sterilised every part of her body. It had a soothing effect on her, almost hypnotic. She gave no thought to the fact that she was pregnant, or for the safety of her embryonic baby growing inside of her. The medical department had already assured her that this process held no danger for her, or her baby.

Suddenly the room reverted to its former state, everything changed with such urgency that it made Mary flinch as she came back to reality. There was a series of clicks, and the door automatically opened to reveal the briefing room. As she entered, six faces turned to greet her, she returned their greeting and sat down at the one remaining desk. All the people assembled here were to be the crew of Mission 1472 Alpha.

The seven colleagues sat in silence as they each filled out documents which sworn them to secrecy about their mission, a secrecy which by law would last two years after the conclusion of the mission. This was a standard document signed by all participants. When they had all finished they were collected together and placed in the hyperbaric chamber which was located in the glass wall in front of them. Mary sat quietly studying the others, in an attempt to get a feel for the people who she would be spending the next three weeks of her life with. At the front of the room, with his back towards her, was the captain of the mission, Jason Daniels. She had worked alongside him twice before. He was a hard task master but at the same time fair, always open to new suggestions and willing to spend time to sort out any problems that the crew may have. She had, in the past, had time to converse with the captain on a semi social level and had discovered a little of his history. He had twice received the medal of honour for bravery; in fact he was one of the most highly decorated private contract pilots in the service. He was also quite unique amongst this crew in so much as he had managed to combine his military life with a highly successful sports career. Being one of the worlds leading practitioners of 'Hung Quan' he enjoyed the status of superstar. Hung Quan was one of the most popularly watched sports on the television networks. It involves a mixture of ancient martial arts combined with modem day hand held weaponry. Unfortunately Daniels status in this field did not preclude him from his military commitments. The law was very specific about their ongoing conscription policies and it had never seemed to bother him. Mary quite suspected that this part of his life bought some modicum of relief from his other roll totally within the public eye.

If Jason Daniels had worked his way through the ranks to his present position, the man sitting next to him was quite the opposite. Marius hatch was a small squat man who carried a little too much weight, his hair was beginning to thin about his crown and his complexion bore the tell tale scars of a juvenile skin complaint. This however did not distract from his brilliance within his field. He was a well studied man, a man who had attained every possible academic award in the fields of quantum mechanics and quantum physics. He was also very learned in all of the fields that would be necessary on this mission. He had passed through the academy in half the time it took for any normal cadet to do so. Subsequently he had entered service at a highly elevated position, and at twenty seven years of age he was already the youngest commander in the service. Even though he was obviously the right man for the job, Mary had always found difficulty getting along with this man. She reasoned that it was because he was on a higher intellectual level than the rest. He himself found it difficult finding common ground with other people on which to converse. In a certain sort of way she felt sorry for Marius, she considered that his intellect had made him a lonely man.

She found herself musing over the other three men in the team. She had neither worked with, nor even met any of them before now. Firstly she considered Matthew Watkins. By his appearance, she judged him to be about her own age. His physique, nor his features gave anything away about him. He seemed pretty average in appearance, however she did know one thing about him, about all of her colleagues, that was the fact that if any of them were not expert in their field or totally dependable they would not be here now. Each of them held impeccable credentials, and all were veterans of at least five previous flights. John De Vie cleared his throat. This diverted Mary's attention away from the meteorologist to the geologist. John De Vie, or as his name tag implied J.D., was in her estimation, the odd one of the bunch. He had almost casually draped himself over the chair, one leg was completely obscuring one of the arms of the chair, and his arm was rested on the back supporting his upper body. His deep golden hair was neatly tied back into a pony tail and his face had not been shaved. This gave him, she thought, an interesting air. He would probably be the most fascinating member of the crew she would get to know. She hoped that he would be a refreshing change from the average type of astronaut she was used to working with.

Sometimes the mere sight of a person, or the way in which they present themselves, their looks, or even just their general demeanour, causes some people to take an instant dislike to others. Travis Wheatley was one of these people. Since Mary had first entered the room she had been evaluating the others, generally she could find no reason to dislike any of them, but, there was something about Travis that she had taken an instant dislike to. He was probably a very nice person. Maybe he was a little misunderstood but somehow Mary didn't think so. He had, what she considered to be, a shifty face. He had very thin lips and piercing brown eyes which picked up every reflection of every light in the room. His eyebrows were pencil thin, almost plucked and shaped. His hair was short well groomed and of a colour that she had never seen before, it was the richest, brightest shade of red she had ever seen.

This would be the first mission she had been on where there had been another woman in the crew. About this, she had mixed feelings. Normally she had been used to being the one whom the male members of the crew would pussy foot around, she was not sure how she would react to the fact that she now had to share her spotlight. On the other hand however, it may be that she could use her as a confidant, someone who would at least understand that sometimes it is comforting talk to another woman.

Anne Homer was the medic, she was single and possessed the looks of a model, the type you see in every glamour magazine. This in itself did not make Mary feel threatened in any way, Mary was a happily married, pregnant woman who was not unattractive in her own right. Anne rose to her feet and asked Mary if she would like a refill for her now empty glass. Mary said she would, and watched as Anne walked across the room to the water dispenser. When she returned Mary commented on the elegance of Anne's wardrobe. They laughed, and a friendly conversation was struck up. The room was filled with the sound of quiet conversation as the crew chatted amongst themselves.

The far wall of the room, located directly in front of the crew, was made entirely out of glass. It created a corridor with the extreme back wall. In this corridor were placed three desks and three chairs. On the desks were note pads, pencils, and glasses of water. Set into each desk there was a computer terminal and a screen which was linked directly to screens that were placed in front of each crew member, and to two screens that were suspended behind the glass wall, facing out into the room. All of these screens were accessed by the control corridor.

The light in the corridor flickered to life and the door to the left opened. In through the door walked three men, who proceeded to take their places behind the desk. Each of them placed a folder onto the desks and began to log on to the computer system. Whilst this was happening all of the crew, including the laid back J.D. sat upright in their seats and prepared themselves for the mission briefing.

The person who was to conduct this meeting was Over Commander Lyle Harrison. He had been in

Alpha 1472

overall command of the Alpha section for many years and was used to briefing crews on mission objectives. This one was different for him, for the crew, for everyone.

Alpha division was set to specifically deal with first contact situations, which to date had never occurred, and for the exploration of new found planets and asteroids, which from time to time came into the range of their planet. Lyle Harrison was the consummate leader. He took an obsessive interest in any, and all of the missions findings and discoveries. This time he was more excited than he had ever been, he was about to give the briefing of a lifetime. Outwardly he remained calm, relaxed and authoritative. He wanted desperately to be part of the crew but his age had prevented him from being included. This did not however dull his commitment to the project. He sipped his water, looked at the assembled crew, put on his glasses and began to address the awaiting astronauts.

"Good morning everyone, as you already know I am over Commander Lyle Harrison. To my left is Major Peter Hooton, and to my right is major general Tom Stewart. These two officers will, during this mission, be your first point contact. All matters regarding anything will first be discussed with your captain, and he in turn will relay any findings, problems, or requirements to mission control via these two men. "Now let's get down to business. You have probably heard the rumours which have been circulating that you are about to visit a planet which has never been visited before. Well I can now confirm that these rumours are in

Alpha 1472

fact not true. Interstellar cartography has confirmed that the planet that is now in range of our own, is one that was visited during the infancy of our space programme. It was the first time that we had ever lost anyone during an interplanetary mission. The three man crew of 106 Alpha did not return however the records show that they did manage to relay vital information about the planet. We believe, from their findings that the surface of the planet is able to sustain life as we know it. Long range sensors show that it supports an atmosphere and there are signs of extensive vegetation and desert regions. As yet we have picked up no radio transmissions, nor do we expect to, so we must assume that either there is no life as we would recognise it, or that if there is life, it is only at a stage of early development. Until you discover more about what you are up against, you will have to be on your guard. The planet is approaching us from the gamma quadrant and will only be in range for three hundred and sixty hours, so we must assimilate as much information as we can in as shorter space of time as is possible. This is a once in a lifetime opportunity that we must make the most of, we will only have one shot at this". He turned his attention to the computer terminal and began to extract the information he now needed. "I would now like you to turn your attention to your monitors. As you can see from the simulation, this is the trajectory of the planet. Alpha 1472 will launch 96 hours before it is in actual range and will rendezvous at this point... This is the first point at which we will be in optimum range for a landing attempt. As our orbit passes through this system, provided that you manage to locate a suitable landing site for your first orbit, you will have precisely three hundred and ten hours to assimilate and collate as much information as possible. This will leave only two hours for you to affect a successful take off from the planet, and as you are all aware break free from its gravitational pull".

With a click of his mouse he halted the computer simulation that was in progress on the screens "At this point we will once again be out of range. I have no need to tell you just how important this mission is. This will be the one that will have the most far reaching implications for the future of every single person on this planet. The information that you bring back with you could be the building block of technological, medical, meteorological, and geological advancements that will see us through into the next millennium and beyond."

"If you look in the envelope on your desks you will find a ROM disk. On each of these disks are the parameters of your individual missions. I know that there is, within reach of you all, the ability for cooperation, and we are relying on that to maximise the information yield from this mission. I have personally hand picked each of you for this mission. I selected you because I believe that you are the best people for the job. It will be the adventure of a lifetime, and I have no doubt that you will all go down in the annals of history, and be spoken about long after this mission is over. This is precisely why failure is not an option".

"If you have any questions, and I would be

disappointed if there were not, all of them should now be addressed through major Hooton and major general Stewart. All that remains for me to do is wish you good luck and a safe return". With these words he stood to attention, saluted the crew and left the room. Major general Stewart rose to his feet and began to address them. "Good morning" he began "All the listening stations around the world have been concentrating maximum efforts on this project since telemetry alerted us to the approach of the planet we have labelled Epsilon Omega, and to date there has been no confirmation of any type of manufactured radio waves. Further to this, observation has not been able to detect any unnatural satellites orbiting the planet. From these two facts, we have to assume that Epsilon Omega has no form of defence, we further have to assume that if there is any type of civilisation present on the planet, it is either at one end of the evolutionary scale or the other, that is to say, they are beyond the need for defence or communication, and it is also likely that they are probably also beyond the need for space travel. However we tend to dismiss this as being the case. We are more in favour of the other end of the scale, a pre industrial society. This being the case, I must stress the importance of non involvement. Under no circumstances will there be any contact of any kind with any intelligent life form that may be present.

Unfortunately mission Alpha 106 made no transmissions back to this planet after entering the atmosphere of Epsilon Omega so, we can have no knowledge of any life form that may exist there. We do know however that the atmosphere has a high probability of being able to support our biological needs. There is no way to even speculate as to the fate of Alpha 106, but we are confident that any problems encountered by them were not a direct consequence of the planet itself.

If you would all like to go through to the relax room we have provided relaxation terminals for each of you. There is also sustenance and refreshments available... Take care to review your mission thoroughly. Report back here at precisely 1300 hours. For now ladies and gentlemen, that will be all". The two officers collected their paperwork and left the room. The crew did likewise and retired to the relax room.

The table at the far end of the relax room was laid with a complete meal. The crew all took their places on the stools that surrounded the table. As they were about to start their meal captain Daniels called for their attention. "Listen everyone, this will be the last proper meal we will be having, and I for one would like to enjoy it in peace. So, I don't want to hear anything about the mission. Now let's eat." His words put everyone at ease, and the next half hour was a welcome break in the already intense time that lay ahead of them. They sat, and for the duration of the meal they engaged in polite, but friendly conversations. The captain had realised that they needed this time to get to know each other, after all they were going to be confined together in a relatively small environment for a long time.

Upon completing their meal the crew moved over to the comfort of the easy chairs that were arranged in a circle, alongside each chair was situated a computer screen and a terminal. In silence each of the crew sat studying and absorbing the information provided for them on their ROM discs. Most of the material held on the discs was of a standard nature but because of the importance of this mission, there was certain information specific to each of them that differed from any other orders they had received before. They sat and worked on their mission briefs for hours, until one by one, they reclined in their seats, each displaying an air of accomplishment. At 1250 hours captain Daniels, having waited until everyone had completed their own evaluation of the tasks ahead, cleared his throat and said to everyone,

"Right, now we all know what is expected of us, I now have to ask you. You have all read the last paragraph held within the file marked **Vital, Read Last!,** and this is the absolute last chance you will have to withdraw from the mission, I am obliged to point out certain facts to you. If you decide to withdraw there will be no adverse remarks placed on your records, nor will it affect any future missions that you may be considered for. Since Alpha 106, there have been no significant problems in space, so all of the departments within the programme assure us that there will be no unforeseen problems with this mission. Bearing in mind these facts I must now ask you to make a decision, do any of you wish to withdraw from this mission?" he paused and waited for an answer. Each of the crew sat and reflected upon the final paragraph which read... *Finally and most* *importantly, the mission upon which you are about to embark, is one, of the nature, which our world has never known before. It is a mission in which there may be a possibility of first contact with an alien civilisation. If this should be the case then certain parameters must be adhered to. We will assume that there is life on Epsilon Omega. Should this life form be at an evolutionary stage that has not yet reached the advancement of our own, we must be aware of its future advancement. To these ends it is imperative that there be absolutely no contact of any kind with any intelligent being encountered. It would be unfair of us as a civilisation to influence the natural evolution, and learning process of another world. If, in the unlikely event that beings encountered should display the same physiological attributes to our own there are provisions within your orders to allow you to interact with them in an effort to establish their level of advancement. In the event of craft malfunction, resulting in the termination of the mission on Epsilon Omega the aforementioned parameters will remain in force. To achieve this we have, for the first time, on any craft installed a self destruction device. This device can only be activated by the input of three of the secret pin numbers given to each of the crew. One of these numbers must be that of the captain, or of the second in command. This drastic measure is important to preserve the integrity of whatever we may find. It is imperative that you understand the implications of this device. Once activated, the self destruct mechanism cannot be aborted. In the event of the need to implement this device, your final orders from control are to prevent the contamination of the planet and its inhabitants, the self destruct device will not be activated until all seven of the crew are secured within the vehicle. There must be no evidence left on the planet to suggest that it has been visited by anyone or anything that is not endemic to that environment.*

Each of the crew sat and considered this paragraph, silently anticipating the others, each expecting one or more of their number to decline the mission. After a few moments it was clear that there were to be no objections to being included in the mission. The captain looked at each of them in turn.

"I will take that as being a resounding acceptance of all of the conditions laid out in your orders, and invite all of you back into the briefing room." When they had all re-taken their seats, the door was automatically closed, and they could hear a pronounced hiss as the room was hermetically sealed. The room then went through the same process as the final entry room. The lights dimmed to the familiar purple glow and began to hum. This process was the final procedure in the sterilisation programme. From this point onwards they would have no direct contact with the outside world. For this mission it had been decided that it would be prudent to minimise any risk of cross contamination between worlds.

After a short wait the two officers who had been there earlier, returned to the corridor and took their seats. All of the crew were now irrevocably committed to the mission, and this was to be the final time they would see anyone before their return.

The clock on the wall was reading 1300 hours as Major General Stewart, and Major Hooton rose to their feet. They stood to attention and saluted the crew, Major Hooton spoke, "On behalf of the entire staff of this facility we wish you a safe journey and a speedy return" The crew stood to attention and returned the salute. The officers and the crew sat down. Major General Stewart reached over to his terminal and pressed the key marked activate. The entire corridor containing the two officers slid silently to the left, as it did it revealed the panoramic view of the launch pad. By this time the shuttle that was to take them out of the confines of their planet was standing proud on its supports. All around the area the hustle and bustle of support vehicles could be seen. As the room travelled slowly towards the shuttle, Mary thought that this was like watching a huge television screen. To her, it felt like she was watching a film. It had a strange fictional quality to it, a quality that suggested that this was not really happening, that somehow it was all a dream. In the night sky she could see a myriad of stars, as she scanned the skies she gave a heavy sigh. Soon she would be a very small part of that theatre.

Her attention was drawn to the carnival that was now being played out in front of her. The speakers inside of their room had now been patched through to mission control, as they came on line the first words that the crew heard were those of the countdown operator.

"T minus one hour, four minutes and twenty seven seconds"

With these words the clocks in front of them changed from reading present time, to give a countdown time displayed in hours, minutes and seconds.

As the room approached the shuttle, activity in the area intensified. They could see final fuelling of the craft taking place, and an army of ground staff making last minute checks that were a familiar sight to anyone who had made this short trip before. The nearer they came to the shuttle, the more they could make out the finer details on the craft. The lighting that was illuminating the area was not as intense as the lights that were picking out the shuttle; they gave a magical, almost surreal air to the craft. Upon arriving at the base of the support structure, the room came to a steady but firm standstill. Outside the room they could hear the sound of ground staff making ready for the next part of their journey. To the sides of the room that they were in, had been attached the mechanism that was to take it upwards though the gantry, towards the opening into the shuttle command positions. As they rose into the air, spotlights followed the room. All that could be seen at this distance by the crew was the topside of the shuttle. Either side, they could see out into the night sky. As they travelled upwards the legend on the side of this great vehicle came into view. As it became fully visible, each of the crew found themselves breathing in, expanding their chests with a feeling of intense pride, and a sense of supreme adventure, wondering what the next few weeks would bring.

All of them sat for a while and read the legend it simply read...

1472 ALPHA
PRIDE OF GOD

2. The journey.

Upon reaching the top of the structure, the room came slowly to a halt. From the sides of the room a curtain began to extend towards the shuttle, as it did so, the night sky that had been visible either side of the ship became obscured. The curtain had created a walkway through to the entrance hatch, which was now clearly visible at the other end. The space that had been created now went through the sterilisation process. As the crew waited they could feel themselves becoming more and more impatient, this time the purple lights seemed to last for an eternity. The glass panel that had formed the front wall of the room was now silently lowered. The only barrier remaining between them and space was the door which was about to open before them.

A feeling of excited anticipation seized them. It was the type of feeling that at one time or another we have all experienced, the kind of feeling one gets when one walks into a new house for the first time, or sits behind the wheel of a brand new car. As they made their way onto the flight deck of the shuttle, the first thing that struck them was the newness, the cleanliness, the smell, and the small confines in which they would be working. All of these factors somehow heightened the adventure and excitement.

Mary stood, poised at the edge of the door, "In you go Mary" said Captain Daniels. He was to be the last crew member to enter the shuttle, it was his responsibility to lock and secure the door. Mary reached up and made a grab for the ladder, actually getting into the shuttle was a problem all of its own. Although she was physically fit, she had always found difficulty traversing the short distance between the hatch, and her workstation. This was a task that was confounded even further by the present angle of the shuttle, and gravity itself. However, once they were in orbit the weightlessness of space would eliminate these problems. Captain Daniels effortlessly clambered into the cabin and was now lying on top of the ladder. Reaching through the rungs he pulled the door closed and pulled down on the triangular lever which activated the locking mechanism. The sound of heavy bolts falling into position could be heard, followed by the hiss of the entire cabin becoming pressurised. He then reached above his head, and in one swift movement had pulled himself into his own position.

They had now reached the point of no return. They were sealed in the capsule, and the next time they would leave the shuttle they would be on Epsilon Omega.

The crew, now firmly secured into their seats, began to methodically press buttons on the consoles in front of them. As they did so, each section of the cockpit illuminated and sprang into life, the communication systems came on line.

"T minus fifteen minutes and counting, all systems show green"

By this time there was no inner excitement felt by

Alpha 1472

the crew. To anyone observing the activities now in progress, it would appear that no attention was being paid to any of the communications being made between mission control and themselves. This, however, was not the case. As each of them went through their final checks to ensure that their stations were operating correctly, their senses were working in overdrive, every sight and every sound was being digested, and nothing was missed. From the very second that the door had been secured, the ground crews had been working feverishly to remove all of the superstructures that had been supporting the shuttle, and now it stood alone, towering into the night sky. It was indeed a monument to modern technology.

"T minus twelve minutes. All ground staff to vacate the area, repeat all ground staff to vacate the area"

With this announcement all of the people who had been working around the base of the shuttle got into their support vehicles, and a stream of headlights was seen driving away from the area. Within two minutes, there was no one there. The shuttle stood alone, floodlit in and eerie silence. The scene inside the cockpit was a complete contrast. The countdown operator had just announced that there was only ten minutes before lift off. Mission control went into its final check sequence. Five minutes later, Daniels opened a communication channel to control

"All checks finalized and completed, everything on board 1472 Alpha reads A,OK and we show green at all stations. "We are entering final preparations and waiting go, over" "Roger that 1472" Came the reply. With this captain Daniels turned his attention to the crew and instructed them to prepare for take off. Complying with his orders, they secured all safety harnesses attached to their seats, and placed their heads into the contoured headrests. With all of the checks and preparations now completed, the crew lay motionless in their seats and awaited the inevitable.

"All final checks and preparations complete, all systems show green, we are ready for go and counting from 15... 14... 13... 12... 11... Ignition... 9... 8... 7... All systems still read green...5...releasing docking clamps ... 3... 2 ...1 ... we have lift off at 1400 hours, 1472 Alpha is clear of the launch pad and on her way, we have go, good luck to you all"

Over the speakers, the crew could hear cheers and celebrations from mission control as they seared through the night sky towards space. As the beast rose into the night, they could feel their faces being pulled and contorted under the immense G forces that were being exerted upon their bodies. Through the roar of the engines they could hear the sound of the operations back at mission control.

"Vector calculations are now complete, opening window sub sector Alpha 92, grid 74."

With this conformation, the series of satellites that orbited the planet, systematically begun to shut down creating a window through which the shuttle would pass. Within seconds the craft rolled over and passed through the unseen portal. Ground control then re-activated the grid to seal the window. Everyone on the ground, and indeed around the world watched via television as they ascended through the patchy cloud cover and disappeared from view. After a few minutes the only evidence left of the shuttle was the tell tale plume of smoke arcing off into space.

Before departing for Epsilon Omega, mission control had scheduled them for two orbits of the planet; these were to be made under the guidance of the computers back on the ground. This gave the crew chance to sit and look through the window and marvel at the sight of their world passing by below them. Positioned around the globe was a network of sophisticated satellites, each one interlinked and interdependent of the next. All of them were travelling in a precise geostationary orbit five hundred miles above the planets surface. This network had been in place since the sun of the planet had turned supernova. It had been a time when the future of the planet was in jeopardy. The resulting affect of the stars collapse was to throw them into deep space, placing it on an elliptical orbit of immense proportions. Many hardships ensued, tidal waves, hurricanes and finally an ice age set in. during the time between the holocaust and the installation of the first network, which had been patchy at best, the satellites that they had managed to launch gave only minimal coverage for the planet. As time progressed and technology advanced, the system was updated regularly. The network was, in time redesigned and upgraded to cover many purposes, not least to provide an atmosphere for the stricken planet. At the heart of each satellite lay a nuclear reactor which provided each unit with enough power to create ample light and heat to sustain the, now artificial atmosphere. The weather for the planet was now controlled through the vast computer network housed within the offices of the meteorological centers around the world. Now, thankfully the only thing that was necessary to maintain coverage was an ongoing program of maintenance and replacement.

In recent years, problems had begun to return to the planet. At first scientists believed that the fault lay with the network that had for so long, protected them. However, extensive research had revealed that the source of their meteorological and geological discrepancies were the direct result of a slowing in the rotation rate of the planet itself. To correct the problem it had been decided that a radical new addition the network had to be introduced. The space facing side of each unit had been fitted with a directional neutron particle beam, which when activated, gave the planet the propulsion it needed to maintain the optimum rate of spin. It had also been found that the newly upgraded system now yielded unexpected benefits that were of extreme interest to the Alpha division. This was planetary defence. Another reason for the existence of the Alpha division was to minimize the effect of space debris entering their atmosphere and falling to the surface. This problem had until recently been the main course for the loss of many lives each year. With the advent of the particle beams, this was no longer a threat. By aiming the beams at the oncoming obstruction they had found that it was quite easy to destroy it before it posed any real threat. This was a function that the network was called upon to perform at regular intervals due to the orbit that they now occupied. The main function for Alpha had always been to prove it's capabilities for repelling any attack from life forms, although this had never been called upon. On the surface, of course the network was all but taken for granted, it was not until you were in orbit around the globe, could you appreciate the sheer magnitude of what it was that provided the basic necessities of life.

The shuttle was now in orbit, with its topside facing towards the planet. All of its movements and functions were being closely monitored from the ground. The final checks on the thousands of sensors which were housed in the outer shell were also being carried out. These would be the last major system checks that would be required before departure. Having now completed two orbits of the planet, it was time for them to begin their long journey to rendezvous with Epsilon Omega, Daniels contacted control.

"This is 1472 Alpha to control, over."

The time had come for him and his crew to assume control of the vessel.

"This is mission control, everything shows green, you are now cleared to break orbit. To the crew of 1742 Alpha we wish you good luck. Over and out" Captain Daniels addressed his navigator,

"Mary, plot and lay in a course to intercept Epsilon Omega"

Alpha 1472

Mary had already calculated the point at which orbit would be broken and the interception trajectory necessary, and with a few clicks on her terminal fed it into the navigation systems. Because there is no right way up in space it was a relatively simple matter to break orbit. The trajectory of the shuttle leveled out and it gracefully dipped away from the planet. Once they were clear of the gravitational pull, everyone could relax. They all released the safety harnesses that had held them securely in their chairs, and began to float freely around the cabin. The only person still in his place was Captain Daniels, as he was busy setting the auto pilot that would guide them for the next four days. Having done this he proceeded to join the others, who by this time had made their way into the sleeping area. His last task was to extinguish all unnecessary lighting. As he closed the door he took one last look into the cockpit. The red glow that emanated from the single light set into the roof, coupled with the illuminations given off by the constant flickering of the control panels gave it a serene almost simulated quality. He closed and secured the door.

The crew was now on route to rendezvous with Epsilon Omega, and with all of their preliminary functions completed, they now had time to relax before preparing for the bulk of their journey.

J.D, Mathew, Watkins and Travis Wheatley, chose to watch the television monitor. They were still in transmission range of the networks and were still able to receive live broadcasts from the surface. J.D. was almost childlike in his reactions when he had realized that they were in time to watch one of the more popular light variety programs on channel 6.

"Oh the great presto he has got to be the best magician ever"

When she realized what the choice of viewing would be Mary groaned. Although she was interested in magic, she did at times find that the airtime devoted to it by the television companies a little overpowering. As J.D. Mathew and Travis settled themselves in front of the screen, Anne and Mary busied themselves preparing drinks.

The pilot and co pilot had elected to sit near to computer terminals and were now each becoming engrossed in two totally different ROM publications. The captain had selected to further his knowledge of the martial arts and meditation techniques, whilst Marius Hatch was passing his downtime studying the technical data and specifications of the ship in which they were now travelling.

Mary and Anne passed out drinks amongst the crew and then retired to the back of the cabin and began to become more acquainted with each other. It was the first real chance they had had for any form of social communication and they had both been looking forward to this time.

They had been en route for approximately two hours when Captain Daniels had decided that it was time for them to get into their sleeping modules. Each of the crew began to busy themselves securing all loose items that were free floating around the cabin. Having done this they proceeded to strip down to their underwear and stow their overalls in their personal lockers. One by one they harnessed themselves into their modules and closed the glass covers. With the closure of each cover came a hiss as each one was hermetically sealed. As the seventh and final capsule was secured doctor Anne Homer opened a small door which was set at the head of her capsule. When it was opened it revealed a small control panel. She then proceeded to activate the system that would flood each module with the odorless gas that would trigger their endorphin release. Within minutes all seven of them were asleep.

As they slept, the onboard computer began to systematically shut down all nonessential functions including life support, these systems would not be needed as each individual capsule housed its own. Finally all lighting was extinguished. Their lives were now dependant on the computer and on ground control. The shuttle was now in almost complete darkness and silent. The only noise that could be heard was the deep quiet rumble of the engines as they continued to power their way towards their destination.

Somewhere in the history of every civilization, there were documented cases of people who possess certain uncanny abilities, abilities which seem fantastic and implausible, yet however preposterous they appear to be, they were the basis of a technique which had enabled long haul space travel to become reality. During the early days of space travel, the agency had found that although the craft they were using had the speed and capabilities to travel from asteroid to asteroid, the crews were becoming over fatigued by the duration and the conditions of extended space travel. Consequently, upon arrival at a new asteroid, exploratory work that had been planned was being severely hampered, and very basic mistakes were being made due to the emotional and physical state of the crews. To overcome these problems, scientists began looking into all avenues to find a way to induce a prolonged sleep status within a crew member, allowing him or her to awaken at their destination refreshed and alert. Their search for the answer had led them to a tribe of people whose ancestry spanned many, many millennia. Their way of life was based solely upon the belief that they and they alone controlled their minds bodies and their destiny. Through the almost total devotion they had towards their lifestyle, they had perfected an art of meditation that had allowed them to develop a technique of self induced coma. The more practiced amongst them could vary the length of their sleep state at will, slowing down all of their metabolic functions to an absolute minimum for survival. Whilst in this state other members of the tribe would take their lifeless bodies and lay them upon a ceremonial alter in the middle of the village to await their return to the redivivus or the rebirth. To the scientists this was very impressive, but at the same time it was impractical to expect that any astronaut would be able to master this feat of self control that had took these people many lifetimes to perfect. The real breakthrough had come when the tribal elders had agreed to a small research facility being set up within their village with the express intention of studying this phenomenon. After many years of intensive investigations, the elusive secret had been uncovered. It had been found that the tribesmen had developed the ability to stimulate their brain into producing certain endorphins, which, once released into their systems, effectively closed down all non essential functions. The most surprising finding was that the endorphins detected were not unique to the tribesmen; they were in fact present in everyone, albeit in a dormant state. Armed with their findings, the scientists returned to their laboratories to develop ways to utilize their new found knowledge. It did not take long, however, for them to realize that they only possessed half of the key, and that it would be many years before they could take advantage of this technique.

The next step had proved to be the most dangerous, and the most sensitive. It was research that had been conducted behind closed doors, a top secret project that had been kept from the media and the public for fear of the impassioned response that it would provoke.

It had produced, within its volunteers, a most unwanted side effect. During the efforts to produce a trigger mechanism to release the sleep endorphins all of the experiments had resulted in either the death or comatose state of its subject. The basic problem had come about due to the initial success of the 'operation trigger'. Everyone connected with the operation had thought that it would be a simple pharmaceutical problem. Thanks to the tribesmen, the project researchers had been able to produce a derivative of a plant that was indigenous to the mountain regions. The drug that had been produced from the hyssop plant had proved highly effective in triggering the desired release. The real problem was that once the trigger device had stimulated the brain, the gland responsible continued via self stimulation, to produce the endorphin. Consequently, the facility had been filled with wards full of sleeping patients. What was needed was a second drug. to halt the production and allow the body to cleanse itself and revive the subject.

The second reviving drug had been discovered quite by accident. The agency had always taken great care when selecting the guinea pig volunteers who would receive the treatment, however, on one occasion one of the volunteers had not been screened correctly. He was the only one ever to have been taken into the program who still had a living relative. The relative, who had been thought dead, turned out to be the man's brother.' He had been working for the government and had been involved in covert operations; working in such environments had facilitated several changes of identity, much to the extent that his true identity had all but been lost. Upon returning to civilian life, he had felt the need to try to pick up some of the pieces of his former life, and by using his connections within the various government departments, he had discovered that he was not the only member of his family and further than that his brother had been placed in the program by the hospital that had been treating him. Having left the world of espionage he now found himself doing the same type of work for himself. His investigations had led him to the research establishment of the space program, where by now his brother was incarcerated and comatose in the overcrowded observation ward. Using the skills he had gained during his time as an undercover operative, he had decided to mount a rescue bid to save his brother. His prowess in this field had allowed him to slip in and out of the facility and execute his rescue virtually unnoticed. Carrying his lifeless brother, fireman style, he cautiously made his bid for freedom. He had barely cleared the perimeter fence when the alarm was raised. Bundling his brother into his getaway vehicle he sped away in the direction of the city. He was aware that they were being perused, and what ensued was a cat and mouse game of capture and evasion. Finally they had found refuge in a perfume warehouse on the outskirts of one of the industrial zones. The rescuer and his charge had found a place to go to ground, and there they lay in a storage hopper of raw materials. It was uncomfortable, but it was, for the moment, safe. The decision had been made for them to stay here, in hiding, until the coast was clear for them to move on. They had been there several hours when, unseemingly, the life began to return to the unconscious brother. The other having researched the condition, knew that this was not possible. But there it was, happening before his eyes. His thought turned for a while to all of the other patients he had seen lying in the ward, and in that instant he knew that if the others stood any chance of recovery they had to return, regardless of the consequences he may have to face.

After the furore of their return had died down and investigations were complete, scientists had finally found the missing part to their puzzle. The antidote was held within the raw materials of the perfume.

They sped silently through the blackness of space towards their target. The automatic guidance system would be operative for the next four days. It would hold them to a course which was almost a complete replica of the orbit on which their own planet was travelling. By journeying ahead of the planet, they would in effect create a time span as their planet came into and out of range of Epsilon Omega. This window would allow for vital surface research to be carried out before the shuttle would have to take off and assume a trajectory that would allow them to catch up with their departing home world.

It had been four days since they had departed from home, and during that time the shuttle had travelled through the vastness of space under the control of the on board navigational computer. In the darkness of the flight deck it had continued to make minor adjustments in the guidance of the craft ensuring that, when the crew returned they would be exactly where they expected they would be. The entire craft was still, dark and silent. The engines continued their dull roar. The crew slept.

1472 Alpha was a new generation space vehicle, the first of its kind. It was able to travel at speeds greater than had ever been achieved before. This was largely due to the breakthrough of anti matter reactor engines which afforded greater power output and incredibly reduced fuel payload. Consequently, they were now travelling faster than anyone had ever travelled before.

The dark, silent, serenity of things came to an abrupt end as the entire shuttle sprang to life. Oxygen circulated around the vessel, environment controls began to heat the cabins and lighting systems flickered to life. It was time for the crew to be revived. Each of the seven capsules was flooded with the antidote gas, and all of the locking restraints which had held the crew stable and the glass covers were released. One by one the crew experienced their own 'redivisus' and before long they were all awake, and ready to resume their journey.

When they had all been fully revived, they proceeded to take a meal and to freshen themselves before the real purpose of their mission was to begin.

Mary had been busy calculating all of the variables required for the approach, the landing and subsequently the take off. For her, this would be the most important part of her personal mission.

Having completed her brief, she contacted Captain Daniels

"Captain, this is Mary. I'm ready with my results now"

The captain informed the rest of the crew who spun their chairs around to face the circle of monitors which occupied the centre of the command deck. As Mary began to address her colleagues the monitors displayed the simulation she had created.

"Right, this is our present position, in two hours we will be taking up orbit around Epsilon Omega. Here is our planet which is now three days behind us, at its present speed it will pass through this system and be out of range in ten days. This gives us a maximum time on the surface of six days and seven hours precisely. I can't, at this moment, say where we will be landing, not until the captain and Mr. Hatch have evaluated the terrain and the predisposition of the planet. All of my figures are based upon the information thus far, obtained by J.D"

The crew's attention now turned to the geologist, J.D. who now leaned forwards in his chair.

"The system we are now in is one of nine planets orbiting a single sun. The one that we are interested in is this one, third out. I estimate that the system is some four and a half billion years old, and completely stable. I have been observing Epsilon Omega and by calculating its rotation around the sun, in conjunction with its axial rotation rate, it would appear that, because of the size and mass of this planet in comparison to our own, we share a similar time scale. Now, when our planet passes though this system, it will pass between the orbits of the fifth and sixth planet and avoid this asteroid belt here. As it makes its pass both the largest planet and the ringed planet will be on this side of the sun, allowing safe passage for the home world. It is fortunate that the third planet is the only one that seems capable of supporting life. Projected interference reports suggest that the distance between Epsilon Omega and passage orbit will result in only minor disturbance to this system".

As each of them outlined their findings the monitors were displaying the various points that they were making. Mathew Watkins was the next to report.

"Taking into account the density and mass of this sun in direct comparison to that of our former system, the size of Epsilon Omega, its distance from the sun and the intensity of the sun, its reasonable for us to assume a similar distribution of the temperate zones we will encounter will be much the same as we would find on our own planet. At present we are not close enough for me to produce an accurate assessment of the atmospheric condition present on the planet, but, from long range, it would appear that this will be a place that will well suit the needs of life as we know it to be. If you look at the weather systems now in progress, you will see several large windows of non clouded activity, I would suggest that if, at closer inspection these areas are free from turbulence or wind systems, that one of these areas would be ideal for a landing attempt".

Captain Daniels acknowledged all of them and turned the briefing over to Marius Hatch.

"What I am proposing now, will ultimately decide the type of landing we will be affecting. I propose that once in orbit we will complete three circuits around the globe, eventually, using the flight path that I have recommended, we will have successfully quadrated the sphere giving us a complete panoramic view of the terrain. Once we have evaluated the potential for landing sites, we will then be in a position to choose the method by which we will touch down". The captain then addressed everyone,

"Does anyone have any objections to any of the reports made, or do any of you have anything to add"

No one spoke,

"O.k. then, Mr Hatch, please make ready your orbital path, and Mr Watkins, prepare to fire a series of probes through the atmosphere as we make our passes. As we can plainly see there does not appear to be any form of satellites in or above the outer atmosphere and as yet the only radio emissions detected are all of a natural occurrence. Well so far it seems that we shouldn't have any problems here so let's get to it"

As they neared the planet, everyone was carrying out their duties in clockwork, precise fashion. Mary had fed into the computer the flight path given to her by Marius Hatch and was preparing to take them into their first orbit when she heard J.D.'s voice.

"Oh oh Captain, we seem to have a little problem"

"Go ahead J.D." He said. "Well, I'm not sure but the surveillance and infrared cameras have detected signs of civilisation down there and it seems to be…."

He pressed a few buttons on his console to confirm what he had found,

"….quite widespread and fairly advanced" Mathew Watkins interrupted.

"Yes sir I can also confirm that"

Captain Daniels turned to his co-pilot and instructed

him to send a message back to ground control to inform them of their findings. Having done that, he called another conference. Everyone once again turned to face the centre.

"Unfortunately we now have a dilemma on our hands. Because we now have a first contact situation with a race that has, we assume, not yet even mastered basic communication or transmission skills, our entire mission must take on a radically new dimension. Because we believe in a policy of non interference, it is imperative that we are not visually detected during the landing or take off. I can show you the options that are now open to us. This is option one. We approach from a high orbit and take a direct descent path to the surface, however, if we take this option, to minimise detection we would have to travel at approximately twice the normal approach speed and would need three times the landing strip length that we would normally require. Moreover, upon landing we would have to find a way to camouflage the craft as to avoid its discovery. Because of the time factor involved this would obviously be a last choice situation."

Hatch fidgeted in his seat before outlining the second option.

"Option two is equally as risky. I am now authorized to release a part of your briefing programme that you have not yet seen. Please pay particular attention to the simulation that you are now about to watch. I will talk you through it. This is a touchdown method that, up until yet, has not been tried. Captain Daniels and I have simulated this type of landing on numerous occasions, but this will be the first actual attempt. Firstly it will require our navigator to select a suitable site. The parameters for this site are held within her document brief. Having decided upon the ideal place we will then place 1472 into high geostationary orbit above the site and commence descent. The descent will take the form of a descending spiral, utilising a circumference of fifteen point three miles. As we approach the surface, the spiral will, under computer guidance, change course to match the axial rotation of the planet. At the point where we pass through the magnetosphere into the exosphere all engine power will be placed on standby, effectively cutting all propulsion. The remainder of the descent will be an unpowered glide. The only time that the engines will be used will be for course corrective purposes. The attempt will take place on the dark side of the planet, whilst the area around the landing site is experiencing their night time phase. On a spiral descent there will be less likelihood of any life forms witnessing our arrival. The second phase of option two is another innovative manoeuvre. The actual landing will take place in one of the seas of this planet. During the final circuit of the descent spiral this craft will perform a yaw manoeuvre, thus bringing the wing horizon to an angle of forty five degrees to the level state. This will have the effect of allowing the wing surfaces to become hydrofoils, enabling us to continue our course sub aquatically. Once under the surface, navigation would switch to sonar detection to find us a suitable resting place.

This option is the one that the agency prefers. However, the final decision rests with the captain". The captain sat and considered the options, and for the few moments he took over his deliberations, everyone sat, all eyes fixed firmly upon him, awaiting his decision. He knew that aborting the mission was not an option and that he had to choose the best option to ensure success. Finally he raised his head, regarded each of the crew and announced his decision.

"Taking into account the non interactive policy, I don't see much choice. We will have to go with option two. Mary, take us into orbit and scan for possible landing sites. Apart from that people, its business as usual"

At this, everyone resumed their position and duties. During the orbital phase a series of meteorological probes were shot through the atmosphere. The information that was relayed back had confirmed that the atmosphere was well within acceptable parameters to sustain their needs. They had all breathed a sigh of relief at the prospect that they would have no need for the breathing apparatus that they had half expected would, as usual, hamper progress on the surface.

All of the monitoring and surveillance systems were operating the navigation station and within the space of an hour, Mary had at her disposal a complete topographical display of the entire surface and was now selecting possible landing sites. She was taking into account that, where there are signs of civilisation, it would be more than probable that an area of such demographics would yield greater rewards for the mission.

She had selected nine possible locations, but the one she favoured most, was the one which lay thirty two point eight degrees inside the northern hemisphere. It was a small inland body of water situated in an area which offered both desert and vegetated regions. The probes had confirmed that the current temperature in the region was above what they were used to, but it was well within the prescribed comfort zone.

Mary had fed the complicated data for the descent into the navigation computer, and they had all secured themselves into their seats. She had positioned the craft in its final orbit. The cabin crew silently went about their business; no one spoke, each of them held certain trepidation towards the impending attempt.

"Twenty seconds to inception" Hatch said.

They could feel their tension levels rising, apprehension was at fever pitch as they physically felt the craft veer off into the descent.

"Manoeuvre commitment confirmed"

They were now irrevocably committed to the landing pattern.

The shuttle had completed three circuits of the dark outer atmosphere and had begun to enter the exosphere. All of the sensors on the outer shell of the craft were busy collecting all possible information they could, about this alien environment. They were now firmly under the influence of the gravitational forces of the planet and it was at this point, that the engines were cut. The action of switching the engines to standby seemed to create an audible void. The familiar deep rumble had now been replaced by virtual silence. They were gliding unpowered through the night sky. As they fell through the various atmospheric layers Mathew Watkins shouted out the different attributes he was discovering. At the same time each of the crew was in turn reporting from their respective stations in much the same manner. This had the effect of creating a highly organised cascade of vocal information exchanges concerning the descent and their present surrounding.

"Thermosphere confirmed"...."altitude 270.5"...."life signs stable"...."hull temperature rising"...."heat shield holding stable"...."spiral adjust on line.. .now..."..."mesosphere confirmed"... "Altitude *53.9* levelling out to fifteen degrees".... "Hull temperature stable"

"Shields stable"..."detecting moisture at altitude 49.1"..."stratosphere confirmed"..."altitude 30.4" "target located and locked in...now"..."life signs show stable"..."troposphere confirmed"... "Altitude 9, *8.5,* 8, initiating yaw manoeuvre, impact in 6, *5,* 4, 3, 2, 1,"

As the shuttle crashed through the surface of the water, all of the crew were violently jarred in their seats. The impact had been much worse than any of them had anticipated, but once they were submerged, everything went into slow motion as the inertial dampers bought them to a full stop.

After a few moments Mary had managed to recover from the splash down and, having switched to sonar was now busy scanning for a suitable place for the shuttle to rest for the next few days. It was not long before she had located the ideal site. Confirming her find with the captain and the co-pilot, she inputted the information into her terminal and with a triumphant final stab at the controls, leaned back in her seat and left the two officers to begin the final phase of the landing.

As they descended through the black waters, the visibility through the cockpit windows was nil. It was as if the window surface had been blacked out. Travis Wheatley leaned over his control panels and activated the outside lighting systems. As soon as he had done this, their field of vision was instantly extended to allow them to see everything picked up within the beams of the lights. It was a whole new world, a strange, silent, aquatic theatre of which they were now a part. As they went deeper and deeper, Travis was feverishly typing at his terminal, making as many notes about this environment as he could. His terminal was time linked to cameras positioned around the shuttle. He would revise these later to make a more detailed study. As the captain guided them through the waters to their resting place, everyone sat and marvelled the wonders they were now witnessing. The deep blue exterior played host to a myriad of different life forms, each of them of interest to Wheatley, who was becoming agitated by the intense rush of information, he wanted to slow things down in order to have more time to collate all of the data he was receiving. Unfortunately for him, the descent rate had been predetermined and was now near its end. In the final moments of their descent, Captain Daniels bought the craft to within six feet of their resting place. Hovering over the ledge they had selected. This was the last stage of the landing procedure. The co-pilot announced that it was time to create the moorings that would hold them firm for the duration of their stay. At the flick of a switch, six, six foot bolts shot from around the shuttle's underside with such force that they embedded themselves into the igneous rock that made up this plateau. Each of the bolts was attached to cables which led back to the craft. The winches began to pull them into the rock and before long they were securely anchored into position. "Craft secured at 0200 hours all system checks complete, good job everybody" said the captain.

All engines were cut and everyone sat back and breathed a sigh of relief. As they looked through the windows into the calm waters, they could see that they had come to rest on a plateau that led to a vast precipice that fell away into the dark abyss below.

All of the excitement connected with the landing was abating and they were now finding time to reflect upon what they had just achieved, and upon where they now were.

They had finally reached their goal, and now they were actually on Epsilon Omega, ready to begin their great adventure.

3. A brave new world.

Time on Epsilon Omega was at a premium and there was to be no time for the luxury of a rest period, even after what they had all experienced. The medic, Anne Homer reached for her med kit and proceeded to inject all of the crew members in turn with an inoculation of sleep inhibitor, this would ensure that they would be able to take advantage of every single minute of their stay here. They could sleep on the return journey. It was now time to prepare for the job that they had been sent here for.

The first probe that was actually deployed from the surface was released from the topmost part of the shuttle. It was sent to the surface attached to a cable. As it ascended, the crew prepared for the more detailed assignations that were to follow. The up coming assignments were outlined in their individual briefs, all of which the captain had released to them now that they were on the surface. As the probe reached the surface, the six glass petals unfolded around the sensor mechanism of the probe and relayed vital information back to the shuttle.

"Well, it seems that we now have confirmation that the atmosphere of this planet is within acceptable levels to support all of our life support needs" Said Marius Hatch,

"Oxygen levels normal, hydrogen levels normal,

nitrogen levels normal and carcinogens minimal, so all in all it seems that we have a green light to go for all of the experiments that we have scheduled." The captain confirmed this and retracted the probe. The next few hours would be critical, they were about to encounter who knew what. Each of them had obviously given this matter some thought. They wondered, would the inhabitants of this world be civilized, or would they be little more than savages? Would this world yield great, invaluable information and research material? Or, would it be a virtual barren wasteland? Would their lives be at risk? Or, would they return to the home world safe? These and many more questions played on their minds. Whatever the questions may have been, they would find their answers over the next few hours.

Each of the crew had read their final briefs and was well aware of what was expected from them, and as if by clockwork they set about their individual tasks.

As second in command, Marius Hatch had been designated to be the first one of them to sample the fresh air of the new planet, an honour that he was well looking forward to. With this first task now imminent he, along with J.D and Travis made his way out of the cockpit area, through the relaxation lounge, and through to the rear of the vessel into the workstation areas where all of the major equipment and stores were located for the mission.

At the extreme rear of the shuttle was the pressurised release room where all of the comings and goings from the shuttle would take place. As

Marius climbed into his protection suit, J.D. and Travis Harnessed one of the individual release pods to the crane mechanism and rolled it into position in the release room. When he was fully suited, Marius made his way into the room and into the release pod. He stood there in the small glass structure and allowed himself a moment to consider what was going to happen during the next few minutes. He was to be the first of his species to breathe the air of a different planet. He knew that this was indeed an honour and in all likelihood his name alone would probably stand out in the history books for years to come as the first. He knew that no one was any more important to this mission than anyone else but he was also aware of the naivety of the media and of the history makers, after all someone's name had to represent the first, and it might as well be the name of Marius Hatch as anyone else's.

After collecting himself, he knew that he was ready and gave the signal to the other two who had now positioned themselves at the control panel. On his signal J.D. pressed the button.

"Inner door sealed and secure, equalising inner and outer pressure.....pressures equalised, flooding escape chamber"

As J.D. commentated on the procedures the actions were played out before him. It took approximately four minutes for the inner chamber to become fully flooded and through the clear water he could clearly see Hatch in his pressure suit patiently waiting to be released into the open sea.

"Inner chamber now completely flooded, opening outer doors" With these words he activated the main outer doors that led to the outside and to the surface of this strange new world.

Two doors, the perfect shape of the body of the shuttle swung silently upwards and outward, opening the escape chamber to the sea. Pressing down on one of the control peddles with his foot; Marius activated the winch mechanism that would allow the escape pod to rise to the waters surface.

Now that he was free of the confines of the ship, all of his ponderings had now disappeared, and he was now taking in the wonders of the environment in which he now found himself. Cocooned in this glass box, little bigger than himself, he was, in effect, travelling upwards in a bubble. He could see virtually nothing except what was highlighted in the beam of his torch light, an occasional fish or some vegetation would pass in and out of view. He felt a little trepidatious as to what he might see or what might see him; after all he was effectively alone in a strange environment, who knew what was lurking in these depths.

The journey seemed to take for ever but in reality it was little more than a few minutes, and as the pod neared its destination and broke the water line Marius watched as the clear saltwater ran down the outside of the glass in rivulets, leaving the unit standing on the surface of the sea. He then reached for the control pad located on his left arm and opened a communication channel to the shuttle.

"I have reached the surface and I am ready to commence environment testing, over"

In his earpiece he could hear the captain's voice, "Roger Mr Hatch, carry on"

With that he looked down at his feet and located the pedal to open the escape pod. He found himself feeling a little apprehensive as the glass panel above his head slid backwards and folded down against the back wall of the pod, and as the sides sank into and below the surface of the water. He felt a little disorientated as he stood in the night air alone in the dark. He was a single, solitary figure, standing on a vast sea, alone and vulnerable. He once again reached for the control panel on his left arm and started about confirming the status of the atmosphere. Systematically he checked the air content to verify that it was indeed suitable to sustain their needs, having done that he reported back to the captain.

"Confirming the status of the atmosphere sir, I am now going to remove my breathing apparatus" With this he proceeded to remove the small mask that had covered his nose and mouth. Slowly, he closed his eyes and took one long, deep breath in. At the apex of his breath he opened his eyes and allowed the feeling of total relief to consume him. Now breathing freely and deeply he started to take in his surroundings.

To all intent and purpose, he was now standing freely on the surface of the ocean looking around, he could see nothing but the vast emptiness of the night. The only thing visible was the feint outline of land which was picked out by small, almost barely visible orange flecks of light that he could see spaced sporadically along the shoreline. In his estimation they were about one to one and a half miles away from his present position. It was impossible to ascertain any more information about this place without more technical equipment, but that would have to wait. He looked up to the sky and could see all of the stars twinkling against a black velvety backdrop. Knowing that he would soon be back up there heading for home, he could not wait to start the mission investigations, finish the job and return to normal life. He was aware of the warm night air on his skin and although he was aware that there was much work to be done over the next few days, he wished that he could savour this quiet solitude for a little time longer. He took one more, large sigh of resignation and looked down, located the pedal and pressed it. As he did the glass walls silently slid back into place and the roof repositioned itself. The pod then sank silently back into the water and started the fifty meter journey back to the shuttle.

The cable dragged the pod back to the release room and as it entered, the outer doors swung back into place and sealed him back inside the shuttle. Once the water had been evacuated from the room, Hatch stepped out of the pod and back into the inner room.

"I was monitoring your ascent and I can tell you that we detected no major undercurrents, the natural swell of this ocean is well within working limits so we can now use the pods freely, no need for the safety cable. Also, we have been unable to locate any creature that would pose a threat to us whilst in the pods" J.D. reported. Marius asked whether the information had been inputted into the computer general information file, J.D. said that it had and the three men retired back into the main body of the shuttle.

Back in the cockpit the crew were busy constantly inputting all of the data they were receiving from all of the sensors around the vessel. They were still receiving information from the probes they had released from orbit. Captain Daniels called another briefing conference. They all spun their seats around and faced the centre consoles.

"Right, well so far all of the information we have received holds no surprises, it's more or less what the boffins at home told us to expect. What we do know is quite interesting. Air samples from the probes show no sign of industrial development, no depletion in the ozone layer, and there are no unexpected amounts of toxins in the atmosphere, so we have to assume that the peoples of this planet have not yet reached a point where they indulge in processes of industrial mass production or nuclear usage. Now, we don't know what to expect here so, firstly I think that we should send just two crew members ashore to reconnoitre the area and to report back their findings via the earcoms. No weapons will be issued on this soirée; we don't want any accidents with the locals, so whoever goes will have to be extra vigilant. The earcoms are equipped with universal translators however; they will be of little use until the mainframe has sampled enough of the local language to formulate a basis for translation, the more we hear, the more we will be able to communicate. This will be a covert observation mission, what we are looking for is information concerning normal day to day living and activities here, for example, the clothes they wear, the food they eat, daily activities that sort of thing. Don't forget, the more we know the easier it will be for us to integrate with them without detection. We only have fourteen days so we have to do this quickly and above all we must not disturb the population of this area. We cannot afford to influence them or the environment in any way. The team must remain incognito. Try to get close enough to sample the language, take photographs and generally observe. Do not try to take any samples. This can wait until we can move more freely without danger of detection. I have decided that the first team should consist of Mary and J.D. Daybreak occurs in two hours, computers have given us a possible idea of what type of clothing may be appropriate but in reality we have no idea so my suggestion is that you go with computer simulation and just play it by ear.

So you have less than two hours to prepare check your equipment, make sure that your earcoms and your cameras work, one of you will have to manufacture clothing so decide who and I will check in with you before the off. Travis, take over from Mary and Anne, you cover J.D. Any more questions...well let's get back to work" With this they all resumed their duties.

Mary and J.D. sat in the work room away from the others, and for a while just stared at each other. After a short while Mary started to snigger with excitement quickly followed by J.D. They spun around in their chairs like two schoolchildren, but this was a small extravagance they thought they could afford. Mary was the first to speak,

"Ok if you check the earcoms and cameras I will start to make the clothes" J.D. agreed and the two set to work.

The earcoms that J.D. was now checking were small inter auditory devices that fitted within the ear cavity, virtually undetectable to the eye. They were inserted using a small pole screwed into the outer casing. Once inserted the pole was unscrewed thereby releasing tiny holding clamps that secured the device within the ear canal. The small securing clamps that made tight contact inside the ear allowed the device to decipher the natural vibration of the skull and lower jaw, and convert it into a signal that could easily be transmitted back to control, or to each and every member of the ground force team. Because the device sat within the ear canal, it in turn could also receive, and transmit to control, and the others, any sound within the natural hearing range. J.D. inserted his earcom and continued testing. When he had relayed the test signal from the computer back to himself and he was satisfied, he handed Mary's to her. She put down the material with which she was working and inserted hers into her left ear. He then sent the computer test signal to Mary.

She found it incredibly weird listening to the dismembered voice, it was difficult trying to decide which direction the sound was coming from, it was like having voices in your head, a strange sensation that took a little time to get used to. At this point J.D. spoke. "How does that feel?"

Mary was a little startled as he spoke, it was strange to see him next to her yet hear him inside her head. The volume had to be adjusted to suit Mary, but everything seemed to be fine.

By this time Mary had almost finished one of the sets of clothes and J.D. had started on the cameras.

The first sets of clothes that Mary had completed were, to say the least, not what one would call the height of fashion. They were dour and colourless, made from a rough type of fabric that would without doubt irritate the skin. They had none of the fine finishing of tailored clothes, no hem lines and no button holes. To all intent and purpose they were very roughly made drapes, constructed to the computers design. Mary cringed, J.D. sniggered. He took the clothes and tried to locate somewhere to place one of the cameras. This was not as easy as he had thought it would be. Under his breath he said,

"Where the fuck can I put this thing"

"I heard that" said Mary pointing to her ear, "Oops, sorry I guess I had better be more careful what I say in future"

Jokingly Mary tutted and carried on with the other clothes.

J.D. had located the first camera on the neckline of Mary's tunic and although it was clearly visible they had to gamble that it would not be detected, after all, all information collected so far indicated that the people here had never seen a camera before. Fitting the second camera was easier. This was placed in the rope that secured the headwear that was part of his garb. Just as they were completing their tests Captain Daniels came into the room, and enquired if they were ready. They told him that they only had to get changed and they would be ready to go.

They stood as if on parade in front of Daniels, he inspected them and although he had no idea of what he was looking for he had to assume that, from the computer simulation, they looked fine and indeed as far as any of them could tell, they did. With this, the captain gave them the go ahead and they were on their way.

Travis and Hatch were waiting for them in the control area of the release room and had already positioned two escape pods ready for their departure. Mary and J.D. positioned themselves in the pods and waited for the room to become flooded. These pods were different from the one used by Marius Hatch. They were not tethered by a cable; they were free roaming pods which gave the operator more freedom. They were designed as submersible transport units and were controlled by the use of foot holes which were recessed in the floor of each pod, and were used in much the same way as one would use a surf board, or skis but much more complex. As they waited they looked at each other and each could sense the excitement coming from the other. The water level rose around them and control started to go through the final checks for the earcoms and cameras. On the cockpit Anne Homer could see them both on different monitors. One monitor showed the overall view of the release room and another two displayed the view seen from each of the individual cameras secreted within the costumes of the team. Yet another monitor showed the outside of the shuttle. Eventually the room was filled with water and an orange light came on to signify that the pressure within the room was now the same as outside. Seconds later the outer doors swung open. When they were completely open a second, green light was illuminated. After a few last minute checks Captain Daniels gave them the all clear to go. With the order given both Mary and J.D. grasped the glass handles on the front wall of the pods and transferred most of their weight onto their heels, then, slowly at first, both pods began to rise out of the shuttle. Once clear of the vessel they were free and in total control of the pods. Looking up they could see the blue iridescent outline of the rising sun playing upon the surface of the ocean, and the higher they rose in the water the more they could see around them. These waters teemed with life, a multitude of fish species, as many different shapes and sizes one could imagine. As they broke the surface they only allowed the uppermost few inches of the pods to protrude out of the water. In the distance they could see some vessels out at sea not far from the shoreline, although their purpose was unclear from this distance, they assumed that they were fishermen going about their early morning business. Either side of the glass handles were located small glasslike controls for the pods. They inputted the approximate distance and direction that would take them to the shore and re submerged.

They travelled towards the shore a few inches below the surface of the water to avoid detection, and as they reached their goal, sensors on the underside of the pods bought them to a gentle halt. Once again they raised the pods a few inches above

Alpha 1472

the surface of the water to observe the coastline. What they saw was a beautiful unspoiled beach flanked by soaring cliffs. The waves were gently lapping against the base of the cliffs and a slight breeze was causing the palm trees to wave majestically almost as if in a gesture of welcome. Looking around they could see no one, it seemed to be a totally deserted part of the coastline, this, of course, suited their purpose perfectly. Once they were satisfied that their arrival had gone undetected they raised the pods fully out onto the surface and opened them to their full extent. The roofs of the pods were first to open, then the sides slid silently into the sea. Once in the sea the sides and the roof raised themselves to lie alongside the base forming a much more stable platform for its occupant to work from, it also allowed the craft to come much closer to the shoreline. Using the foot controls the pair brought their craft into shore, as they did so they were extra vigilant, eyes scanned all around for anyone who would see these strange figures gliding effortlessly on the surface of the water. When they got as close to the beach as they could possibly get, they deactivated the pods which then sank the six or so inches to the sea bed, and anchored themselves in place. As they stepped out of the foot holes and into the water they were aware of a continual series of high pitched beeps in their earcoms. This was the locating beacon that would enable them to return to the pods when this particular mission was over. The pair then walked the short distance to the beach, and for the first time since leaving home, they stood on solid ground.

4. Observation.

As they emerged from the shallow water they could feel the warm fine sand cling to their wet feet, it felt good and as much as they would like to have lingered for a while, they knew they had to find cover. At this stage they could not afford to be discovered, at least not until they had seen some of the locals and confirmed that their clothing and appearance would fit in. Along the beach they could see a small outcrop of rocks which they thought may afford them a more sheltered place to hide and to plan their reconnoitre. As they ran along the beach the beeping sound in their ears slowed in frequency until it completely stopped. They could feel their feet drying on the sand and by the time they were safely hidden amongst the outcrop they were completely dry.

The outcrop was a collection of huge jagged boulders that had, sometime in history, been part of a major landslide from the surrounding cliffs. This, however, was not a part of recent history and there was no danger of further subsidence from this rock formation. J.D. was fascinated by the structure of the rocks and spent a few minutes inspecting them. As he came around the back of one particularly huge outcrop, he came across a small cave which stretched back into the cliff base some ten to fifteen feet or so, the cave roof was about seven feet tall and the cave was completely dry.

"Mary, come here"

As he spoke Mary heard him perfectly in her ear and started around the outcrop to meet him. When she found him he was inside the cave with his arms outstretched displaying his find.

"Are you guys getting this" he asked,

"Yes indeed, it looks like an ideal place to use as a shore base" answered Travis, who was bringing the find to the attention of the captain. Daniels looked at the monitors and agreed. "Good find guys"

It was time for them to move on, and so, cautiously they made their way to the back of the beach scrambled over a small hill and began to make their way inland. They had travelled approximately five hundred meters when they were contacted from the shuttle.

"Ok guys its time for you to split up now so decide who is going which way and we will keep in touch individually, J.D., Anne is going to monitor you and Mary you have me" said Travis. With this Mary and J.D. shook hands and started to walk in different directions. Of course they would still be in contact via the earcoms but for the first time they suddenly felt very alone.

As he walked between the trees looking for some sort of path to follow, J.D. was taking in all of his surroundings, the trees, the plants, the little creatures that were flying around, when all of a sudden he disturbed a somewhat larger creature which ran though the undergrowth disturbing the surrounding foliage and giving out a warning shriek. Almost simultaneously J.D. let out a shout of his own and it was obvious that it was a yell of fear. Instantly his head was filled with at least three other voices,

"JD……what's happening? Are you alright? Speak to me……JD"

Somewhat breathless he explained what had happened, told everyone to calm down and realised that although he was feeling somewhat foolish, they had all just had a minor wake up call to the fact that they were in a strange place, and should be on their guard at all times. He bent down, grasped his knees, took two or three deep breaths, stood up shook his head and continued on his way.

The further inland he walked, the more he noticed that the lush greenery was becoming thinner and thinner until finally it almost disappeared completely. He found himself standing on the edge of a topographically different area. In front of him the scene was barren, a rock strewn desert landscape that stretched out in all directions as far as the eye could see. He stood motionless for a while; the sun was starting to get hot, what he wouldn't do for a pair of decent sunglasses, shading his eyes. He scanned the horizon, trying to decide which direction he should go. He bent down and picked up a small handful of sand and threw it up into the air, some of the grains caught on the light gentle wind and flew off just to his right 'well that's as good a direction as any' he thought, and started to walk in the same direction that the breeze was blowing. As he walked the day grew hotter.

He had been travelling for about an hour when he came to the foot of the hill. It was not steep; it just seemed to go on forever, upwards. Thinking to himself that he should have chosen a different direction he started to climb. As he did, the sand under his feet gave way and each step was diminished as his stride sank backwards. The short journey was arduous and exhausting, it seemed never ending, one step forwards, one slide back. But as he reached the top he was rewarded. The summit of the hill gradually gave way to a view that thrilled him beyond. He got to the absolute apex and lay down on his front and observed.

"Can you hear me guys"

He felt a little stupid alone on this sandy hill, no one for miles around talking to himself.

"Loud and clear, go ahead"

"I've come across a big town or city or something can you see it"

The shuttle confirmed that they could and waited for J.D. to speak.

"Could you zoom in on the town and tell me if the clothes we have are going to fit in"

Control tried to get a good picture of the town from the camera located in the headwear that J.D. was wearing.

"John we can't get a good picture unless you can keep your head still"

With that comment J.D. placed his fist in the sand and placed his other fist on top of the first and then placed his chin on top, "Is that better?"

The shuttle said that it was, and that they would apply anti- judder to the images to see if they could get a better image to work from. They had been filming for about forty five seconds when J.D. asked if they had enough to determine whether the computer projection was accurate enough for them to pass undetected amongst the indigenous community. Control confirmed that they had, and that the clothes which they now wore were good enough to pass. He then asked them to describe what they had seen in more detail.

"O.K. well the town that you have found is nothing remarkable, it seems to be little more than a collection of roughly built houses, no particular layout to the town, no discernable road structures and no visible signs of mechanised industry whatsoever. The houses are, in the main, one storey simple dwellings that seem to be built around one larger building that seems to be the centre of the town; we think that this building could be the main authority, if any, of the community, but at this point this is only supposition. It's….err…it seems a little early to see any people but you can relax the ones that we have seen appear to be exactly the same as us two arms, two legs etc..Oh, and only one head which is a pretty good sign. Stand by we are just trying to increase the definition of the images. Here we go, there are some people there that seem to be dressed exactly the same way that you are john, and well, I don't believe it they have the same long hair and, hang on, they seem also to have facial growth like you. John you are going to have no problem fitting in here."

With that J.D. stood up brushed the sand from the front of his robe and started down towards the town.

Mary had been walking in the opposite direction and had heard all of what had been transpiring between J.D. and base. The more she had walked and listened, the more she had become settled, mentally, about the way that they would fit in amongst the locals. By now she was just strolling along taking in all of the smells and views of her surroundings, and although it was quite barren it held a certain fascination for her, somehow it felt comfortable and for want of a better word it uncannily felt like home. This was a feeling that she could not explain to herself, she had certainly never been here before, or even been in a place that remotely resembled her present surroundings, but nevertheless it felt strangely familiar, comfortable. She seemed to have been walking for ages, nothing changing, nothing different, the same landscape, the same lack of vegetation and the same desert. Almost ready to resign herself to the fact that she would find nothing, she stopped in her tracks. In the distance, somewhere, she thought that she had heard something. It seemed to be almost musical, a ringing, clanging sound. She stood motionless, took one deep breath and held it, to prevent her breathing affecting her hearing. After a few seconds she closed her eyes and covered them with her hand and tried to focus all of her concentration on finding the direction of the sound. When she thought that she had located the direction she opened her eyes, briefly looked towards the area in which she thought that the sound was coming from and started off in that direction. As she walked, the sound started to get louder and more distinct. She could now hear that the sound was that of muted bells, the sound that one would expect from bells that were not well formed, exactly like the ones that hung around the necks of animals back at home, and indeed the closer to the sound she came, the more the sound fitted her image. Mary rounded a small outcrop of rock and almost found herself in the middle of a small group of goats. Some of the animals were startled by Mary's sudden appearance and darted off in different directions. One of them caught Mary on her side in his efforts to escape, and sent Mary careering to the ground. Almost as soon as she had hit the floor a figure appeared towering above her, reaching out his outstretched arm to help her to her feet, his face was full of concern for her wellbeing. As he helped her up he was talking to Mary but his words meant nothing to her. His language was one that she nor any of the others had ever heard before, and as he spoke to her the voice recognition software aboard the shuttle was recording and analyzing every syllable trying to formulate some sort of phonetic structure and meaning, searching for anything that the computers could use to begin the basis of a translation for this strange tongue. In the cockpit the main screen had now been designated solely to the purpose in hand. This unexpected encounter had brought forward the need to translate, and as quickly as it had happened, the crew had rearranged the monitors to accommodate this new situation. The views from the cameras that the shore based crew were carrying had been split screen on the big monitor, but now they were being displayed on the smaller screens situated either side of the main central screen. Mary's saviour was still talking to her and still making no sense whatsoever. Travis was watching him on the left-hand side screen and as he was talking the centre screen was feverishly flashing through all known language structures and phonetics to try to construct some form of communication. The man looked somewhat dishevelled. He was unshaven and had long dark hair. The robe in which he was dressed was almost exactly the same as the one which J.D. was wearing, but this one was a faded chalk blue and was somewhat more worn and shabby. Mary noticed that he had a certain unpleasant odour, it was, she decided, a cross between the animals which he tended and a whiff of poor hygiene, a pronounced smell of stale sweat. It was not an overpowering smell but Mary was aware of it. He continued to talk to her.

"Are you guys getting this" asked Mary "because I could sure do with some help here?"

As she spoke Travis could see the quizzical look on the strangers face, it was obvious that he could understand Mary no more than she could him. Travis assured her that the computer was working on the problem but at this moment they needed more conversation to work with. In her ear she could hear J.D. asking if she was alright and if she felt that she was in any danger. She answered him and said that she didn't think that this person was any threat to her. Because she was speaking out loud to J.D. the stranger thought that she was speaking to him, which bought forth more of the strange language, and the computer continued to work. The stranger had sat Mary down on a nearby rock and had started to tend her minor wounds. She had scratched herself on her wrist during the fall and the area had begun to go red, small droplets of blood began to seep though the skin and rest in small globules on the surface. The man held Mary's hand gently and inspected the damage; he said some words and reached for a soft animal skin container that was slung over his head and hung around his side. Looking around he could find nothing to use to clean the wound and so he took the small hide top off the container and poured some of the water onto a corner of his robe and started to bathe the wound. He seemed unconcerned at the sight of Mary's blood and so from this she had deducted that he was seeing nothing out of the ordinary.

"Well it seems that we have the same colour blood"

She said, and the man smiled at her almost as if he understood. Anne Homer agreed. Travis's voice came into her ear telling her that the computer needed more conversation. Mary tried to assist as much as she could by talking to the man. Feeling a little stupid she pointed to herself and said 'Mary'. She then patted her chest and repeated her name. The man looked at her a little confused and shrugged his shoulders. She was not going to give up and so she repeated the action of patting her chest and repeating her name, each time she did so, she pointed at him using a questioning gesture, and asking his name. after about five or six times the man finally realized what Mary was asking and a look of realisation spread across his face, he then said that his name was Aaron and found great pleasure in the fact that, albeit for one word, they had been able to communicate. He then lifted the water container and offered it to Mary and gestured that she should take a drink. Not wanting to offend her new friend she accepted and thanked him. The more that he spoke to Mary, the more the computers were finding translatable words, and each word that the computers thought was recognisable was highlighted on the screen highlighting usable words in orange. These words would take their place in the dictionary that would eventually become the main means of communication with these people. The words on the screen were only computer guesses and were subject to change at any time. Once the computer was satisfied that a particular word was an exact translation the orange light immediately turned to green, and would be locked into the memory. There was no way of knowing when they would have a fully working language bank to refer to, and so, it was imperative that they sample as much conversation as possible.

After he had finished bathing her wound and they had had their fill of the water, Aaron rose to his feet from where he had been sitting, next to Mary. He held out his hand to her and beckoned her to follow him; she stood up and spoke,

"I think he wants me to go with him what should I do"

As she spoke Aaron half nodded, half bowed his head and held out his hand in front of him beckoning some more.

In her ear she could hear Travis telling her to stand by for further instructions. This was a decision he had not got the authority to make, and so he pressed the button that opened the ship wide communication channel.

"Captain, this is Travis, you might want to get in here we have a situation that requires your immediate attention"

Within seconds the captains' voice came through the speakers.

"I'm on my way"

As Captain Daniels walked into the cockpit he could see the image on the screen of the stranger trying to beckon Mary to follow him somewhere. Quickly Travis briefed Daniels on what had happened and told him that Mary needed a decision.

"Mary, this is Captain Daniels. Do you feel that this man means you any harm?"

"No sir, he has been tending the wound that I received when I fell and he has been talking to me for ages. He seems genuine enough, he isn't armed and in any case if he was going to do anything I think he would have done it by now"

As she spoke to the captain, the man looked around to see who it was that she was talking to. He seemed a little confused as he listened to Mary's conversation; he felt that she was talking to someone, but to whom? He knew that it wasn't himself, and the more she spoke, the more he looked around.

"I think that this could be an invaluable opportunity for us, I don't believe that we should waste this chance sir"

Daniels thought for a second,

"Ok Mary but if you get into any trouble we will

get DeVie to you as soon as we can"

Mary thanked the captain and assured him that she would be careful. She then turned to Aaron and said,

"Ok then Aaron, let's go"

He seemed quite pleased that Mary had accepted his invitation, and they started walking along the rough path that had obviously been etched into the ground by the feet of countless goats over countless years. As they walked Mary listened to Aaron talk, he had a soft, warm, welcoming voice that did not seem to fit his rough exterior. She felt comfortable with the whole situation. It was as if for some reason she belonged in this primitive hot environment. Although it seemed that she was not paying any attention to him she was listening carefully to see if she could find any part of his language that sounded familiar to her. But this language base was far too difficult for her to even try to understand, she would have to wait for the computers to decipher and translate it into their own.

Although he had been talking for a long time, and it was obvious to him that Mary had understood nothing of what he had been saying, Aaron continued, probably in the hope that she may understand something and that they would be able to communicate, he was patient, and the way in which he spoke was slow and methodical, and Mary was very attentive to his words.

"Ok Mary here we go"

Watkins said in her ear.

"the computer hasn't yet managed to come up with

a complete language base we need much, much more for that but we have a few basic words that we think may just fit the bill. So, if you are ready I want you to say this, and repeat everything I say syllable for syllable, we don't want any confusion that may get you into trouble are you ready"

Mary said that she was and cleared her throat. "Right, as far as we can make out this should say 'could I have some more water please'. So here we go"

Watkins then repeated the line in the foreign tongue.

"Could I have some more water please?"

Mary cleared her throat once again and said the line as clearly and as slowly as she could.

"Please, some more water I could have"

Aaron suddenly stopped, said something, smiled and reached for the water container and offered it to Mary. The translation was grammatically incorrect but it had the desired effect and in her ear she could hear people congratulating each other and herself. After she had taken a drink she handed the water back to Aaron and they continued on their way. Mary, on behalf of the whole mission had a feeling of excitement and achievement and a general sense that they had made an important breakthrough. The more the computers heard, the better the communication between this race and theirs would become.

J.D. had been listening to the conversation between Mary and the ship, and as he approached the village he did so with a slight smile on his face. He stood for a while on the outskirts of the town, there were only a few houses here, roughly built structures of mud and clay which consisted of a downstairs level and one more level built on top. There seemed to be no specific design to these houses, every one was as individual as the next. Every one exhibited a difference in the building technique that could only have come from the person or persons who constructed them. For the moment he could see no one around. It was quiet and peaceful, and he doubted for the moment that this part of the town was inhabited.

Beyond the outskirts he could clearly see the rest of the town which was built on a hill, and now that he was nearer he observed that the higher up the hill one looked, the better constructed the buildings were. The entire town seemed to be crowned by one impressive looking structure, its design and construction was far superior to the ones further down the hill and it was far more opulent than any he could see in the town. He started to approach and as he did, the solitary figure of a man appeared from one of the dwellings. On the monitors the crew had spotted him and had decided to let J.D. exercise his prowess in the native language. "Ok John, something simple, try this 'Good Morning' and don't forget get it exact"

J.D waved at the man and said "Good morning"

The man yawned, waved back and repeated exactly what J.D. had said. Everyone felt that they were making progress.

They seemed to fit in well, their clothes and their general demeanour did not seem to cause any adverse reactions from the local inhabitants and they had started to feel quite comfortable being here amongst them. J.D. had been wandering around the town for a couple of hours generally observing the people going about their day to day business, it was almost like being an unseen observer allowing him to sit and watch lives revolve around himself as he casually mingled among them.

Occasionally he would nod his head towards someone and greet them with the 'good morning' phrase which was always returned. And other times he would just walk right past a person and look over his shoulder as they passed him, content simply to let that person walk away, oblivious to whom he really was.

At the end of the street he now found himself on, he could see that there was a small gathering of people walking purposefully in one direction, he decided that this was something he should investigate, and so, he followed the throng as they walked towards the large building at the top of the town. As the procession continued, more and more people seemed to join, and soon the gathering had turned into a crowd. The reason for this behaviour soon became apparent as he turned the last corner and found himself standing at the entrance to quite a fair sized market gathering. The hustle and bustle was really quite amazing; it seemed that every inhabitant of the town was here in this one place. It was vibrant and noisy; the air was filled with people eagerly bartering with the stallholders for the best price they could get to purchase their wares. This was the ideal opportunity for the computers to absorb as much of the local language as it could in one easy session. As he walked deeper into the market he was surprised at the speed of life here, it was a complete contrast to anything he had seen that morning, people seemed passionate to the point of fighting to get exactly what they needed for the day. At the centre of the market there stood a stone trough filled with water, around this trough some asses were tethered and were drinking, totally untroubled by what was happening around them. J.D. sat on the ground near the animals and leaned against the cool stone; he sat, and watched for hours. As he observed and listened, so did the computers, and on board the shuttle the main screen flashed orange and green as more and more words were being recognised. Just as he had started to tire of sitting in one place for so long a man kicked his leg and asked how much he wanted for his animals? Before he could get a translation from the shuttle another man had intervened quite angrily and started to shout quickly and irately in his language. John was caught in the middle of an unpleasant exchange and was being shoved from side to side, this scuffle had not gone unnoticed by the people who were within the vicinity. The shuttle was feverishly trying to translate what was happening to J.D. and advised him to get out of there as soon as he could. They told him to use the word 'sorry' as often as he could and make his exit as fast as possible. He did so but not without more abuse and pushing. Eventually he did escape and moved himself to another part of the market. From where he now was, he could still see the furore of the argument and by now it had attracted the attention of some different people, people he had not encountered until now. These men were dressed totally different to anyone he had seen up until now. They wore red, short, lightweight robes under a metal breastplate, on their feet they had sandals which were held in place with leather thongs crisscrossing up their calves. On their heads they wore metal helmets, topped with a black feather crest and hanging at their sides were short swords, whilst some of their number carried long sharpened poles. As the men approached the unrest, two of them drew their swords from out of their scabbards and almost instantaneously the argument was quelled. This was a new and unexpected development for the crew and J.D. was advised to leave the market and find somewhere quieter to continue his observations.

As he walked briskly out of the market and back along the same street by which he made he entrance earlier, he said out loud,

"Will someone please tell me what just happened back there and who the hell were those weird guys with all of the hardware?"

Travis answered him,

"Ok don't say anything just carry on walking and I will try to explain. It seems that the big guy who kicked you wanted to buy your animals and the other guy must have thought that you were trying to make a quick buck by selling something that wasn't yours. That seemed to start the argument, from what we could see here, you got out just in time because the other guys looked like they were the law in town, From the reaction of the people around they are not someone you want to mess with. The strange thing is though, the guys in the uniforms don't seem to have the same facial structure as the rest of the people here, and it's almost as if they are an entirely different breed. We really don't know what's going on yet, but if you see any more of these guys keep well away. To date they seem to be the only threat here. For now take a break and get yourself together, we will replay the video we got and see if we can come up with anything else"

J.D. agreed and found himself a stone bench in the shade of a building and sat down.

"Are you alright"

It was Mary. He assured her that he was fine, and then described to her what the armed men were wearing and told her to be on her guard.

The day had grown hot and he was thirsty. Through the open window near where he was sitting he could hear voices laughing and jeering. He could not understand any of what was being said, but it did not seem to be the normal jovial banter of friends. It was almost as if someone was being belittled, or ridiculed. He tried to pay no attention, he was quite happy to relax and let the computers do all of the listening for him. He was idly running his foot through the dry sand on the floor when he noticed a small disc of metal. He bent down, picked it up and examined it closer. It was a coin, roughly made; it bore the head of a person on one side and on the other was the complete figure of another, each image was circled with strange writings. It was not a perfect disc, it seemed to have been pressed or cast with a circle in mind but the finished product fell well short of the aim. As he looked at the coin a man came out of the building where he was sitting and said something to him. The shuttle spoke to J.D.

"He has just asked you what he can get for you. Say this,' what do you have?"

J.D. did what he was told, and the man read out a list of things that he had,

"well my friend it seems that you have found the local pub, say this 'I'll have a glass of your best please' and lets hope that the coin you found is enough to pay for it"

Within minutes J.D. was drinking the most disgusting drink he had ever had, but for some strange reason he found himself enjoying it. The banter continued inside for the entire time that he sat with his drink; there was much laughter and a fair amount of protestation, albeit from one voice. He finished the beverage, which left a strange taste in his mouth, stood up and placed the cup where he had been sitting, beside it he placed the coin and walked away from the tavern to see what else he could find. The innkeeper went out to collect the empty pot and collect his pay, whether it was enough or not was irrelevant, J.D. didn't stay to find out.

"Listen guys, the captain thinks that you have done enough for today and wants you to return to base so, make your way back as soon as you can" As soon as he heard Travis, J.D. immediately started to backtrack through the town and began to head back to the shore. The heat of the sun had begun to die down now, and as he walked he found time to reflect on the day, as he began his journey back to the shuttle.

Mary asked for a translation to allow her to make her departure from her host, she had had a nice relaxing day, which had bought a welcome break from the close confines of the last few days. Aaron had turned out to be the perfect companion he was kind and welcoming. They had spent most of the day at his house. After returning with the goats he had corralled them into a field and then had taken Mary to meet his wife Beth, and their newborn child who they had named Luke. Mary could see that they were a loving, content family who had been eager to entertain their guest in the best way they knew how, and although the language barrier was a problem, it did not stop these people from accepting her into their home.

The house was simple, it consisted of two floors, downstairs was virtually two rooms one which was open to the outside and another, which to all intent and purpose was nothing more than a store room. The upstairs section of the house was also two rooms. One room was where the family slept and the other was where they lived, cooked, and spent most of their day. Mary had been entertained for most of the day on the roof section which was covered by a rough canopy, which gave much needed shade from the searing heat of the midday sun. On the roof there were a few rustic built chairs and a table, and throughout the whole house the walls were bare accept for the few pots and pans in the kitchen area, and the few trinkets which had been attached here and there to break up the starkness of the decor. She almost didn't want to leave, she felt really quite comfortable with these people and thanks to the sporadic translation she was receiving, had managed to gain quite an insight into the day to day life of a local herder, but the time had come for her to take her leave of them, so she made her excuses and having received her translation she told them that it was time to go and she thanked them for their hospitality. They in turn invited her to return at any time. Aaron offered to walk her back to the place where they had met but she declined, thanked them once again, took her leave and started back to rendezvous with J.D.

As she approached the beach she could see J.D. leaning against the rock formation they had first seen when they came ashore. She waved at him and he waved back and said hello, and although they were still quite a distance apart, the novelty of the earpieces still held a great fascination for them both. Walking across the sandy beach, she was in no hurry, she could talk to john, and at the same time enjoy these last few moments before returning to the shuttle. The closer she came to the sea the stronger she could hear the homing signal in her ear, it was not uncomfortable but it was there. They chatted for a while and then decided that it was time to return. They walked along the sea line and as they did, the signal became stronger and faster until it reached a pitch and speed that told them that they had reached the place where they had left the escape pods. After carefully looking around to see whether they could see anyone, they walked into the sea, located the pods, and placed their feet back into the foot controls. As soon as their feet were properly located the homing signal stopped and the platform rose to the surface. They then manoeuvred the pods back out to sea raised the sides and started back to the shuttle.

5. Ridicule.

Joseph walked into the tavern for his usual daily few drinks. He looked no different from any of the other men here, but when he arrived nearly all of the customers greeted him with a friendly wave or shook his hand. He had made his way through the crowd of people at the inn. He had already noticed that there were more people here than there would normally be. He thought that maybe they were celebrating something that he had forgotten, or had not been invited to, either way he was a little confused by the fact that his quiet afternoon sabbatical had been invaded by all of these people. Of course he knew all of them, but to find them here at this time of day was most unusual.

"Busier than usual Joshua" he said to the innkeeper,

"Morning Joseph, the usual is it" Joseph nodded his head and waited for his drink and an explanation for all the people.

"Yes, its great for business, I must get old Eli to come in every day he is really funny"

Joseph was now more confused than before. Joshua composed himself and told him to listen. He turned around and leaned on the bar with both of his elbows and grasped his fingers together around his stomach.

"Eli, Eli, Joseph is here now tell him what you

have been telling us"

Joshua handed another drink to Eli and encouraged him to recount his adventures.

"Oh Joseph, you should have been there, I've never seen anything like it before in my life."

At this, the entire bar broke out into fits of laughter.

Eli was known to drink a little, and it was generally accepted that since he had arrived in town he had been very secretive about his past. No one knew if he had any family or where he came from. He was an inoffensive sort of bloke who had got to know people around town and had chosen this particular inn to spend as much free time as he could. He lived alone on the outskirts of town, and for a living he would do almost any work that was offered to him on a casual basis. His hygiene was probably not the best, but all in all he was accepted for who he was.

"Joseph, it was like nothing I've ever seen. I left here last night and, ok, I probably did have one more than I should have, but I wasn't drunk. I know when I've had enough but last night I was just merry. It was a hot evening and I wasn't ready to go home, I just needed to go for a short walk to clear my head, so I could get a good night sleep. I was supposed to be at Joab's smithy this morning to work for him today."

He looked over at Joab who raised his glass in agreement and laughed.

"I didn't go because I never got a wink of sleep last night after what I saw. I went out through town past my house and walked down to the sea. I wasn't going to be long; I only had a little oil in my lamp.

Anyway I got to the beach and I sat on the big rock, you know the one I mean, the one I always sit on when I'm thinking. Well it wasn't long before I fell asleep. I suppose I'd been out for about…well not long, when I woke up my lamp had gone out, but it was a clear night and the moon was full so it was still kind of bright out there so it didn't matter. But the thing is… I saw something that was not of this earth, I don't know what it was but it was definitely not from here."

At this there was more laughter which Joshua interrupted and said,

"Hold on, hold on, fellows, please Carry on Eli"
Eli took a large mouthful of his drink and continued.

"Listen, I know you think that I am a little nut's and that it sounds stupid, but I know what I saw. It was fantastic. I woke up and just sat there staring at the sky there wasn't a cloud up there it was as clear as anything, it was beautiful, all of the stars twinkling in the night. Then I saw it. At first I had no idea what it was, in fact I still don't. So I sat there and watched. At first I thought it was just a shooting star but as I watched it got bigger and bigger and it was coming towards me. I was starting to get worried then all of a sudden it changed direction and started to go in circles and as it did, it set on fire, not for long just a little while. The light from the fire lit up all of the sea and then it went dark again. There was a long cloud where it had been, and for a while I lost sight of it. When I saw it again it was heading straight for the sea. Then suddenly there was a great splash and it was gone. I think its down under the water somewhere, but I don't really know"

By the time he had finished his story the entire bar was in uproar, for most of them it was the funniest thing they had ever heard.

At this Joshua went outside. He was gone for a few minutes, and then he returned to pour a drink for a customer who had stayed outside. When he returned for the second time he stood back next to Joseph and asked if he had missed anything whilst he had been serving the stranger, Joseph said that he hadn't and Joshua told Joseph about the newcomer outside. "A really strange man with an equally strange accent, probably from out of town"

He then turned his attention back to Eli.

"So Eli, what exactly did it look like then" he asked.

"Well...its hard to describe it was like... erm...like...like a chariot, yes that's it, like a chariot on fire, screaming through the sky". This description bought about the loudest round of laughter yet. He continued,

"Yes screaming through the sky heading towards the sea and when it hit it was like a hundred pure white horses jumping for the sky"

By now the laughter was louder than ever and Eli had realised that he had got a captive audience and if he milked the situation he could get free drinks all day. By now his imagination was kicking into high gear. He needed to prolong this situation and so he started to elaborate.

"And then...and then I found myself being lifted by a strange force into the sky, towards the heavens.

I could not resist, I fought but it was useless, I just carried on going up. I could see all of the town and the next. I shouted and shouted but no one heard me. It must have been hours before the great unseen hand bought me back to the shore and set me down on the beach. I was so frightened I just ran and ran. I even left my lantern on the beach" he paused for a while, thought to himself and then said out loud, "must get a new one…" he continued, "and the next thing I knew I was sitting outside waiting for Joshua to open".

Everyone in the bar just laughed, Eli knew that he had gone too far with the hand thing but he had said it now and he already felt too foolish to even try to take it back.

"I know you don't believe me and I'm not asking you to, but I know what I saw and I tell you, it was not of this land, it was something beyond anything we know about, and I for one am going to be watching everything from now on".
With this the innkeeper went outside again to see if the stranger required any more to drink. When he returned he had a big smile on his face, he went back behind the bar and spoke to Joseph.

"Today just gets better and better"

"How come" asked Joseph,

"Well you know the stranger I was on about outside, he only had one drink and look what he left for payment"

He flipped the coin in the air put it between his teeth and then slipped into his purse.

"Oh happy day"

6. Taking stock.

Both Mary and J.D. had taken time to shower and freshen up after returning to the shuttle and were now seated, alongside the rest of the crew, around the monitors in the cockpit. It was a relaxed atmosphere for a debriefing session, each of them had drinks and snacks on their tables and for the moment they were engaging in friendly chit chat which continued until Captain Daniels joined them and brought the meeting to order.

"For a first outing I think we have had a highly successful day, however, reviewing the data and watching the playback from both cameras there is one major area of concern that we need to address. In this region there seems to be people who to all intent, seem to be the indigenous inhabitants of this land. From Mary's experience, and the general outlook of things observed by J.D. they seem to be a peaceful, pre industrial race, with no signs of any technology whatsoever. The general consensus among the crew is that these people, if we do not provoke them, will cause us no problems. But the other ones that you nearly fell foul of J.D. are a bit of a mystery at the moment. They seem to be the law givers of this nation, their uniform type of dress would indicate either some form of police, or military organisation exists here and so, we all need to be on our guard when we are interacting with anyone here. Don't forget we do not know the laws here and I don't want any one falling foul of them. Worst case scenario would be being taken into custody and missing our departure. We only have one chance and we can't afford to wait for anybody.

Both Mr Hatch and Mr Watkins have now deployed the signal booster dish which is now floating sub surface directly above us, and now we have direct contact with home. The signal is not as good at the moment as we would have hoped but Mr Hatch assures me that it is possible to further boost the signal, and will resume work on this problem after this meeting.

Mr Watkins you have been working closely with the translation banks what is the status at the moment."

The captain then handed the meeting over to Travis.

"Well, we have had a great day and we have a forty five percent working translation base, not quite enough for the computer to go automatic yet. I have it set at seventy five percent. The translations are not yet perfect but the computer has extrapolated enough of the local language to give us a working structure, obviously the more we hear the better things will get. There were a few anomalies and these occurred when we encountered the military type guys, there were a few odd words that did not fit in with the language structure that is being used by most of the inhabitants. We will keep our eye on these but early theories include the fact that these are people from an entirely different region which means that with their air of authority, it is entirely possible that they are, or once in recent history, were an invading force, and that they form part of some sort of military rule in this area. But this at the moment is only a theory. I believe that our next visit ashore will give us enough for the translations to become automated."

It also seems that our arrival did not go completely unnoticed. From the conversations that were overheard when JD was outside the inn, it would seem that one individual witnessed our arrival. However, we have been lucky on this occasion because his story has been ridiculed by the locals and we do not expect any repercussions from this unfortunate incident".

"Thank you Mr Watkins, any questions anyone." Asked the captain and when no one offered any he continued.

"Whilst john was ashore I asked Anne to take over the geology station and I think she has some findings, Anne"

Although Anne homer was the medic for this mission she was also a fine geologist and taking over the geology duties was almost second nature to her. She cleared her throat and addressed the rest of the crew. "Thank you sir, I've been examining the topography of the area we are now in. The ledge on which we are now resting is a solid bedrock and as such is quite stable, however the cliff face which rises to the port side of the shuttle has several large boulders which are not so stable, they shouldn't however give us any problems but we should be aware that they are there, and caution should be exercised at all times. It would take quite a force to dislodge them and unless we experience an earthquake or similar, we should be OK. The monitors do not indicate any seismic activity at this time, nor have I detected any wave movements that would worry us. I will ask J.D. to check my findings to confirm that things are alright."

The captain thanked Anne for her research and indicated that John should check things out. He then turned his attention to Marius Hatch.

"Mr Hatch do you have anything to add at this time." hatch said that he did not, and the captain then instructed him to draw up a duty roster for the coming day. J.D. raised his hand, he was acknowledged, and the captain invited his comments.

"One thing sir, I think that it was lucky that I found that coin today, and it may be useful for any of us out there to be able to purchase things should we need them, if nothing else it would help us to integrate a little better."

There were general nods from around the circle and the captain agreed that it would indeed be a good idea. The problem was how to obtain these coins. It was not a good idea to steal them, they couldn't go to a bank, and they knew no one they could borrow any from. A lively discussion ensued culminating in the suggestion that they should try to manufacture their own. The few coins that they might need for the next few days would hardly affect the economy of this planet and although it was in effect forgery, it was something that Daniels thought he could sanction in this instance. He gave the job of making the coins to Travis, and said that he would confirm the use of them through control when he spoke to them later. He also added that when Travis was making the coins he should use the images recorded that day by J.D.'s camera to ensure that whatever they used was as authentic as was possible, they could ill afford to be questioned on their use by the authorities. They had to minimise the risk of detection, whilst they were here. His final instruction for this meeting was that they should each transfer all of the data collected this day to the T file, ready for transfer back to control. Daniels then asked one final time if there was anything else, and bought the meeting to an end with a few welcome words to the crew.

"Well if that is all, I think you have all deserved a couple of hours to yourselves, we will resume duties at 20.00 hours ship time"

With this he stood up and retired to his private quarters. The rest of the crew went into the recreation area and each chose their own form of relaxation.

In his quarters, Daniels slipped off his boots and sat at his desk. The room was small but functional; the walls were padded, as was the rest of the ship and the only concession to home comforts was a family photograph taped above the computer terminal. He punched a few keys on the keyboard and the screen flickered into life. On screen were several icons one of which was named captain. He touched the icon on the screen which in turn opened another file containing more icons. When he touched the communication icon he was presented with a security panel requesting a code. On the keyboard he punched in a security number which would connect him to control back home. Within seconds the speakers began crackling into life. He had no problems with the others hearing his conversations, this room was completely soundproof. "1472 Alpha to control, are you receiving me over"

He waited for a few seconds before repeating himself, again he received no answer. He tried a third time and this time he was rewarded with an answer from home. The reception was sporadic at best, it was almost unintelligible and he struggled to hear the person at the other end. He tried to make a few adjustments to clear the signal but until Hatch had refined the settings, he knew that this was probably the best that he could hope for

"1472 this is command, awaiting your report over"

At least he had some sort of communication with them and because this is exactly what had been expected, he had prepared a video report to be sent with the transmission reports that they were expecting. The first thing that he did was to transmit the daily report, should this line of communication break down there would be no way to get the information back home. As soon as this was done he asked to speak to Major Hooton or Major General Stewart. The person on the other end said that he should stand by, and transferred the communication to Major Hooton.

"Hooton here, go ahead Daniels" Was the reply or at least he though that was the reply. The channel was so bad that most of what was said was eaten up by static interference which caused the message to break up and crackle. As frustrating as it was it was the best they had at the moment.

"I hope you can hear me sir, we have encountered a minor problem here, nothing drastic just a little something we overlooked. The people of this planet use a form of currency to purchase goods and services. We at present, do not have any of this currency, but we think we can manufacture it right here on board. I need your permission to go ahead and use the coins we make. Its all in my report but on this one I need an answer within the next few hours, or at least before our next visit ashore"

For a while it seemed that the entire system went dead, Daniels was just about to make further adjustments when the speakers sprang back into life startling him just a little.

"Can't give you an ans...n that one at the mo...nt. we will get b...ou later with an answer...con...t..."

He had trouble deciphering this last communication and had to replay it several times to decide that it was 'can't give you an answer on that one at the moment. We will get back to you later with an answer. Control out. Once he was satisfied, he severed the link with control and switched the computer to standby mode, swung his feet onto his couch, closed his eyes and relaxed.

Generally the shuttle was quiet at the moment, all of the crew had chosen pastimes that made little or no noise, the only person that was conspicuous by his absence was Marius Hatch. Everyone else had taken the captains advice and used the time to relax; Hatch was the only one working. He wanted to get the communications network up and running perfectly. He paid no attention to the others relaxing, and felt no desire or need to follow their lead, and no anger towards them for not wanting to work. This was just the way he was, and probably would always be. He was just one of the few individuals who did everything by the book, and beyond.

As they relaxed the atmosphere was good, everyone was doing their own thing. Mary and Anne had once again made drinks for everyone, and had taken one through to Hatch, who had been working in the cockpit area. The two women were now sitting in comfortable chairs chatting.

"I know I saw it on the monitor but what is it really like out there" asked Anne. Mary gave a little thought to what she would tell her.

"Its like nothing I have ever seen or experienced. The first thing you notice is the air. It smells so clean, fresh, and when you breathe it its like you want to breathe it forever. It fills your lungs and you just know it's so clean, no pollutants whatsoever. It's worth going just for the air. And the water is crystal clear; when we stepped off the pods it was so warm like a comfortable bath. And the beach, oh the beach is fantastic, no one around for miles and great open stretches of the most golden sands I have ever seen. It was like having your own private place with no one to bother you. The sun is hot around midday, but I for one could learn to cope with that. Away from the beach it's a bit barren and dusty and that makes you feel a bit dirty, let me tell you. I really needed that shower when I got back. But all in all it was a magical experience."

Anne was hanging on every word, and the more she listened the more she wanted to go. She then asked Mary about the people and the town.

"Well the town is nothing to look at, just a load of mud huts really but the people, well the ones I met, were great. We had a real problem with the language but even though, you could tell that they were genuine. They gave me a feeling of belonging, it was if I was a long lost friend or relative or something. They didn't need a lot, it was as if, this is their life and they were content to be who they are, Simple folk with simple needs. They had their little family and to see them together was a joy, you could tell that they really wanted to be with each other, it made me think of my David. I am enjoying this mission but I can't wait to get back home."

Anne agreed that she was looking forward to the return journey also. For a while the two women sat in silence thinking about what Mary had just said. Anne turned to Mary and almost in a whisper said.

"So how long is before you hear the pitter-patter." Mary blushed and smiled at the same time.

"We found out just before David's birthday so next year we will either go out for a meal or spend his birthday in the delivery suite"

They both laughed and Anne said that either way it would be a great present for him.

At this, the captain's voice came over the intercom "Sorry people but we have a lot to prepare for tomorrow so back to work. Daniels, out."

With this, the recreation area was cleared and everyone returned to their duties.

7. Obtaining the past.

He sat for a while in his quarters contemplating his next move. Things were certainly running smoothly to this point, but he was eager to push on with the mission. Because he, and consequently the crew, already had their mission briefs, they had plenty to be getting on with. There was, however, an element of the mission which was on a strictly need to know basis and to find out exactly what this was, he had to be in touch with control back on the home world as often as possible.

He reached over to his computer terminal and was just about to make contact when they actually contacted him.

"Ground control to Daniels over"

It seemed an abrupt impersonal greeting from home but it was efficient and to the point. Daniels replied, and was informed that the conversation was being passed to Major Hooton and that he was to stand by.

"Hello Jason this is Peter how is it all going"

Suddenly the conversation had taken on a more personable air which relaxed Daniels. He relaxed onto his bunk to take the rest of the call and as he did so, he told Hooton that all was well and things were going to schedule.

"Is this a secure call" Hooton asked. Jason leaned over to his console and activated the privacy button which bypassed all records of this conversation being recorded and stored on the computers. Having done so, he assured Hooton that they were indeed now having a private conversation.

"OK, here's the deal. The currency thing is probably an unnecessary evil but we have no objections so there are no problems there, you can go ahead with that one but there is something more pressing. I am going to give you a code that will release a mission brief held within your own orders. To access this you will need to click on the mission logo on the opening screen while holding down the numbers 1472. This will present you with a login screen where you will enter this code

'1472/106/daniels/recovery'

I need you to read these new orders and get back to me. Do you understand?"

He assured him that he did and signed off. Feeling that this could take some time, he got up from his bunk and made himself a drink, then sat at his desk to see what had, up until now, been kept from him.

He inserted his ROM into the computer and was almost immediately presented with the opening screen and the mission logo. It was a representation of the ship featuring two ellipses to represent the separate orbits of the two worlds with 'Alpha 1472'. Underneath the image, was the exact same logo that had been embroidered onto their uniforms? Firstly he placed his cursor over the logo and before clicking it, he made sure that he had the numbers 1, 4, 7 and 2 firmly depressed. It was a little awkward but when he was comfortable that he had the correct combination he clicked the logo. The computer whirred and clicked and after a few seconds he entered his code and the screen revealed its secrets. The familiar face of Major Peter Hooton appeared, over his face was superimposed a small play button. Daniels took a sip of his drink, placed it thoughtfully on the desk and began to watch the video.

"Captain Daniels this recording is for your eyes only, what you are about to told is top secret and should not be discussed with any member of your crew. I am sure that as a matter of course you have researched all of the Alpha missions and have found nothing untoward since the 106 mission. 106 were reported as being one of the most tragic accidents of our space program since its inception. This, however, was not strictly true. Yes it is true that no-one returned, and it is also true that we lost three good men who have since become legends. But what became of them is unknown and this forms part of your new mission. We have known, for generations that Epsilon Omega falls within our orbit path every two and a half thousand years or so, and 106 was in fact your predecessor. Their mission brief was very different from yours. They were a crew of three who had joined the academy from orphanages across the globe. They were, originally kids who showed outstanding degrees of learning, and for their age they were leaps and bounds ahead of their contemporaries. The Alpha project had been alerted to their abilities, and after extensive checks to determine that they had no families; they were taken into the project. At first there were six of them selected but only the best three were selected to stay with the project. The corps took these kids and nurtured them through their education, grooming them specifically for the 106 mission. By the time Epsilon Omega was due to enter our orbit the crew were aged about twenty one years old. They had been kept segregated from society, the only thing they knew, was how to do the job they had been selected for. You see, Jason, Alpha 106 was always meant to be a one way ticket; there was no return for this crew. I know that you are sitting there a little confused by this but all will become apparent".

Daniels paused the playback and took another sip of his drink which by now had become a little tepid. He knew that there was a part of this mission about to rear up that he had not expected. He reached over and restarted the video.

"At the time that 106 was due to embark upon its mission our world was going through a little turmoil, there was unrest and our governments were finding things a little hard to control. The people needed heroes, something to look up to, and something to give people common ground and more importantly the populous needed a focus. The crew of 106 were just that. Not only did they become an integral part of our history, they also had a specific purpose to fulfil. This is the main reason that this must remain confidential. If the truth were to be revealed it would mean re-writing all of the history books, not to mention the general world wide feeling if people found out that for millennia they had been lied to. But enough of that back to the purpose of 106. To all intent and purpose the crew were little more than scribes, their sole purpose was to observe and to keep a diary on their findings. They were to find out as much about this planet as was possible and to create records. The problem we have is that we do not know whether they survived or whether they really did perish as history would have us believe. Their take off from this planet went according to plan and we maintained contact right up until the point they had initiated their landing procedure. Their craft orbited Epsilon Omega as planned, and they committed themselves to enter into the atmosphere. Two minutes into the manoeuvre we lost all communications. What happened, no one knows and all future connection to Alpha 106 was lost, so we have no idea what became of them. What we do know is what their mission brief was. Their brief was to simply document everything they could about the planet. There was another problem however, the life expectancy of the crew was at best 120 years, and so to continue the mission, the second part of their brief was to recruit new members to the crew from the indigenous peoples to continue their work. What we need to find out now is if they actually survived and just how good those kids were.

This is how it works. When you have finished with this report you will contact me and I will give you your next set of instructions. They will in no way detract from the mission as it stands…consider this a little extra adventure".

Daniels watched as the words 'End Report' flashed across the screen. He picked up his cup and drank the rest of his drink, which by now was cold. Walking from his quarters into the main rest room his mind was full of what he had just heard. He refilled his cup and quietly spoke to Hatch,

"Listen, something has come up that I have to deal with urgently so I don't want to be disturbed for the next hour or so. Any problems you are in command".

Hatch acknowledged the order without question and returned to what he was doing.

As he entered his quarters he turned and secured the door then sat at his desk to contact command. Very soon a secure link with Major Peter Hooton was established.

"Hello Jason, are you ready for your instructions". He asked. Daniels said that he was and sat back in his seat to receive his orders for the new part of the mission.

"OK, this is a need to know situation so the fewer people aware of this information the better. We have selected John De Vie and Mathew Watkins to be your operatives for this, so as soon as we are finished you will have to brief them and for god's sake make sure that they understand the importance of secrecy, and the delicate nature of what you are about to undertake.

The original mission instructions were that all records made should be sealed and stowed safely away from discovery. Into each of the containers used there should be placed a homing beacon and that the containers should be hermetically sealed to protect against deterioration, so if there are any surviving documents they should still be in a readable state. Now, we are aware that the crew were not equipped with enough beacons to last a millennia, but we are hoping that enough survived to allow us to get a lock on them, and for you to recover the information. To make this happen we have installed into Alpha 1472 a device which will deliver a long range tracking device into a geo-stationary orbit above your position. The firing mechanism for this probe runs directly through the heart of the ship. The probe is pre-programmed and all you need to do is to activate it. Once in orbit it will transmit data to the mainframe. This data can only be accessed by us, and by yourself. Once the beacons have been located you will despatch your team to make the recovery. We are aware that you will need specialised equipment that you believe that you are not carrying, but if you take a look in the aft equipment room of the shuttle, you will find a floor panel located to the far back left of the room next to the departure chamber. Lift the floor covering and unscrew the floor plate this will reveal a locker that has a computerised locking device it is only accessible by inserting your dog tag, and your thumbprint. This locker contains all of the equipment that we think you will need for the mission. A lot of this tack is brand new and so on each of JD's and Watkins mission ROMs' there is detailed instruction to their use. The release code is the same as yours was. Their codes are held within your orders, as are the firing codes and instructions for the probe. The probe will stay in orbit for as long as we need it and then you will destroy the probe when you leave. Do you have any questions at this time?"

Daniels said that he did not, bid his commander

farewell and began to set about his task.

The two crewmen were busying themselves with various tasks concerning the forthcoming shore based foray when the captain's voice came over the intercom.

"JD, Watkins could you please come to my quarters immediately"

Without hesitation the two men stopped what they were doing and headed towards the captain's room. JD knocked on the door and they were requested to enter. Once they were inside Daniels told them to shut the door and motioned them to take a seat on his bunk. The room was hardly big enough for one, let alone to hold a meeting in but this was the most private place on the ship. When they were seated Daniels stood up turned around and locked the door, then re-took his seat, and began to address the men.

"I'm sorry to have to talk to you here but what I am about to tell you must go no further. I have to remind you that you have both signed the standard secrecy contract at the start of this mission. We know that you did not think that this would extend to your fellow crew members but you have been selected for an extra mission that may or may not have far reaching consequences for our entire world".

With this he began to outline his previous conversation with the Major, and briefed them on what would be expected of them.

They would be expected to locate any documents that may exist, to open any containers, and to digitize all of the information held within. The document would then be resealed and left in situ for future generations. The information that they would obtain would become part of a highly protected library of information that had been compiled by the military since the dawn of time. As he spoke to them, Daniels activated the launch procedure for the probe. As he pressed the button the entire craft was subjected to a mild shudder which prompted Hatch to communicate with the captain.

"Sir we have just experienced something that has caused the ship..." Daniels interrupted him mid sentence, "Yes sorry Marius that was me just doing some adjustments, orders from command, should have warned you first" the conversation paused for a second, then Hatch said, "roger that sir....out" Neither Daniels nor Hatch believed for a second that it was the truth, but Marius had to accept the feeble explanation.

Daniels continued the briefing,

"The one strange thing is the fish. For some reason the way the original crew were instructed to identify each other was with the call sign fish, fish one, fish two, fish three, we don't know why, it may be something or nothing, but I am to brief you on everything that we know"

At the end of the meeting the captain gave each of them their release codes for the extra information held within their ROM discs and told them how to access the extra files. Finally, he asked if there were any questions. JD spoke first,

"How are we to keep this from the rest of the crew? This is a pretty small place sir"

"And how are we to get the equipment off the

ship?" added Watkins. Daniels said that they should leave these details to him and that they were just to concentrate on their mission ahead. Most of everything they needed to know was contained within their brief.

"We will meet one more time before your depart, so if that is all, you two have some homework to do"

With this the two men left the captain's quarters and returned to their own.

It seemed that the fact that JD and Watkins were billeted together was far from a coincidence. They entered their room and each sat behind their monitors and began to study their briefings. They sat in silence for about an hour, each of them ingesting all of the information they would need. They finished reading at about the same time, closed down the programme sat back in their chairs and looked at each other; neither of them could believe the web of lies and untruths that had been propagated by their governments and their military. Little was said between them they were both aware that anyone could be listening to any conversation they may or may not have. They simply contacted their captain and arranged their final meeting.

When they were all together again behind closed doors Daniels addressed them for the last time.

"The equipment locker is located under the floor panel to the left of the release pods, I have contacted command and added new release codes to the locking device. You are to load the contents into one of the pods and you two will travel in the other. I know that it will be a tight squeeze but we have no other option. You will travel under the cover of darkness, get your kit ashore and take it to the cave you found JD. Get yourselves set and await further instructions."

As he spoke a communiqué came through from command. Daniels answered the call.

"Jason, this is Peter are you alone"

He said that he was with JD and Watkins, the Major was OK with this, it could save a little time.

"We have just received information from the probe and its good news we are picking up a signal, very feint but its there and it is about one hundred and thirty clicks south of your position so if you are ready you have a green light to commence your mission, good luck guys Hooton out"

Although the communication was short and abrupt they knew that command was probably a hive of urgent activity and that time was indeed short.

The two men were instructed to go directly to the departure bay and ready themselves to leave. Daniels was to call an emergency meeting of all other staff in the main control room of the shuttle to provide a diversion while JD and Watkins left the vessel. Everyone knew their roles and on the captain's orders they began.

While the rest were being occupied by Daniels the two men located the locker and JD inserted his dog tag into the slot. He then offered his thumb to the small screen and the locker clicked and then slowly opened. They knew from their brief exactly what was inside, and they set to loading its contents into the first pod. When it was done they set the controls to tandem and got themselves into the other. It was indeed a tight squeeze but they managed it with little room to spare. The short journey was going to be uncomfortable but it would only last a short time. When they were ready JD pressed the button to automate the departure. They were on their way.

8. Recovery.

They had arrived on the shore, stowed their equipment in the cave and were walking back to where they had left the pods. There was about thirty minutes until sunrise and a light breeze was in the air. They could feel the effects of the gentle wind below their knees where they had been standing in the water. It had produced a chilling effect causing the small hairs on their legs to stand on end as the water evaporated. In the distance they could see the sky changing colour, becoming ever lighter as daytime replaced the night. It would soon be light enough for them to start out on this new part of the adventure. Watkins pressed the remote control in his hand which signalled the pods to automatically return to the shuttle, and then they returned to the cave.

They busied themselves preparing for the journey. Unpacking several cases they first assembled the mountain bikes that had been provided. They were lightweight, alloy framed with power assisted motion units which allowed for speedier travel over all terrains. The bikes had been finished in strange paintwork that seemed to reflect their surroundings; it was, for a mountain bike, brilliant camouflage. Alongside the bikes there was a multitude of gadgets, some that would be of use, some that would be surplus to requirements, however, all of them would be taken to ensure that any situation could be successfully dealt with.

In their earcoms they were contacted from the ship.

"JD, Watkins, this is Daniels, I have routed communications so that only we three can hear the conversation, we can hear everyone else but they cannot hear us. I need you to set out in the next twenty minutes. You need to push the bikes and wear local dress until you are sure you are beyond anyone's sight. I have patched the location of the documents through to your wrist locators, so if you activate them now you will get a general idea of the direction in which you need to travel. Are you ready to go on my mark?" Asked the captain. The two travellers said that they were and waited for the signal. While they were waiting they dressed themselves in the robes that were usual for this area. In what seemed like the blink of an eye they could hear the captain's voice in their ears. It was the command to leave, and with that they were on their way.

Their senses were heightened as they left the comparative security of the cave; they were of course fearful of being discovered even before they had begun. They started out along a well worn path in the direction indicated by their location devices. From any distance it should have looked like two men strolling along a path on an early morning stroll. Closer, however, it would have been clear that it was two men pushing strange contraptions which would have immediately raised anyone's suspicions. Fortunately there was no one in sight, which in itself calmed them somewhat.

One hour into their journey they came to an outcrop

of rocks which was enough to conceal them from any prying eyes that may have been around. The bikes were propped up against one large boulder and the two men crouched down, both on one knee. They pulled up the sleeve of their robes to reveal the locators and switched them to scanning mode. This mode detected heat sources within the vicinity. What they were searching for were heat signatures of ninety eight point six degrees which they knew was the body temperature of the local inhabitants. Having found no signatures present they began to discard their robes. Placing them into a security bag, they secreted them just under the surface of the sand, signals from the probe had suggested that the terrain they would be travelling through was unpopulated and they would not need this costume, also, the weight of the garments would slow them down. They set a location point of their clothing on their wrist pieces. They now stood dressed in knee length, tight fitting shorts, tight short sleeved shirts, peaked caps, sunglasses and backpacks. Having set their wrist locators to automatically scan for heat signals, they set out. Mounting their bikes, they began to pedal their way across the desert terrain. After they had gained a good speed they activated the cruise control from the switch on the handlebar and the cycles took over the arduous task of transporting them onwards. The power pack should give them about twelve hours of power.

The heat was searing as they approached midday they had not experienced such temperatures but they continued on towards their goal. The signal strength on their locators was getting stronger and the estimated time of arrival was now reading forty five minutes. Thanks to their mode of transport they had made good time and believed that they would have ample time to complete their mission. The plan was for them to stay and work overnight, and through the next day, returning back to the shuttle on the following evening. Although they had been chatting to each other during their journey, they had had no need to contact the ship. It was kind of liberating just talking to each other without the rest of the crew being privy to what was being said. They could, however, hear all that had been going on with the other crew members throughout the day and were aware of the progress being made. It was time for them to make a progress report, and so, they attempted to contact Daniels. There was no reply. They made several attempts, still no reply. They would continue on their way until the captain was free. After all, theirs was a simple mission, locate and record documents. What could go wrong?

Three strangers had spotted JD and Watkins and had been tracking them for about an hour. They had unwittingly evaded the heat sensors by making sure that their body signature was concealed behind rock surfaces thus avoiding detection. The two travellers had no idea that they were being observed. They had arrived to within two hundred metres of their goal and had dismounted from their cycles, and propped them up against a rock face. Standing a couple of meters away from the outcrop they stood, consulting their locators and were just about to attempt to make contact with the shuttle when the first of the strangers pounced. He had made his way to a ledge above their position seconds before, and leaped down onto them. Both of their locators recognised his signal and set off alarms to alert them of his presence, but it was too late he was already in mid flight and moments later he was upon them. The force with which he knocked them to the ground was enough to render Watkins momentarily unconscious. JD struggled with his assailant and eventually made his escape. As he ran away from the attacker he reached for his belt and detached his tazer and fired it into the man's torso. He instantly went into muscular spasm and collapsed to the ground. JD turned to go to the aid of Watkins but before he could reach him the two other men appeared as if from nowhere. One of them ran to attack Watkins and the other was heading for J.D.

J.D took a stance in the sand and prepared himself to receive the attacker. The captain's voice came into his ear.

"What is happening…report"

JD stood there face to face with the other man and quietly said,

"Sir, we are under attack. Stand by"

Daniels could hear the panic in his voice but was helpless to assist, he had no choice but to wait and listen to the ensuing commotion.

It was a stand off. Neither man willing to commit to the attack. Neither sure of the others weaknesses, or of their strengths. Moments passed like minutes when suddenly the stranger ran towards John. J.D. managed to dodge the first attack, or so he thought.

As they passed, the assailant deftly dropped to the ground, as he did so his legs entwined with J.D.'s and brought him to the ground. With the next expert manoeuvre the man had flipped himself onto John's back and had grabbed his head. J.D. was now completely pinned to the ground face down, one hand firmly gripping the back of his head and the other held tightly against his mouth. He was both immobilised and mute. It felt as though this attacker was poised to twist his neck and snap his spinal column. He was helpless, and in blind panic he reached out into the sand and for some reason he drew the crude outline of a fish. He could feel the tension on his neck, as it was twisted to its full extent, the pain was almost unbearable, and then, slowly the pressure was released and the hand which had held the mouth was repositioned to allow J.D. to breathe and to talk.

Demandingly, the man asked what this sign was. J.D. had no idea what was being asked of him. Suddenly in his ear he heard the welcome voice of the captain.

"FISH, just say fish"

JD then heard a second voice, much calmer and matter of fact. It was that of Marius Hatch,

"Captain the computer seems to have a workable translation in place I am about to switch to automatic response"

Instantly the captain snapped back, "Do it, Do it now!"

Without thinking Hatch switched the computer to automatic.

Suddenly J.D. could hear what his attacker was

saying; the computer would extrapolate the translation and provide appropriate answers. J.D. lay there, still immobilised and said to the shuttle.

"How do I say, it's the sign, the sign of God the sign of Alpha"

Instantly the computer had heard his request, and had translated the sentence. Using a calm, sampled voice it then relayed the translation back to his earpiece. In turn J.D. repeated this to his assailant who slowly released him. J.D. checked himself and went to assist Watkins.

J.D. had helped Watkins into the shade of the outcrop, and had given him some water when he turned his attention to the men who were tending their associate who had been hit with the tazer gun. He was a little groggy but otherwise was unhurt. After asking the computer for a translation he addressed the three men.

"Now, you guys are a just a little bit too skilful to be common criminals. So, just exactly who are you?"

The men looked at each other inquisitively, and then one of them nodded to the others. Then one of them spoke.

"We are the keepers".

The crewmen looked confused.

"The keepers? The keepers of what?" Asked Watkins. The three men became agitated, and the tone of their voices became more abrupt and angry.

"No more questions. Not until we know exactly who you are, why you are dressed in this manner, and what you are doing in this area"

To answer these questions they had to consult with

their superior. They told the men to wait while they conferred with each other, then they would answer all of their questions.

The conversation that took place between Daniel and the other two was not that of a superior talking to his subordinates, it had more of an air of three people equally discussing the options of the situation. The two obvious options were, whether they should disclose the purpose of their mission and to reveal who they were. Or, keep their identity secret and create a web of deception for these men. The first option would certainly leave no doubt in the minds of these people what they were up against, and of course by not lying they were less likely to contradict each other in their stories. Between them they had decided that the truth would be the best policy. Daniels gave them carte blanch to proceed in any way they deemed fit, but he would be listening and would intervene if they disclosed anything that he felt was unnecessary.

They turned their attention towards the three men who had been listening to their conversation. They were aware that there had been an unseen third party involved, and were slowly beginning to piece together a hypothesis of their own. Before J.D. had the chance to speak, one of the men addressed him.

"We have listened to you talking. You speak in the old tongue"

J.D. and Watkins were taken aback. They knew from this simple statement that they were talking to people who knew much more than they had at first thought. Watkins made the opening gambit in the conversation by asking who they were and what they were the keepers of. The men explained that they were part of an ancient order of specially selected people who gave their lives to the cause. Selection to the order was made at a very early age. Orphaned children would be taken in and raised by the custodians in the ways of the sect. From all of the children cared for by them, only the very devout would be selected to become members of the hierarchy, sworn to protect the faith. The rest would be free to find their own path with the assistance of the keepers. The order of the keepers had been in existence for many centuries and many generations.

The three men stopped talking, rose to their feet and walked a short way, away from J.D. and Watkins who remained seated around the base of the rock. After their impromptu meeting the men returned and sat back on the ground forming a small circle with the other two. They had decided between themselves that they had said enough at this juncture, and that it was time for the others to reveal a little about who they were and what they were doing in this region.

JD glanced at Watkins and with his left hand he squeezed his lips. An almost unseen nod was passed between the two, then, J.D. took a deep breath and moved his hand away from his mouth and began to explain. He began with what he thought would be his last sentence,

"We are not of this world"

He expected that this phrase alone would produce some reaction from the men that would end all talks, but to his surprise, he received no untoward reaction. He paused for a while, and then he looked slightly into the air and said, to no one in particular, "Captain could you confirm my translation please?" Daniels confirmed that what he had said had indeed been accurate. He cleared his throat and continued to give answers to their questions. He decided that it would be best if he did not try to blind them with science. Trying to keep his story simple he began. He explained that he was from a world that travelled in the sky and only came near their world once every two thousand, five hundred years or so, and that they were only here for a very short time. He told them that they were here on a mission of great importance to their people and that they had a deadline to meet. As he spoke, the three sat quietly, taking in all that was being told to them, their faces were expressionless. He had thought that what he was telling them would be exciting or shocking or even unbelievable but, there was nothing, no emotion whatsoever. Continuing, he explained that his people had visited their world before many generations ago. Three travellers were left here to observe this place, and to make records of their stay, which were to be collected at this time, and that they were the chosen ones who were to locate the documents. One of the men raised his hand to stop J.D. from speaking. He acknowledged the stranger, stopped speaking and waited to hear what he had to say. What the stranger wanted was a little more conformation as to who they were. What they wanted was information that could not have been made up or supplied by a third party. What they wanted was information about the first mission, information only they would know. J.D. was at a loss as to the answers he should give, he stumbled in his thoughts then offered the fact that their mission number was Alpha 1472, and that the original mission was Alpha 106. At this the three men slowly nodded, almost with an air of confirmation. They also wanted to know the names of the first visitors. Both J.D. and Watkins knew the answer to this question. It was part of their history. Malcolm Keogh, Garry Parr and Balvinder Hasar. At this the men began to smile for the first time since their meeting. There was one more thing they wanted to know. The sign of the fish. Why did J.D. use the sacred sign? J.D. explained that when the first mission was planned, the three visitors had said that they felt like a fish out of water, a phrase on their world which meant someone who is in a situation they are unsuited to, and so this became the word that they used to identify each other.

With this final piece of information, the three men fell to their knees bowing before them pledging their allegiance. The two travellers bid them to stand up and not to do this again. It seemed that from this point onwards they had found at least three allies.

JD spoke to the ship.

"Captain, can you hear me?"

"Go ahead JD"

"Everything is under control here Sir, we can now continue with our mission"

"Very good. Carry on, Daniels out."

9. The catalogue.

Firstly, they had to locate the documents. It never occurred to them to ask the others, they simply activated their wrist locators which indicated that they were within two hundred yards of their goal. They started to scout around to find anything that may give them some indication as to where they were hidden. Eventually Watkins looked at one of the men and gave him a shrug of the shoulders, indicating his frustration. The man sheepishly raised his eyes and pointed skywards. Matthew's eyes followed his gaze and a rather foolish realization came over him. He called to J.D. and indicated where he thought the locators were pointing to. As they stared at the face of the cliff they could see no obvious sign of any place that could conceal what they were looking for. They backed up from the cliff to gain a better vantage point, and at a distance in excess of two hundred, or so metres, they could just see a small dark shadow that was being cast by the angle of the sun. If this was what they had been looking for it had certainly been selected with great thought. It was out of reach of most people, and concealed brilliantly. Returning to the base of the cliff they opened their backpacks and took out some of their equipment. There were four slender tubes which screwed together to form one long tube approximately half of the height of J.D. To the bottom of this Watkins screwed a small gas bottle which he had detached from the cross member of his bike. He then stabbed the base of the bottle into the soft sand and dropped to one knee. Aiming the contraption skywards he hoped to secure a line in the proximity of the shadow they had seen earlier. This would be a one shot chance, missing this would mean an arduous climb to get to the ledge. When he was satisfied with his aim he reached down to the bottle and pressed the fire button. As he pressed there was a loud hiss of gas as the compressed air propelled the anchor skywards. This made everyone flinch, involuntarily. The anchor had embedded itself into the rock about three feet wide and to the right of the ledge. There were now two hanging wires leading from the anchor point to the ground. To one of these they attached an extremely thin high tensile rope which they pulled. As they did so the rope ran up, through the loop and back to where they stood. The next task was to secure these two ends, as one, into the base of the rock. Reaching once more into his back pack John took out a small contraption. It was a handle attached by a cord to a footplate which he clipped onto his shoe. He then attached the handle onto the cable which ran up the mountain side, and slipped his pack onto his back. Activating the handle winch he began to rise up. As he ascended he had to stop on occasions to free him self from where the cable had snagged on the uneven surface. Upon reaching the top of the cable J.D. found that he had a two to three foot reach to land him self on the ledge. The ledge itself looked to be stable but with the reach and the uncertainty of its actual stability, he was a little wary. He paused for a moment to consider how to make the short traverse from the cable to the ledge. With his free hand he reached around his body and detached a line from his back pack. He then clipped the one end of the line into the loop of the anchor and tied the other end around his waist and his legs, thus forming a makeshift safety harness. Having done this he held the cable with his free hand and released his other from the handle that had held him safe. It took him a few minutes to free climb across the gap but shortly he had arrived. From where he now stood he could see why the location of this now apparent cave was the perfect hiding place. It was almost impossible to see from ground level because the entrance to the cave had been built to form an obscuring wall that blended perfectly into the natural mountain side. He slipped off his back pack and once more took a piece of equipment out. This one resembled a gun. Placing the barrel against the rock surface he fired two, more secure anchors into the wall then he dropped a sturdier line to the ground. Watkins told the others to wait where they were, the others would only be a short while, then, he attached another winch to the fresh cable and ascended the cliff. Looking out from the mouth of the cave the view was spectacular. Desert and rocks stretched out as far as the eye could see. But they were not here for the vistas. Armed with their halogen lamps they entered the cave. As they walked in through the small entrance they were met with a mild musty smell, which was not unpleasant. There seemed to be a spicy fragrance to the aroma inside which, although not overpowering, did remind them of the smell one would encounter in places of worship. The chamber in which they now stood was about half of the size of the cave they had used to stow their gear on the shoreline. It had about the same head room but was demonstrably smaller. Stacked along the back wall were a number of earthenware containers. They counted twenty in all and thought that their work here should only take a few hours. They tried to relay this information to Captain Daniels but there was no communication inside the cave. The thickness of the rock had interfered with their earcoms. The only way to contact the ship was to return to the precipice at the front of the cave. Matthew returned to make contact while J.D. further examined the cave. He began by pulling the jars away from the wall, inspecting each one. They all seemed to be intact and each of them was sealed. When Watkins returned, he told J.D. that they had the go ahead. They began to open the first container. The lid had been sealed to the main body using a thick viscose material with a similar consistency to tar. Quite what it was was unclear. It did, however, slow the process. J.D. took a small blow torch from his bag and began to play the flame onto the seal. After a few moments the material began to melt and run down the pots in black rivulets. It took about three or four minutes for the seal to become malleable enough for them to prize off the lid. When it was opened they peered inside and could see that the interior was well packed with rolls of parchment. The two smiled at each other and began to remove the contents. The parchment felt fresh and pliable, not at all what one would expect from a centuries old document. Either the seal performed extremely well or this artefact was not as old as they were expecting. They unrolled the first document and spread it across the floor. Watkins stood far enough away so that he could get it all within the screen of his digital camera. There was a bright flash from the camera which illuminated the whole cave. The first piece was done. J.D. rolled it back up and placed it aside. They repeated the process until they had documented the entire first container, then they repacked it and rolled it back into its original place. Watkins went to the precipice and transmitted the records back to the ship. He returned to find John sitting on top of the containers, stroking his top lip, contemplating. Matthew asked what was wrong. He said that he wasn't sure but something didn't feel right. To him the documents felt too new to be what they were looking for. Watkins agreed and went to his bag. He took out a small box and waved it in the direction of JD. "Let's test its age" he suggested, and asked John to get him a sample. He re opened the first container and using his knife cut a piece from the corner of one of the documents and passed it to Watkins who placed it into the machine. After a few minutes their suspicions were confirmed. The documents they were examining were no more than a few years old at best. J.D. pointed out that these twenty containers could not possibly be the result of over two and a half thousand years of documentation. They left the cave and made their way back to the men who were still waiting at the base of the cliff.

The five men sat in a small circle, JD and Watkins needed some more information, urgently. They told the men what they had found and explained that it was not feasible that their findings could possibly be the result of two millennia. They insisted that everything they were seeking was indeed held within that cave. One of them took the lead and began to tell them the story.

"We know that what you seek is in the cave, it has been our sacred place for many, many centuries. We are the keepers. We are nine strong and we belong to three great tribes. Three of us from each tribe are sworn to protect and defend the cave against all comers. We have known of your arrival since the beginning and have been expecting you. We did not know exactly when, but it has been written that it would be around this period. You see, our tribes were founded by the people of your original crew. History tells us that they were sent from the skies to be with us and to observe, document and record for future generations. The kings of our tribes are bestowed with the original names of your peoples and once every year on the anniversary of 'the visit' a delegation chosen by the kings themselves make the pilgrimage to this place to deposit the scriptures for the preceding year. Each of the collections from each tribe are placed together and taken to the cave. It has been this way for countless generations, it has always been here, and we and our predecessors have always protected them. There is no other place, these are our sacred grounds. So, if what you seek is not where you seek it, maybe you need to look deeper for what you desire"

This last comment confused John and Matthew, but they were convinced that what they needed was back in the cave and so they started back up the cliff. They re-entered the cave and activated their hand held torches. Looking around they could not see anything that was out of the ordinary, it was just a simple cave. They decided to check the walls. Each of them started at the wall near the entrance and worked their way around the perimeter in different directions. They tapped the surface with hammers, tapping high and low as they went. Having checked nearly the entire wall without finding anything untoward they met on the far side of the cave. They were just about to give in when the final tap sounded with a different timbre. Both of them stopped immediately and looked at each other for a moment. Watkins tapped in the same place again, then two or three inches to the right and then back in the same place. There was definitely a distinct difference to the tone of the two places. Stepping back from the wall they tried to visually detect a difference in the wall surface, but there was none to be seen. What to do? It was evident that they had to find out what was behind the wall, but how to achieve this presented a minor problem. At first they tried to attack it with their small picks, and although they did find that the wall was a degree softer in this place, it was also obvious that it would take them far too long to break through. Whoever had sealed this newly discovered entrance had been master builders; it was strong and undetectable from the natural rock surface. After consultation with their commanding officer, it had been decided to use explosives to break through. They moved the containers in this first cave to the far wall near the entrance in an attempt to save them from any damage. Having done this they began to examine the far wall in more detail. They tapped around the area and managed to locate the approximate area of the sealed opening. Judging the centre of this they attached a small, round metal container. On this container there was a small read out and a couple of buttons. Watkins asked J.D. how long he thought, and J.D. said that he didn't know but suggested about twenty seconds. This agreed, Matthew set the timer, waited for his partner to leave the cave and activated the device. He then ran across the cave, out of the entrance and onto the small precipice where J.D. was waiting. They huddled together waiting for the explosion, trying to make the best use of the limited cover they had on the ledge. The ten seconds that were left before the detonation seemed to pass slowly, then, almost without warning, the device exploded, sending a dust cloud rocketing out of the entrance. They shielded their faces to protect them from any flying debris. Then all went quiet. For a few seconds, from within the cave they could hear rocks falling but soon this too became silent. From the foot of the cliff the commotion had stirred the three men who demanded to know what had happened. J.D. shouted down to them that everything was alright and they would explain when they descended the cliff. They waited until the dust had settled somewhat and went back into the cave. Switching on their lights on, they could now see a second entrance in the back wall. The explosion had torn out the false section, perfectly leaving the debris strewn across the floor. Picking their way through the rubble they entered. What they found astounded them. It was a second room that they estimated to be at least twice the size of the first, and it was packed floor to ceiling with containers. They took a little time to estimate how many there were and then returned to make their report. Standing on the ledge they began to talk to Daniels, "Sir, we have discovered at least one inner chamber to this cave. It has got about a thousand more containers inside. We reckon that if these guys have been bringing one a year then there must be at least one more chamber here. There is no way we are going to be able to record all of them in the time that we have. What do you suggest?"

Daniels thought for a while. This was an eventuality he was not prepared for. He told them to stand by; He would contact the home world for further instructions. They acknowledged this and sat on the ledge to rest for a while. After a short while they decided that they should try to save a little time later by investigating the new cave. They decided to do this in ten minute shifts to enable one of them to remain in contact with the ship. J.D. took the first shift and entered into the caves.

Once again he picked his way through the debris and went into the second cave. Taking out his hammer he started to knock at the exposed walls. There was not a lot of wall to knock at in this chamber; the containers were lined up leaving only an aisle between them. Being in the cave alone was eerie. He knew that Watkins was just outside, but he felt alone and vulnerable. The back wall was lit from the bright glow of his torch and he was intently aware of the complete blackness behind him. Despite his uneasiness he continued to tap at the walls. Before long he had located a second change in tone of the wall, indicating yet another possible chamber. Armed with this discovery he returned to his compatriot.

As he drew nearer to the entrance, the static cleared in his earcom and he became party to the conversation that was now taking place between Matthew and the ship. He interrupted the conversation,

"Sorry to butt in sir but it seems that there may be another room further back"

The conversation came to a halt, while Daniels pondered this latest revelation. About thirty seconds had passed before he spoke again. He asked how long they would estimate it would take them to catalogue one of the containers. They discussed the mechanics of removing the lids, taking out the documents, photographing them and replacing them into the containers, and decided that each one would take between fifteen to twenty minutes. The captain said that the top brass had decided that this was unacceptable. It had been agreed that they were to break open, by whatever means necessary, sample batches from across the range of containers. This would give them a sporadic documentation across the ages. The rest of the containers were to be left intact. This was going to be a very, very long night and they figured that if they could solicit help from the men below they could catalogue much more than would be possible on their own, so, they descended the cliff face once again to talk to the men.

Firstly they explained the explosions that were heard. Secondly, and more importantly, they tried to illicit their help to catalogue the contents of the cave. The men listened to their request and then flat down refused their assistance. The refusal was not from any malicious intent. It was simply that their laws forbade them to enter the sacred place. The only people who were allowed to enter the cave were the elders and their entourages. Both J.D. and Watkins spent ten minutes pleading with the men, but they were adamant that they were not going to go against their laws. It soon became apparent that no amount of begging or pleading was about to change their minds. Having accepted the situation, they began to make their way back to the cave.

The first task was to blast their way through the newly discovered entrance. This presented a problem because the containers were stacked near to, and either side of the place they needed to clear. What they decided to do was to use two lower impact charges placed centrally at the top and the bottom of the area. The charges would be set to explode at a two second interval hopefully sending a shockwave through the rock and minimise the spread of the detonation. They set the charges and retreated to the safety of the other chamber. This time it was less of a shock to the system. The charges went off as planned and they returned to survey the damage. On their return they noticed that six of the containers nearest to the door had been damaged and that the entrance to the next chamber was now open. This room was about the same size as the second and was packed much the same. They made their way to the back wall. Their intention was to check to see if this was the final room. As they approached they saw something written on the wall. As they dusted away the fine layer of debris that had collected on the wall over the centuries they slowly revealed the writing. It read. In this place are the journals of the crew of Alpha flight 106. We have through the years tried to complete our mission to the best of our ability. We hope that whoever finds these documents makes good use of them. May God live within us for ever. At the bottom of the inscription were the signatures of the three original crewmen. Malcolm Keogh, Garry Parr and Balvinder Hasar.

As they read this legend, they both held a feeling of pride, and although they never knew the men personally they could not help but wonder what had become of their ancestral compatriots and what their lives must have been like. J.D. lifted his camera and took a photograph of the wall. After a few moments of quiet contemplation he looked at Watkins and took a deep breath through his nose and held for a few seconds. When he exhaled he said that it was time to get to work, Watkins agreed and they began to formulate a plan of action.

By this time they calculated that they had 30 hours left to complete their task and return to the ship.

They had already worked out that they could complete one container every fifteen minutes, so they decided to divide the two inner chambers into 120 equal parts and take one vase at each of these points thus giving them an average cross section of records across two millennia. This was the best that they could achieve given the time constraints they were working against.

While the two crewmen were busy marking out their plan of action the captain was equally busy on board the ship. He had decided to contact the home world with the news that their objective had been reached, and that given the time constraints of the mission, it had been decided to take a chronological sample across the millennia to digitise and transmit back home. What everyone had realised was that one hundred and twenty or so samples across two and a half thousand years of information would not be nearly enough to give an accurate cross section across the two millenniums since the records began. At best, they would get a snapshot of life every eighty five years or so. In effect they would see the social advancements of a society after the event and not as an ongoing documentary.

Captain Daniels had been liaising with his commanding officers to reorganise the entire mission brief to accommodate the collection of as much of the information as possible. When the new schedule had been agreed and passed, Daniels had the task of telling J.D. and Watkins their new orders. He was not looking forward to this.

In their ear pieces they heard the captain "This is Daniels are you receiving me, over?" he waited for the reply but the two men were at the far side of the chambers and were just finishing marking out where they were going to take the samples from. When they had completed the task they decided to go back to the entrance for a breath of fresh air before they began to open the jars. As they were approaching the daylight the signal from the ship became clear in their ears. "…cieving me, over.

JD made the reply and said that they had to find a way to communicate while they were deep inside the rooms. They all agreed to work on the problem, then, Daniels began to drop the bombshell.

"Taking the timescale of this planet into account we have 14 days before we have to make our departure and I am sorry to tell you guys that it has been decided to change the mission parameters to allow you to stay at your present location to facilitate the collection of as much information as possible". They looked at each other and instantly they could sense the feelings that the other was experiencing. The instant they heard the news, J.D. slapped his hand to his forehead, turned towards the wall and out of frustration he kicked at the softer sandstone which dislodged a sizable chunk of rock that flew out of cave and fell down to where the guardians were still waiting. They knew that apart from this task they had effectively been cut from the mission and that they were now nothing more than librarians.

"You are going to need the help of your new friends. I know that they will not be able to assist in the caves but you will need provisions while you are there and if you can persuade them to supply you, that would be one problem you won't have to deal with. What we need is for you to collate as much of the information as you can. If you finish beforehand, great but if not just get as much as you possible can. I know you are both disappointed by this but this is the core of the entire mission, our world needs this information and you two are it now. I will of course be here for whatever you need. So, sorry but orders are orders. I will talk to you later. Daniels out."

The two men stood there for a while in total disbelief. J.D slowly started to shake his head from side to side. He was frustrated and wanted to shout and swear. Although he knew that Daniels was not to blame, he needed someone to direct his anger towards. He wanted to curse but he was acutely aware that anything he said could be heard through the earpieces. Watkins could see his frustration and reached out to offer him comfort; J.D. shrugged off his attempt and stormed back into the cave where he knew that he could not be heard by the captain…. Then he cursed.

After he had relieved himself of his inner anger and had managed to compose his thoughts and resign himself to the situation, he and Watkins started back to talk to the men below.

When they returned there were only two of the three men there, they asked as to his whereabouts and were told that he had been dispatched to inform the elders of their arrival. They thought nothing of this and began to ask if they would hopefully help with the provisions situation for the next two weeks. After much discussion it was agreed that they would help but there was something in the conversation that made J.D. and Watkins feel that there was more not being said than was being said. For now, however, this was the best that they could hope for. At least they would be fed while they worked. The next two weeks would be gruelling, all work and no rest. At least the sleep inhibiter would allow them to utilise the maximum work hours available to them.

Agreements made, the two men started back up the cliff face to begin their task.

10. Revelation.

The day started much the same as the previous one with one inescapable difference. Everyone was busying themselves with the preparations for the coming shore expeditions. The crew were obviously confused by the absence of JD and Watkins, all of them wanted to know where they were but none were to willing to ask the question. Although they were eager to find out, they were all prepared to wait to hear officially from the captain. Hatch's voice came over the intercom to announce that it was time for the morning brief. Whatever was happening came to an immediate halt and they made their way to the cockpit to attend the meeting.

They were all seated when the captain appeared at the door of his quarters. From here he could hear the muffled sound of the conversations taking place among the crew. He interlaced his fingers and cupped them over his head which he tilted back, and although it would appear that he was looking at the roof of the corridor, he was in fact looking into space, considering how much of the present situation he should reveal to the crew. He knew that his orders were strictly need to know, but he trusted all of his crew and felt a certain amount of unease about not revealing to them the true nature of the mission. He breathed a deep sigh, and decided that at this moment it would probably be a wiser course to follow his orders and keep them in the dark for now. Collecting himself he entered the cockpit. He bid good morning to the assembled gathering and took his seat. He took a few seconds to prepare himself then he began to address his crew.

"Well...you have all obviously noticed that John and Matthew are not with us this morning. In fact, as you are all aware, they are not even on board. The fact of the matter is that they have been sent on a highly sensitive mission unfortunately, at this time, I am not at liberty to discuss with you the nature of what is happening but you need to know that this is not my decision, it is the directive from home and for now, I would appreciate it if you could just accept that this is a necessary step and if at some point in the future I can reveal more to you, rest assured, that I will."

Having delivered this news he felt almost as if he had, by his restrictions on divulging any information, betrayed his loyal crew. It was an irrational feeling because the people who sat before him were professionals who knew that the captain's orders were final. He handed the meeting over to Hatch, who would outline the daily schedule to the others.

"Mary we would like you to go back to the same place that you went yesterday but this time, take Anne with you."

Anne acknowledged the selection with a gentle nod and a whispered thank you. Inside she was buzzing. Although they had only been here for a short time, the fact that others had already been ashore and she had been confined to the shuttle only able to observe via the screens, had made the waiting all the more anxious. But now she was to go and experience this new planet for herself.

"We need you to accompany Mary to visit the same people as yesterday. We need to know the physiology of these people. Try to be inconspicuous in your investigations. Do not alarm the inhabitants, take your mini kit and take as many readings and stats as you can. Mary it's up to you to keep their attention while Anne does her job, and keep them talking so we can keep updating the translator. I will be taking over from McVie; My job today will be geology, fauna and flora. Travis will be with me and we will maintain a position near the shore base so any problems I will be nearby to provide assistance."

He handed the meeting back to the captain who bought it to a close by saying that the communications between crewmembers had been re-routed and they would not be able to hear or contact J.D. or Watkins, and if he became at liberty to let them know anything else he would. With this the crew readied themselves for the day ahead.

Four of the available eight pods were being used on this occasion and were ready to take them to the surface. There were just two more pods sat in their housing bay positions, seeing this made her wonder once more what J.D. and Matthew were up to. Anne could feel the excitement inside of her. She wanted to giggle or scream or something but she knew that this would not be the professional thing to do. As she stepped into the pod she could feel the cold smooth floor on her feet it was a stark difference to the rough non slip flooring which ran throughout the rest of the shuttle. She played her toes on the floor as she waited to be released into the ocean. Within a few minutes the wait was over and they were on their way.

Until this point Travis had felt almost superfluous to the mission. His role so far had consisted of general duties, manning the computers, readying materials for soirees, and generally being available for anything that might need to be done. Now, however, although his role had not changed he felt that he was becoming more a part of what was going on. He had been quietly studying his fellow crewmen, becoming more familiar with their idiosyncrasies, trying to evaluate how each individual would react to a given circumstance. His was an important role within the crew, he would report his findings to the captain, assisting him in the assigning of personnel to given tasks during the mission. He was the crew psychologist and he found it easier to do his job if he kept a low profile. He knew most of everything that was happening on board, not however the whereabouts of the two absent crewmen, and this bothered him. Having taken all of this into account, he was also looking forward to leaving the ship for a while and experiencing the comparative freedom of the open air.

Once ashore, and having submerged the pods the party split into two distinct teams. The men headed toward the lush vegetation that bordered the beach area to begin their surveys, and the women started along the same route Mary had taken the day before to revisit the family she had met. She felt that today would be more productive now that they had more of a working translation available to them. The two women chatted as they walked, generally about their surroundings, what had happened yesterday, and issues that related to women in general. They were acutely aware that their every word could be heard by the rest of the crew and as a consequence of this, most of what they wanted to talk about went unsaid except for the occasional questioning glance, and an attempt at an impromptu form of sign language.

The morning sun felt warm against their clothing and even warmer on their bare skin as they made their way. The route was familiar to Mary but a new and exciting experience for Anne. She was taking in all of the sights and smells of her new surroundings, and savouring every moment of being here. There was no possibility of the two getting lost. The previous days journey had been recorded by the computers and was being fed to their ear pieces by the computer in a series of quieter commands by a distinctly different voice from the main translation voice.

"Travel in a northerly direction until the next command then turn due east by five degrees"

Mary heard the instruction but already she was familiar enough with the route from yesterday that she had no need to pay attention to the directions. This seemed so natural to her, so comfortable, almost as if she had found a natural second home. The computer had been switched to automatic allowing it to accept voice commands from the crew, and Mary spoke to it.

"Computer, discontinue route commands for Homer and Emmanuel" she said. A computer voice answered her. "Route commands disabled for Homer and Emmanuel" Anne asked why she had done that. Mary shrugged her shoulders and said "I just know the way, follow me"

As they approached the clearing where she had first met Aaron they could hear the bells which hung around the goats necks gently clanging as the animals grazed. Aaron immediately recognised Mary as she walked around the flock and greeted her by holding both of her hands and bowing his head towards her. As he straightened his body Mary reciprocated the bow and asked how he was and inquired as to the well being of his wife Beth. He said that all was well and invited the two women back to his house once again. On the short journey, introductions were made for Anne who was introduced as Mary's sister. The party arrived at the house and as they walked up to the door Aaron called out to his wife who came to the upstairs window holding the baby in her arms. She beckoned them to enter and join her on the upper level. Duly, they went in. It was unusual for the couple to receive visitors twice in two days and even more rare for it to be the same stranger twice in succession, but it was a welcome diversion and Beth was glad to see them. She was introduced to Anne who immediately took an interest in the infant, Luke. As a medic she had realised that if she could examine the baby she could gain much more information in a shorter space of time than trying to surreptitiously get the information from either of the parents. They were treated to refreshments and retired to the roof top where they sat and chatted together, courtesy of the on board translators. They had been talking for about half an hour when Anne in her native tongue said "Computer, translate, May I" almost instantly the reply came into her ear. She stood up and crossed the room to where Beth was sitting and used the translation while gesturing towards Luke. Beth smiled and said of course, she then handed the baby to Anne who went back to where she had been sat and cradled the baby. Luke was no different from any other baby she had examined, maybe he didn't have the same clean baby smell about him but he certainly was not dirty, just different.

Strapped around her upper arm was a medical diagnostic device which would allow her to take all of the readings she needed. Running down the front of her arm there was an ultra fine optic fibre which ran all the way to the tip of her index finger and as she was playing with Luke the device was taking readings from him, pulse, blood pressure, oxygen saturation and temperature. This was all well and good but she needed more. She needed to talk to Mary again.

"Mary, I need a diversion so that I can do a few more tests on Luke, so, when I cough I need you to get Aaron and Beth away. I only need about thirty seconds" Aaron and Beth had no idea what had just been said but they were, by now, getting used to the sporadic conversation and the foreign sounding interspersions that they had been hearing and so paid no undue attention to this. Mary just said OK and waited for the signal. At this stage Beth offered to refill their drinks which they both accepted. When the offer was made Anne recognised an opportunity and motioned to Mary with a cough, realising that she could facilitate Anne she waited for Beth to pour her drink. As she did so Mary feigned a slip which sent the contents of the jug down her dress. In a minor panic that she may have offended her guest, both Beth and Aaron quickly escorted Mary into another part of the house to clean and dry herself. This gave Anne the opportunity she needed. Quickly, she took an attachment from inside her garment and plugged it into the monitor on her arm she then scanned the infant from head to toe. Having done this she deftly put the device back into her dress. Next, using her index finger she swabbed the inside of the baby's mouth to take DNA samples and finally she needed a blood sample. As the others re-entered the room she pricked the baby's heel with a micro pipette for the sample. The prick into the heel caused Luke to cry. To cover her tracks, Anne stood up with the baby and rocked him, trying to calm him. Eventually she could not stop his distress and so she gave him back to his mother who quickly calmed her son. With all of the commotion over and apologies made they sat and talked for a further hour.

Spending time with these people was not uncomfortable, they were warm and welcoming and the two crew members were settled for the day just passing time with a nice family talking about general things that happened in and around their environment. They had found out that the military types that J.D. had encountered the previous day were called Romans, and were part of an invading force that controlled the area. They were told that the Romans were indeed to be feared and respected. This information was monitored by all of the crew, including Watkins and J.D., so everyone was now on guard should they encounter these people in the future. The only time when things became a little awkward was when Aaron or Beth would ask questions about where the two women were from and what their history was. These questions were expertly avoided.

They had been there for about five hours when they heard the captain's voices in their ears.

"This is Daniels here. Something has cropped up that needs all of our attention. I need all of you to return to Alpha as soon as is possible, this does not apply to you John, or you Matthew. The rest of you come home now. Daniels out"

They all knew that for the captain to cut short the day's activities meant that something big had arisen, and that whatever they were doing was now not the priority. The women made their apologies and said that they would re-visit their new friends soon but they had to be elsewhere and had to leave. Aaron and Beth seemed to understand and waved from the door as the two women started back for the beach.

The beach was deserted when they arrived, Hatch and Wheatley had returned to the ship as soon as they had received the message. They located their pods took one last look around to make sure they were not going to be detected and started back for the ship. When they arrived back in the cockpit everyone else was seated in around the centre console waiting for them.

Everyone welcomed them and they took their seats. Daniels had been the only crew on board Alpha that morning, but that had been engineered so that he could co-ordinate the situation with minimum distractions, and so that he could maintain maximum secrecy about what was actually happening. But now the time had come for him to go against orders from the home world. He knew that his orders were need to know but he considered that his crew needed to know. He trusted them and considered that if they were in the picture, then they in turn, would give him their fullest co-operation. He cleared his throat and considered the room for a second before he began.

"OK…so, you are all probably aware that something big has happened, and for the sake of the mission I think that you all need to know what it is. I have been told by the top brass that this is highly confidential and only the people directly involved should be in the picture. So in effect I am about to disobey orders and I am counting on all of you to respect that and keep this confidence to this group, even if you are questioned by higher authorities."

Having heard all of them agree to his request he continued.

"What I am about to tell you will shock you and has the potential to rock the very fabric of everything that our society has been built on since time began."

He paused for a moment and took a sip from his cup. Then he began. "We have all been told throughout history that Alpha 106 was lost during its mission and that there were no survivors. This is not true. 106 was always meant to be a one way mission. It is true that mission control lost contact with the crew and assumed that they were lost, but there was always a chance that they managed to complete what they set out to do. No one really knew until now. Their loss was used politically to calm unrest across the world and it worked, so in a way their loss did us a lot of good. In one way I suppose there has been no deceit, but if people found out that the truth had been manipulated to achieve an end, then can you imagine what would happen?...I can't. Anyway, the thing is, their sole mission brief was to document this planet and to keep a record of their findings for us to collect. We had no idea what we would find but it seems that our ancestors were successful and their records are here in this area. J.D. and Watkins have been dispatched to recover them but there is a problem. The problem is that it will take them up to fourteen days to digitise all of the information that has been left. You see, the original three took their brief to the extreme and have passed their mission on throughout the generations, and now there is over two and a half thousand years of documentation to collect. So what I have decided is to leave John and Matthew there to grab as much as they can and we will share the rest of the mission between us. Now, I know that you will all be taking on more than you signed up for but I hope that I can count on you to step up and allow us to complete. I know that you all have the skills to do this but I need you to pull together to make this happen." He looked at each of them in turn and then asked if they were onside. After a few moments they all agreed and gave him their co-operation to do what they had to do. He then asked for their thoughts. After a while when they had all been contemplating what they had just been told Travis was the first to speak.

"Why don't we send more of us to assist and get the job done sooner?"

The captain dismissed this idea saying that the rest of the mission was equally as important and that they should complete the other elements between them. At this point J.D.'s voice came into the captain's ear.

"Sir, are you near a screen you need to see this"

Daniels stopped the conversation around the table and told everyone that he was about to open communications between all of the crew and instructed them to pay attention to the screens.

"Go ahead John what have you got"

As he spoke the screens began to show what was being seen from the cameras in the head cams of the two men from their vantage point at the mouth of the cave. The third guardian had returned. But he was not alone. From where they stood, they could see a crowd of about three hundred people making their way down the valley towards where they were. Daniels asked Hatch to see if he could zoom one of the cameras to get a closer look at what was heading in their direction, and as he did so they could see that, to all intent and purpose they were being visited by a tribe of men. They could detect no women in the gathering and all of the men were dressed in three distinct types of garb. Furthermore, they could see no evidence of weaponry apart from a few staves. There was no urgency; it was an orderly march in their direction.

J.D. asked if the captain had any orders for them and the captain said that there was no provision for this, and that they were to 'play it by ear' but be careful. This was not comforting to the two men who were by this time being filled with apprehension as to what the next hour would bring.

As they stood looking at the approaching crowd they could hear the two remaining guardians shouting up to them from below. Having attracted their attention they began to beckon to them to come down to the base of the cliff and greet the newcomers. They looked at each other and after deciding that there was no where else to go they reluctantly decided to leave the safety of the cave, and trust their fate to the guardians and their tribe.

Standing at the base of the cliff face they were in two minds whether to try to make a run for their cycles or to stay and see what would ensue. As unsure as they felt, they decided to stay. They stood rooted to the spot, every fibre of their body wanted to run. Every muscle was on the verge of involuntary spasm and they were both experiencing a feeling that they could throw up at any second. But they fought their inner demons and stayed.

The tribe approached, and as they did so they could see that they did so in three separate columns, all wearing what could only be described as a type of primitive uniform to signify the difference between them. The front of the column stopped about ten feet in front of them and stayed there until the rest of the column had caught up. When the entire tribe was lined up, the leading, three men raised their hands in the air and the whole group sat cross legged on the ground. The middle of the three men, who remained standing approached J.D. and Watkins, followed by the other two. All five men stood there together for a while looking at each other. The three newcomers then fell to one knee and with heads bowed they offered their outstretched hands. Held within their hands were three translucent orange blocks. Embedded into each of these blocks was an extremely old piece of fabric. Each of the artefacts that were being displayed differed slightly from the next, but generally speaking, they were the same. As J.D. and Watkins looked down at what the tribesmen were holding the image also appeared on the screens on board Alpha. Everyone stared at the screen in total disbelief. None of the crew was prepared for what they saw. What the tribesmen were offering was the original mission badges of Alpha 106.

11. The truth will out.

"Err…OK, well, that was something that I didn't expect. Captain, I think that this one is a little beyond us where do we go from here?"
Both J.D. and Watkins were confused and for a while no one spoke. All on board Alpha sat in stunned silence. Eventually the captain managed to break his trance like stare from the screen and became suddenly aware of what he was looking at. Quickly, he gathered his thoughts and asked the computer for a translation. Almost instantly it was available and he instructed J.D. to repeat it to the tribesmen.
"Please stand up. Come and join us, we have much to discuss."
There was no time to contact the home world for advice and orders on this situation. This would be a situation where Daniels would have to make decisions based on the developments that would occur during this encounter, he would report later.
The three leaders plus one other joined John and Matthew in a small hollow at the base of the cliff. The shaded area was large enough to seat all six of them in a circle. They sat cross legged and each of the leaders placed their respective artefact in front of them. The fourth member of the delegation placed a box in front of him. At this point there was no indication as to what it held.
So far this had been a day of surprises. Not,

however, as surprising as it was about to get. Daniels instructed J.D. to become the spokesperson and asked him to relay any message that was offered to him. He then asked the computer for another translation.

"My name is John DeVie and this is my colleague Matthew Watkins. We have travelled a great distance to be here today"

The three tribesmen exchanged glances with each other and without speaking they nodded in agreement. Then one of them spoke.

"We know who you are. We have been awaiting your arrival for many generations"

All of the crew were shocked. Shocked to the point that all of them jolted in surprise when they heard the tribesman speaking in their native tongue. It was unexpected and it threw them into a momentary panic. People were checking the systems for errors, checking the earpieces to see if there was any anomalies, or if they really did hear what they thought they heard. The plain truth of the matter was that the crew and these people shared a common language.

Daniels addressed the crew.

"OK, John, Matthew stay calm, do not panic ask them to give you a moment to…to…erm…to give this situation some thought"

They passed on the message and all was agreed. The party sat quietly waiting.

"Everyone else stay calm, let me think." For a while he massaged his eyebrows deep in thought, trying to find the best next move. Suddenly it became clear. "Matthew where are your backpacks?" he asked. Watkins replied that they were in the cave. He was then instructed not to alarm the others but to tell them that he had to retrieve something of great importance from the cave and to go and get them. If he had to, he was to invite one of their party to accompany him. Duly, he made the offer but they all declined saying that whatever he had to do, he had to do, and that they were his servants. This statement confused everyone but at this time nothing was said. With this he went to get their backpacks.

Part of their expedition kit was spare earpieces. Daniels had decided that, with their permission, they would use the spare ear pieces to allow greater communications with the crew. Now that things were calming down they had all realised that this was an opportunity that could not be missed. By the time Matthew returned with the back packs DeVie had already been talking with the tribal leaders and secured their consent to place the devices in their ears.

They took the ear pieces from their back pack and showed them to the people before them who looked at them quizzically. Making hand gestures only, J.D. and Watkins suggested that they insert the devices now to which the elders agreed. At this point everyone of the crew remained silent. They then proceeded to insert ear pieces into the ears of the remaining two at which point one of the elders interjected and prevented the fourth member from being fitted with a device. He waved his hand in front of him indicating that he was not to be privy to what was happening to them, he pointed to the main three of the party which suggested that they, and only they, should use whatever it was. After they had all been fitted with the devices Daniels spoke in a quiet voice and in his own language.

"Do not panic. My name is Captain Jason Daniels"

Despite his request for them to stay calm, the sound of this dismembered voice in their heads was, at first too alien for them to digest and in a minor panic they abruptly got to their feet and started to display outwardly visual signs of panic. This in turn prompted a reaction from the waiting tribes, who started towards the party. Realising that their fellow tribesmen were intent on protecting their leaders using whatever force was necessary, the three leaders quickly composed themselves and held out their outstretched arms in such a way that it quelled any uprising instantly. The mob stopped in its tracks and after a questioning look at their leaders, and the leaders assuring them that all was well, they returned to their crossed legged positions. J.D. and Watkins breathed a sigh of relief, as did the rest of the crew. The leaders re-joined the circle ready to talk. Daniels waited a few moments to allow them to settle themselves and to become more accustom to the strange voices in their heads.

"Don't panic. My name is Jason Daniels and I am the leader of a small band of explorers sent here from the sky to collect the information held within the cave above you. We are seven strong but represent people who number many, many millions. We come from a place called God, and we only have limited time in this place. We therefore beseech you allow us to continue our work. We will, as far as possible, not disturb this place and will leave as soon as our mission is complete. However, we would like to learn more about your people. Who are you, where did you come from and most important why are you here now?"

The middle one of the three chieftains spoke first.

"In time, all will be revealed to you but first we must facilitate your mission. We have selected members from each of our tribes to assist you in your quest. They number thirty six, twelve from each tribe, and are at your disposal to perform whatever duties you see fit. They are sworn to you and are yours to command.

Also, we bring the sacred gift for you. It has been in our care for two millennia but now it is time to relinquish it to its rightful owners."

At this the first elder motioned to the fourth member of their delegation to hand over the box which had sat in front of him since they sat down. Having delivered the package, he was dismissed, and he duly took his place among the ranks. Watkins received the gift and thanked them. The third elder instructed him to open the box which he did. It contained another block of the orange transparent material but this one was different. Contained within the block was a package and clearly visible was a note it read…This is a record of the crew of Alpha 106, it spans a period of sixty years. This disc is the last record of a mission that we consider to be a complete success. To whoever finds this, please use the information wisely and treat the bearers with ultimate respect as they will treat you. We have lived fulfilled lives and have found a home among these people. Do not grieve for us, celebrate our lives. God speed. MK,GP,BH.

Watkins read out the inscription and when he had finished a wave of emotion washed over the crew. It was a proud emotion for a crew that had died over two and a half thousand years earlier. Anne Homer wiped a tear from her eye and said "that's beautiful." Everyone heard what she had said but it was something she meant and felt no embarrassment for saying it. Daniels said that he was going to dispatch Travis to their location to collect the disc so that it could be processed and transferred back to the home world. Now it was time for the elders to tell their story. Before they began they stood up and faced their brethren and motioned that the selected few should now attend and become the workforce for J.D. and Watkins. Now that they had a workforce, the two men returned to the cave and began work in earnest. They would of course be able to hear what the elders had to say via the ear pieces. The three kings sat with their backs to the cliff face looking out onto their tribes and taking the story in turns, they began. "We three tribes are the direct descendants of your original mission to this planet. My name is Melchior, this is Balthazar and this is Gaspar. We are the current kings of our tribes. Our names are inherited when we take our rightful place and directly reflect the original names of our forefathers. Everyone is only known by one name, so, in our history the name of each member of the trinity was shortened to suit. We are each strong nations and from the teachings we have always known that this day would come. We, and generations before us, have been expecting this day for hundreds of years. Our scriptures began on the first day of their arrival and have continued ever since. The place where we are now is the most sacred of all places to our tribes it was selected by your people to be the place at where the records lie. It is called Secacah, and has been protected day and night by specially trained members of our tribes since records began. At this time there are four chambers containing our complete history from day one.

At first there were only the three of them but over time they took wives, had children and attracted followers to their way of life. Before long their community had grown to such an extent that they were attracting attention from outsiders. The attention was not always welcome and for many years the tribe experienced many losses due to malicious attacks from outsiders. It was decided by the trinity that it would be better to split the tribe into three distinct tribes each being led by one of the trinity, and that our ancestors should shun outside contact in favour of a more secluded existence and through this we have lived a peaceful way of life for hundreds of years. We are a simple people who live off the land, and due to the teaching and guidance of our elders throughout the years, we have become self sufficient and have no need of others.

When the great divide happened each tribe set out to find different lands to occupy. It is written that their journeys were long and arduous but eventually all three tribes settled and became rooted to one place. Our tribal network covers a triangular area that is seven days from each other and this place lies at the very centre of our lands.

Throughout the year, our scribes document every part of our daily lives as decreed by the Magi. It is their sole purpose in life and has been so since the beginning. They write about everything from daily happenings to major events and disasters. They keep records of who is born and who dies within our communities and they also keep records of who lives where and what their role in the community is. So, you can imagine that over the period of a year there is a substantial amount of material created. Once every year the documents are sealed in their containers and sealed in the time honoured method and brought to this sacred cave to take their place with all of the other documents. All three tribes attend on the same day and the ceremony always takes place as the sun sets over the mountains. Our priests, and the chosen members of their order place the documents and our guards keep them safe from anyone who would desecrate our history.

Our history and our way of life is governed by the master record. It is a document that has been passed down though the generations from the original copy that was written by the original kings of our tribes, your countrymen. Every twenty years our master record is remade by our scribes and checked by the present king and his court for mistakes. It has remained unchanged for hundreds of years. The master record is exactly the same for all of the tribes ensuring that our history can follow the same divine path. It is our law and our guide. The second appearance has been foreseen since the beginning and as is written in our laws we are your servants, and are duty bound to do your bidding. So mighty ones, command us and we will obey."

Hearing this last sentence Daniels motioned to Hatch to cut the communications with the elders and turned to the rest who had been listening intently to what had been said.

"Well it seems that 106 did more than a good job. They are responsible for an entire community who have lived their lives by the ideals of just three men. Now it seems that to them we are some sort of deities to be worshiped an obeyed." We need to get home involved in this one."

He ordered Hatch to re-establish communications and to talk to them while he talked to high command."

The captain had made contact with base and was talking to Over Commander Lyle Harrison,

"Hello sir sorry to bother you but we have had a very interesting morning here. Things have been moving fast and developments have meant that I have had to make some unorthodox decisions. Firstly, all of the crew have had to be told about the mission DeVie and Watkins were sent on and now things have developed in a way none of us could have imagined." He continued to fill Harrison in on all of the details and Harrison listened without interruption. When he had concluded his report Harrison asked him to stand by, he had to discuss this with his team. Daniels agreed and returned to the rest of his crew. On his return he walked in just as J.D. was making a progress report. He said that they had organised the workforce into several production lines. Two tribesmen were opening each of the containers, while two more were unpacking and laying out the documents. At this stage either J.D. or Watkins would digitise the documents. A further two were charged with re-packing each container and passing them to the final four on the line whose job was to reseal the vessel. At the present rate of production they estimated that the job could be completed within four days. The captain suggested that he may send Mary or Anne to join the effort and maybe speed things up somewhat. At this point Watkins joined the conversation. "Sir, with all due respect we have not seen any women here at all. We have no idea how females fit into this society as I recall from our own history our planet used to be a male dominated society. It may be the same here at their present stage of evolution." The captain spoke to Travis who was en route to join the others. "Travis, did you get all of that?" he said that he did. "Well mister psychologist what do you think would it be a good idea or not. Give me your thoughts."

"Well sir, given what I have observed to date, I would certainly say that Matthew has a valid point. This certainly seems to be a male dominated society. I'm not sure whether the leaders would accept a woman in their midst, there is always a chance that it could affect the work. In my opinion I think that it would be better to leave things as they are for now"

Daniels thought for a moment. He valued the

opinion of Wheatley and took his opinion on board. He decided not to send anyone else for now. Both Anne and Mary felt slightly belittled by this, they were not used to being treated as anything other than an equal. They kept their feelings to themselves and remained silent.

The communication panel in front of Hatch was indicating that a communiqué was coming in from the home world. He informed Daniels who immediately retired to his quarters. Over the intercom came the voice of Harrison.

"Jason, this is Lyle, I have Tom and Peter with me." They all greeted each other then Harrison continued. "First of all I want to say that you have done a great job, we can see that you had no choice in the decisions you have had to make, and we all agree that if we had to advise you we wouldn't have done anything differently. But now, things have taken a turn that was unforeseen and we have to think on our feet. We are going to be here with you for the next few hours to see how this all pans out. We want you to continue running the show while we listen in. We will not interject unless absolutely necessary. Let the crew know what is happening I think your decision to keep everyone informed and in the loop is probably the best course for now. So get back to the deck, we will observe."

He thanked them and returned to his post. As he did so he couldn't help but feel vindicated by the decisions he had made that day.

He motioned again for Hatch to cut communications for the leaders. When this was done he addressed the crew. Having briefed them on the current situation he introduced the commanders who greeted and praised the crew on a great job done thus far. Then he turned his attention to the task at hand. His primary objective was to get field reports from every member of the crew, so that the commanders could be put firmly in the picture as to what was happening on the surface. When he was ready he asked Marius to once again re-connect the link to the leaders. Once the connection had been established he commenced with the field reports.

The three leaders sat patiently listening to all of the reports, and became familiar with all of the voices connected to the seven people they had been told were members of this small band of people who had been sent to be with them. The attention was then turn towards the leaders.

"This is Jason Daniels I would like to speak to one of the three kings." Realising they were being spoken to, the kings looked at each other and decided, quickly, who should be the spokesman.

"Master, this is Gaspar; I am at your service."

Daniels looked at his crewmembers and shook his head slowly. He was uncomfortable with the idea that another being should be subservient to him. Being of lower rank was alright because that was the order of things in the chain of command, but he did not like being revered without reason. He was determined to nip this in the bud before it drove him to distraction. He spoke gently to Gaspar.

"Hello Gaspar, I need for you to do something for me." He said. Gaspar asked what he wanted. "Please stop referring to me or any of my party as master. Simply use our given names. My people will introduce themselves so that you may learn how to address us." He then instructed the crew to introduce themselves one at a time. When they had done so, there was silence. Daniels waited for a reply, but there was none. He thought for a second that there may be a fault with the ear piece that was in Gaspar's ear.

"Gaspar, can you hear me?"

The three kings were looking at each other; their faces were a mix of horror, disbelief, and wonderment. How could people so powerful make such a request? Sheepishly Gaspar began to reply.

"Master, we cannot comply with your request. You are our masters; you are the almighty ones, the ones we have waited for since time was recorded, you and your kind are the very reason for our existence. We are your servants and such, we are honour bound to do your bidding. We could never assume such a position in your presence."

They were uneasy about the request made of them and they stood, uncomfortable, thinking that in some way they may have upset these mighty beings. The captain once again cut communications, then, he addressed his superiors.

"Sirs, would it be permissible to ask these leaders to simply not revere us for the next two weeks, after that they can think of us as they will. But for now, we are finding this really distracting. If we deserved the adulation then maybe it would be ok but we don't. We are just regular people"

The conversation continued between them for half an hour or more, with the home world expressing the opinion that this had been their belief system for generations and that as visitors to this world, they had no right to alter the order of things. The crew would then argue that simply by being here at this time, coupled with the fact that they were now in the company of over three hundred tribesmen who each in their own right were to be witnesses to this event, meant that their belief systems had already been either contaminated or confirmed. The eventual outcome of the debate was that there should be some effort made to make the crew's job as easy as it could be. To assist the crew, Harrison had agreed to speak to the elders in an attempt to make proceedings more formal while they were here. When Harrison had taken the time to prepare himself, the captain spoke to the elders. On this occasion he was speaking to Melchior. This time he was greeted with what had become the usual greeting whenever they spoke.

"I am here oh mighty one, tell me your bidding so that I may serve you better."

Daniels said to him that this type of greeting must stop and that he wanted him to speak to someone who was of an higher authority that he was who would give him the permission to relax more in their presence. Melchior asked where this person was. Without knowing more about their history and what their teaching were, he was at a bit of a loss in explaining this one, so he decided to do a little ground work first. He asked Melchior where he thought that they came from. Melchior answered this question by revealing a little about their history. He said that they had been expecting this visit because it was laid down in the master records that visitors would arrive from beyond the stars, and that they would walk among us for a brief period of time. They would appear as we do but possess a knowledge that was far beyond that of our own. He also said that the original three were benevolent men who were worshiped. They bought a supreme sense of order and organisation to a group of people who were destined to become the three tribes. Their teachings have been passed down through the generations and form our laws. We imagine that we live our lives according to the ways laid down by the divine ones and we hope that we share a similarity to you. It is of course not our place to see ourselves a mighty a you. It has been written over the generations that at the second coming we will submit ourselves to you and do your bidding without question. And so the love we feel for your ancestors, we feel for you.

Daniels felt aware that these three leaders with all of their history, records and teachings, really had no concept of where they were from. He surmised that they had a romantic idea that there was a place beyond the stars that existed as a home to them and the visitors. It was also quite obvious that anything he or any of the crew said to them would change nothing about the way they addressed them. It was time to get Harrison involved.

Harrison had, of course, been monitoring this exchange closely and had decided that this was, in comparison to them, a society in its infancy and as such he must approach them as if talking to, children. Not in a condescending manner, but in a kind fatherly fashion. On his console he typed a message to Daniels to signify that he was ready. The captain spoke to the leaders.

"Your teachings are quite correct, we do come from a place beyond the stars and we have travelled far to be here. Our home is called God and one of our leaders wishes to talk to you. The next voice you will hear will be that of Lyle Harrison"

Almost instantly, Harrison began to speak; there was an anomaly with the communication systems. It was unexplainable at that moment but it had the effect of adding a deep reverb to the communication. There was nothing that could be done about it for now, but the conversation with the elders had to go ahead. As he spoke, Hatch tried to correct the problem without success.

The deep reverberated, surreal voice of Harrison came into their ears and as it did so the three men fell to their knees proclaiming that it was a voice from God. Harrison knew instantly that whatever he said would have little or no influence on these people. After they had calmed down he began to re-address them. His tone was slow and considered.

"Melchior, Gaspar, Balthasar. My name is Lyle Harrison and I am speaking to you from far away in the place we call God. Originally we sent some of our people to your world to learn about you and your peoples. To us, they were very special people, and it seems that they have become very special to you also. They were extraordinary men who appreciated simple things. They did not ask for any special treatment, they only did what they thought was right for the people who were important for them. Your people are such people. Although we are descendants of the three who began your society, we do not require any form of adulation or any special attention. We are grateful for the assistance you show to us, and your help is more that enough. Please treat our representatives as your friends. Address them as you would a brother, a sister or an ally."

When he had finished talking the three men huddled into a small circle, and in a whisper they hurriedly discussed what the voice from God had just said. They were unaware that everything they were saying could be heard by all. Having deliberated about their reply, they addressed the voice. Balthasar spoke,

"Almighty ones, with the greatest respect we can show, we must decline your request," As he spoke he was overcome by a great feeling of trepidation, a fear that he may anger these powerful beings, bringing down retribution on his people. But, somewhat warily, he continued.

"Since our tribes were formed, and records began, our beliefs have been set in stone. This is the way we worship and keep the memory of the original visitors alive. All of our people believe the same. We three are merely the present kings of our tribes, and as such are just the representatives of our great peoples. We cannot ask our people, or be seen by our people to treat or address you in any other way. To us you are the almighty ones, the ones who bought order to our lives, the very source of who we are. We cannot turn our back on our tradition or our people. So with due respect we hope that you will accept that to us, to all of us, you must be worshipped because it is the order of things."

Everyone who could hear, had stopped what they were doing and had listened intently to what the leader had to say. With the greatest compassion, they had realised that these three men were indeed strong, rightful leaders of their people. Everyone felt humbled that a comparatively primitive society could show such fortitude and sense of being. For them it was clear that they had absolutely no right to try to interfere with their beliefs.

From the brief silence that followed, Harrison felt that he was in tune with the thoughts of all of his people on the surface and believed that he was about to speak on their behalf.

"You three men are indeed fine representatives of your nations, and we accept your reasons for not changing the way in which you address us. It was wrong of us to attempt to alter things. You are strong willed and we respect your decisions. You will not hear my voice again, but, know this. I feel honoured to have this opportunity to speak to you. I hope you continue to be strong because I feel that you are, and will continue to be, great leaders who will lead your tribes into great prosperity and wisdom"

With this the three leaders once again fell to their knees and raised their hand to the skies in adoration. Gaspar spoke on their behalf, "Masters, we are, and always will be, your servants. Look down on us and see how we grow. We hope we will live up to your expectations."

12. Celebration.

As the sun began to fall behind the mountain range to the west, it revealed one of the most spectacular sunsets they had ever seen. On their home planet any sunset that may occur was artificially reproduced. To see one occurring naturally was a joy and a wonder. JD had set a camera on a tripod to capture the spectacle. They noticed a remarkable change of temperature as the sun slowly disappeared. They felt a chill which made the hairs on their arms stand up, and cause them to brace against the cold. In reality the temperature had not dropped that dramatically, but compared to the heat of the day it was more than noticeable. They had been taking a break on the parapet of the cave when two separate things occurred at the same time. As they looked to the left of where they were standing they could see the solitary figure of Travis heading in their direction. At the speed he was travelling they estimated that he would arrive in approximately five to ten minutes. The thing that was taking most of their attention could be seen directly in front of them. From this elevated position they could see the three tribes spread out in front of them still sitting in ranks, cross legged. They had been there since their arrival and the two men wondered how they could stay there all day in the searing heat. This was, however, not what had caught their attention. In the distance they could see, coming down the valley, more tribesmen. The new arrivals numbered a further three hundred or so, as far as they could estimate. Watkins took a pair of binoculars from his pack and held them up to get a better look at what was heading their way. The approaching tribesmen looked, to be exactly the same as the ones that presently sat before them. The main difference was that these newcomers were transporting many items of differing sizes. Some were smaller and were carried on the backs of people, supported by pieces of cloth that hung around the top of their heads, effectively creating a support sling. Others were much larger and required teams of men to transport those using long poles much akin to people carrying large stretchers. Matthew handed the binoculars to John so that he could also get a better look at the scene below. They were both curious and began to hypothesise as to the meaning of the new arrivals. Then, they heard a long blast on some sort of instrument. It was a muted but loud sound that they felt sure could be heard for miles around. As soon as the tribesmen who were working in the cave had heard the sound they instantly stopped work and made for the cave opening. Once there they urged J.D. and Watkins to descend the cliff face to join the others. They did not ask why, their curiosity was at such a level that they wanted to know what was happening down below, and so they duly began to make their way down. As they traversed the last few feet to the bottom, Travis arrived on his bike. Although this was a strange sight to all of the tribesmen, none of them broke ranks. They all sat in their places. There was much discussion and pointing amongst them as they marvelled at this new visitor on this strange machine. None of them had ever, or could ever have seen, such a technologically advanced piece of equipment. The sight of this only served to further cement their position as almighty beings in the eyes of their hosts. Travis propped his cycle against the base of the cliff where it seemed to meld into its background which further amazed the on looking tribe. He then went to greet his fellow travellers who briefed him on their progress and drew his attention to the approaching hoard.

The two groups of people merged into one group which now formed a circle around a sizeable stack of the cargo which had been manually carried to this place. Through the crowd came one man who approached the elders. The elders stepped forward to meet the man half way between the crew members and the gathering. He said to the leaders that everything was in place and that they were, with their permission, ready to commence. As soon as he had received their permission he turned to face the crowd who were waiting silently for the signal. He raised his arms into the air and stood in a Y stance and waited until he was sure that he had everyone's attention. When he was sure that he had, he bought his hands together in one resounding clap which seemed to reverberate all around the area. At this point, the up until now quietly ordered tribe sprang into action. Melchior, Gaspar and Balthasar turned and walked back to address the crew.

"Almighty ones, we have awaited your arrival for many generations. To celebrate your presence among us we have prepared a feast in your honour. Tonight we will feast and rejoice. Tomorrow we will double our efforts to complete your quest. But tonight, we must commemorate your company."

J.D. addressed the captain and said that they were sorry, but it looked like they were about to have a party and that it seemed that they had no choice. They would, however, set a series of cameras so that the ship could observe the celebrations. The captain agreed and they waited.

Over the next hour the scene before them was transformed from an open plain into a makeshift camp. A series of large tents had been constructed in the shape of a large horseshoe, the open end of which was facing the cliff face where they stood. A huge fire had been started in the centre of the camp and the orange glow illuminated all of the marquees which seemed to stand out against the dusky night. It was not yet fully dark, and they could see the plume of smoke rising into the evening sky. Butchered animals were bought to the fire and set among the growing embers to begin cooking, alongside several large pots containing more food. The central tent of the horseshoe was simply an open three sided structure with a roof and into this area was placed a number of seats rough hewn from wood and covered with several animal hides. At the base of the cliff where the ground was cooler were placed several large terracotta urns containing some kind of liquid which they assumed was to be the refreshments for the evening.

By the time that the sun had completely set and the dark of the night was truly established, the preparations were complete. The three leaders beckoned J.D., Watkins, and Travis to join them at the feast. As the three men walked towards the gathering the three kings bowed their heads and offered out their arm in a guiding motion as they walked past. They walked through the crowd for the first time and as they did, a path was created through the tribe. They were slowly walking through a group of people who were completely silent. As they passed, each of them bowed their heads. The only sound that could be heard was the crackling of the large fire. They continued walking through the path as it formed. It eventually led to the centre tent where they stood facing the six hundred strong crowd, in an eerie, surreal silence. Within seconds they were joined by the three leaders who took their places behind them. Melchior leaned forward and said to them. "Masters, they are waiting for your permission" J.D. asked what should they say? And he was told to simply tell them to begin. J.D. cleared his throat, glanced around at the others, shrugged, and then announced "Let the festivities begin." The instant the words had left his mouth, the silent scene erupted into joyous mayhem. A cacophony of cheering, whistling, whooping and shouting washed over the crowd. All six of them took their seats in the tent and as they did, tribal drums started to play. The sound of the drums affected the entire tribe who started to dance around the fire in a clockwise direction and sing in unison. As they watched the spectacle that was unfolding before them they were tended on by a series of young tribesmen and women who brought to them food and drink which they laid upon the table that was situated before them. The contents of the banquet was simply astounding, it was astonishing to believe that in such a short space of time they had prepared all of this fare, and indeed the surroundings in which they now found themselves. As the food was laid down the aromas that emanated from the table were mouth-watering. Even before they had sampled anything before them they could almost taste what they were about to eat. After an hour of feasting and watching, the entire tribe stopped dancing and they all raised their hands to the sky and with one almighty roar the ritual dance was over. What followed was a series of individual and group performances, which included sword swallowing, singing, fire eating, individual dances, combat demonstrations and much more. All of the performances were greeted with great applause, and cheering from the rest of the audience who by now were all seated around the horseshoe, and was also indulging in the abundant fare. It took about three to four hours to complete all of the performances. At the conclusion, the entire arena became calm and relatively quiet. Individual groups formed, made up of people from different tribes all meeting within the sub groups that were now amusing themselves. It was a terrific sight to see, all of these people happy to be entertained without any technology.

The six of them sat in the head tent and talked about the tribal history, the laws and the way of life that these people led. Any question asked was eagerly answered. Never once was an untoward question asked of the crew. Their hosts thought that it was beyond their place to be so impertinent, even though their curiosity was boiling over.

They talked for about an hour, and then, there was a lull in the conversation. Melchior saw this as his opportunity. He motioned towards a man who was standing nearby. The man approached and whispered exchanges were made. The man left. He returned minutes later with nine young females. They were paraded in front of the visitors. Each of the girls was about eighteen years of age, and each of them beautiful and blemish free. They all wore the finest silk garments which barely covered. As the silk rested against their skin every contour of their bodies was highlighted under the fine cloth. Melchior turned to the crew members.

"Masters, May we introduce our gift to you. These are the virgins of our tribes, all of their lives they have been prepared for this moment, they are all dedicated to the purpose. Since birth they have been awaiting your arrival and we guarantee their purity, now we offer them to you."

Back on board, the rest had been watching the proceedings and indeed enjoying the evening. But now, things were different. Mary spat out the drink she had and began to laugh. The rest of them also found it amusing, even Hatch found himself indulging in a slight snigger. Watkins let his head roll back and out loud he said "Captain, help." Through a muffled snigger, Daniels asked what the problem was. He had immediately seen this as a chance to inject a much needed shot of levity. He cut the reception to the leader's ear pieces and then he gave the crewmen his advice.

"OK, so let me see. You now have a choice boys. Choice A is to accept the gift of your hosts and take a girl each and do with them what you have to. Now this would definitely appease the elders, because from what I can gather these young women have been bred to remain celibate in case you decided to call. In their culture it is probably an honour for them and their families to be chosen to be one of the 'virgins for the almighties.' Or you have choice B, Which is of course the company line. Now the company line states that any member of the crew experiencing an encounter of the close kind should take care not to inject any of our culture into theirs." This started a wave of giggles that could be heard in the ear pieces. "Now you are the guys on the front line and to be honest, I don't think even I could get there in time to stop you. So, I would like to think that you would use your intellectual manhood and choose option B, but the decision is yours. Just remember, whatever you do we will be listening to make sure that you keep the end up for the corps." At this the entire crew burst into uncontrollable laughter. The choice was obvious, but it was comforting to know that the person who was leading had a sense of humour.

The elders could see the smiles on the faces of their guests and reasoned that they were pleased with their offerings. J.D. said that they could not possibly take them up on their invitation for one of the young ladies. At which point Gaspar said that the offer was not for one of the virgins but there was three for each of them. Once again the laughter re-ignited on board the ship. Travis was the one to decline the offer. The reaction from the elders was not, altogether, unexpected. They believed that they had angered the almighty ones by their offer. Travis and the other two quickly assured them that they were not offended. It was simply not their custom to accept gifts of this nature. They were, of course, flattered by the gift but unfortunately they had to decline to accept. As soon as the words left his mouth, Travis' imagination went into overdrive. He could imagine lying naked upon animal skins in one of the tents with three young naked females draped over and around him, there to cater to his every desire and whim. The entire, erotic scene played out in his mind in an instant. Of all the opportunities he had missed in his life, this was by far, the biggest. The one that he would regret the most, it would have been the one chance he would probably ever have had to fulfil one of his greatest fantasies. As the girls were led away, Travis could almost feel their skin against his own as he watched his dream slipping away. He shook his head and snapped his senses back to reality. What he was unaware of, was the fact that he was not the only one of them experiencing the same, or similar fantasies.

The hour had grown late, and many of the revellers had retired for the night. Some of the more senior members of the tribes had been afforded the luxury of one of the tents. The others had found places around the encampment to settle for the night. One of the more luxurious tents had been reserved for the guests but due to the sleep inhibitor that had been administered to them, they had no real need for its use, but having just disappointed their hosts they did make use of it for an hour of rest, and for a chance to talk about the day's events. Guards had been posted around the perimeter of the encampment and slowly the noises that could be heard abated until the only sound that was left was the crackling embers of the dying fire. Soon the only people awake were the guards and the three crewmen.

13. Completion.

They had been in their tent for about an hour and a half and the rest period had been beneficial to them. They felt refreshed and ready to continue with their task. They were aware that the camp had fallen into silence and assumed that everyone was asleep. For them sleep was not an option, and so, they had decided that it would be better use of their time if they returned to the cave and continued to catalogue the documents. They rose from the beds that they had been relaxing on and quietly left the tent. Cautiously they crossed the horseshoe; they had no desire to disturb the sleeping tribesmen. Picking their way through the sleeping bodies they eventually made their way back to the cliff face. They thought that they had made it undetected, and were just about to begin their ascent when they heard the familiar voice of Gaspar.

"Masters, is your accommodation not to your approval? Have we not made you comfortable? Have we offended you in any way?"

All three of the crew took time to assure him that everything was as it should be and they had been the perfect hosts. The one thing that had raised the suspicions of the elders was the fact that since they offered the virgins to the visitors the voices in their heads had stopped communicating with them. And this alone had made them think that they had angered them in some way. It took some time to appease the elder and to convince him that they had no problems with the tribes. To prove this they had the ship re-establish communications with the elders. It was not a conscious decision to cut communications; it was an oversight during the humorous episode they had enjoyed earlier. As soon as Gaspar could hear the voices in his head once more, his face displayed a slight grin as his eyes closed, simultaneously, he exhaled slowly and his head lowered. It was altogether the look of a man who was comforted. The instant communications had been restored, the other two leaders could hear the voices too. At the time they were sleeping, then suddenly, hearing the disjointed voices they woke in a sudden panic until they realised what they were hearing once again. The rude awakening had brought them sharply to their senses. Coincidentally, they left their respective tents at the same time and headed over to join the others. The others were quickly told what had transpired while they were sleeping and were told that the crewmen were about to go back to the caves to continue the work. Balthazar was concerned that they were not getting the rest that they needed and tried to insist that their duties in the cave could be taken over by some of the tribesmen. He was assured that they did not need sleep. He was sceptical about this, but who was he to question an almighty. He decided to himself that it would be his duty to observe them for any signs of fatigue. The elders had rapidly designed a rota system for the tribesmen, who would assist in the work. There would be a four hourly shift of thirty workers assigned to the task. The work would continue day and night until all of the documents had been digitized. There would also be a catering corps who would keep the workforce fully fed and watered. The organisation for this feat had been expertly conceived and executed by the elders within a few minutes. They ascended the cliff face and entered the cave followed by the first shift of the new workforce, and within ten minutes they had organised the production line and work commenced.

The system they had adopted turned out to be highly efficient and the tribesmen proved to be tireless workers. Almost instinctively these primitive people seemed to grasp what was required of them to complete the task, and everything progressed like clockwork. They were efficient, tidy, courteous and above all accurate and fast.

After the first four hours had lapsed, it was time for a change of shift. Even the change of workforce was a seamless affair. A steady flow of a replacement thirty workers filed into the cave system and systematically took over the position of one of the workers who then proceeded to leave the cave and descend the cliff face. The remarkable thing was that the replacement worker knew exactly what was expected of him and regardless of where any particular worker was within the process, the replacement simply took over at that point, which kept the process constant and unbroken.

Soon after the third shift had begun, the sun began to rise from the east and as it did, one could feel the temperature, once again, rising. The break of day heralded the departure of Travis back to the ship with the storage media. He said his farewells to his fellow crew members and descended to the base of the cliff where he found the three leaders. He thanked them for the entertainment they had provided the previous evening, and also thanked them for the gift of the strange orange block. As he was about to leave the elders fell to one knee and in turn they held his hand and kissed the back, then held it to their forehead for an instant. Having done this they bade him farewell. He went back to his cycle and as he rode off, the entire tribe faced toward him. In unison they fell to their knees and with arms outstretched they bowed majestically in his direction. Travis faced them and returned their bow, and then he mounted his bike and started back in the direction of the ship.

Later that day, during one the shifts Melchior had visited the cave to check on progress and he found himself talking to Watkins. He was curious as to what the devices were that the two men were using. Matthew explained that it was a device that allowed them to record an entire document in the blink of an eye. He was careful not to get too technical because he knew that Melchior would not understand unless it was explained in the simplest of terms. Melchior was none the less intrigued by this wondrous machine. The one thing that occupied his thoughts was not the mechanics of it, but the operation. He wanted to know if this machine was difficult to use. Not thinking Watkins said "hell no, you just point and press" Melchior was confused and repeated "point and press?" immediately he realised his error and thought that a practical demonstration was in order. He waited until the next scroll had been laid out on the floor in front of them and then he showed Melchior exactly what happened. He pointed the camera at the scroll and when it was perfectly located in the view screen he pressed the button. He then held the camera in front of Melchior to show him the image he had just taken. Melchior was in awe. He had never seen such magic. He looked at the perfect reproduction of the scroll and mused over the fact that an exact copy was now in the machine. "Can anyone do this?" he asked. Matthew said that in principal it was a fairly simple task. He then asked if it would be permissible for him to talk to his fellow elders using the ear device. Watkins said that, of course it would be fine for him to do so. For some reason he felt that he should be holding something while he spoke, but he brushed this aside and addressed his compatriots.

"Gaspar, Balthazar, this is Melchior can you hear me?"

It was strange for the two men to hear an unsolicited remark from their friend. Up until now they had only heard him during normal conversation with the crewmen and their unseen colleagues. They acknowledged that fact that they could indeed hear him and asked what he wanted?.

"I have been speaking with Master Watkins and I would like for you to send the scribes to join us in the caves". They had of course heard what Melchior and Watkins had been talking about, but had no idea what was happening. They did, however, agree to send the scribes and duly went to summon their attendance. Within half an hour the scribes had arrived in the caves. Melchior beckoned to Watkins to join him near the mouth of the cave, which he did.

"Master, these are the scribes of our tribes. They and their ancestors have been responsible for the documents which you now see before you. They are amongst the wisest men of our tribes, and I feel sure that if you were to instruct them on the operation of your recording device, they could relieve you of the burden of your task. Matthew thought for a second and then spoke to the captain.

"Sir, what do you think?" he asked. Almost immediately the captain replied.

"Well, it is a relatively simple process so why not give it a go. But make sure that you check occasionally to see that everything is OK"

Watkins, with the permission of his captain, proceeded to instruct the scribes in the operation of his device. They were quick studies and very soon they could use the cameras sufficiently enough to do the task. Once they had mastered the skills they needed, they were incorporated into the workforce, assigned a place in the rota, and took over from J.D. and Watkins.

For the next three days J.D. and Watkins spent the time studying the geological and meteorological traits of the area. They were always escorted by a detail of guards who watched over them wherever they went, and were attended by servants who looked after their food and refreshment needs. Periodically they would return to the caves to check on the progress of the work and to check on the quality of the scribe's camerawork. For the next three days, this is how things progressed.

The sun was directly above them and it was the fourth day of their stay in this valley when they received the call from the elders summoning them to the cave. The task had been completed, and when they arrived back in the cave it was exactly as they had found it. All of the urns had been resealed and restacked in their original places. There were teams of builders repairing the false walls that they had blown up on their arrival, and very soon there would be no evidence that they had ever been here. Once they were satisfied that everything was as it should, and that they had collected all of their gear, they left the cave for what was to be the last time, descended the cliff and congregated at the base with the elders. They told the leaders that now the work was ended, it was time for them to go. However, they would like the opportunity to sit with them for a while before they departed. The elders felt honoured that the almighty ones would want to spend time with them in a social aspect before they left. It was agreed and they retired to one of the tents on the edge of the horseshoe. On their way Melchior told one of his subordinates to begin striking camp. Without the presence of their guests it was time for things to revert to normal for the tribes.

They all sat on the animal skin covered seats around a central table that had been set with a modest meal and drinks. The conversation had been of a general nature until the voice in their ear told them that it was time.

"The time has come for us to take our leave of you and unfortunately we have to take the voices out of your head. Your world is not ready for this type of technology yet, one day you will develop wondrous devices of your own. But for now…" They understood. But before they offered their ear towards Watkins for him to remove the earpiece, they wanted one last chance to say farewell to the voices they had become so accustom to.

"Almighty ones, it has been an honour and a privilege to be a part of your great world for these few days. We are here as your servants and will always remain so. If in the future you need to call on us, we and our progeny will be at your service. We are your humble servants and will always be so. Farewell masters, speed safely to God." It was an emotional speech that affected all of the crew who felt humbled by these simple people who had developed such a devotion to them. Each in turn the crew responded with thanks and farewells to each of the leaders. Matthew then removed the earpieces. There was one last thing they had to do. It seemed unfitting to leave without bestowing a gift on these people and, it was decided that in light of the fact that they had virtually nothing to offer, that they would leave them with a legacy that they felt sure would last for thousands of years.

"We have felt honoured to be in your presence these last few days and would like to leave you with a gift to remember us by." Both of the men reached into their back packs and took out a craft knife. Then carefully, to avoid damaging the gift, they began to pick at the stitching which secured their insignia badges to the flap. Within minutes they were removed and the small remnants of cotton were plucked away from the badge. They then presented them to the three kings. One was given to Melchior, and one to Gaspar. Reaching once more into his bag J.D. produced a third patch which was almost identical to the other two but which bore the name Travis Wheatley. The look on the faces of the elders was beyond gratefulness, it was as if they had been given a whole new world. The crew knew that these patches would be treated the exact same way as were the original ones. They would be encased in orange stone and revered for all time. With this it was time for them to go. As they left the tent they noticed that it was the only one left standing. The entire camp had been struck, and this was the only evidence that there had been a temporary population occupying this valley for the last four days. They made their farewells and started back for the ship.

As they were about to mount their cycles they turned back for one last look. They saw the three kings standing in a line in front of the entire tribe who once again fell to their knees, outstretched their arms and bowed in unison. The crewmen returned the gesture and then left.

14. And on the seventh day.

The journey back to the ship was largely uneventful. After the last few days they were glad of the journey. There was no hurry to return and so they leisurely cycled back using the global positioning to guide them. En route they located their costumes and dressed back into the garb of the area in case there was someone around who may see them. Having done this they continued on their way. The sun was beginning to set when they arrived back at the beach. The heat of the day had passed and they were now standing on the shoreline experiencing a pleasant balmy early evening. They stored the gear that was not being taken back on board at this time in the cave with the rest of the equipment, then, they returned to the shore to allow themselves some free time. Walking in the sea, they had time to reflect on the previous few days. The general consensus was that they had been privileged to have met the tribe who had helped them to shorten their task by so much time. They were amazed at their dedication to their predecessors and astounded that a complete society had developed from the teachings of three of their fellow compatriots. They had been walking for about fifteen minutes when they decided to turn around and make for the ship. Their bodies had now become used to the temperature of the water and to their feet it felt like a tepid bath, the occasional wave demonstrated that the actual temperature was lower than their feet would lead them to believe as it lapped onto a previously dry area of skin. J.D. instructed the computer to activate pod location for DeVie and Watkins, and they began to hear the homing beeps in their earpiece. They quickly located their pods and began back for the ship.

They walked into the cockpit and joined everyone else who had been waiting for them. It was time to debrief the mission. Everyone was fatigued, not tired, fatigued. The sleep inhibitors had done their job and allowed them to continue working around the clock. The body however, needs quality rest to recuperate and their bodies had been used constantly for six days. They all felt slightly irritable and they all needed a rest period. There was no chance of them falling asleep, but there was a real danger that if they overdid the inhibitors, mistakes could be made. Costly and potentially dangerous mistakes.

The first order of business was to download all of the information collected from the caves and to transmit it to the home world. J.D. and Watkins took the cameras out of their bags and handed them to Hatch who began the download process. The amount of data that had been recorded would take many hours to transfer from the cameras and then even more time to transmit. Hatch began by sampling some of the images to check the quality of them; he was more interested in the images taken by the scribes. There was no need for concern; the work undertaken by the inexperienced team was of the same quality as that of J.D. and Matthews.

Having checked everything he began the download, and then he turned his attention to the meeting.

The Captain began debriefing the crew.

"OK, so here we are on day six, according to the rotation of this planet. It has to be said that we have already exceeded all expectations, and now, we are well ahead of schedule. Before any of you get excited, we will not be going home early. This is a one off opportunity and we have to take full advantage of it. While J.D. and Matthew have been otherwise occupied, Mary and Anne have been ashore and have spent time with their friends. Also, they have been making regular soirees into the town and now we have a fully functional translation for the indigenous language. The language base for the language of the Roman inhabitants is slowly growing but at best it is a little sketchy, so wherever possible we need to eavesdrop on these people to increase the database. Remember these people do not seem to be as docile as the locals so, you must always be on your guard when you are near them. We have found out that the money we have been manufacturing is of a predominately high denomination, so we have obtained samples of other coins and have begun to make smaller, more manageable values. You will all be issued with a supply of these coins for your next visit ashore. Mr Hatch has managed to liberate the storage device from the orange resin casing, but the connection is so primitive we have not as yet been able to connect it to our computers. The boffins back at home are working on the problem and hopefully we will soon be able to take a look at what it contains. Anne reports no medical anomalies; this atmosphere seems to suit our physiology perfectly. Finally, we have all exceed the regulation usage of the sleep inhibitor, so, tonight we will all, with the exception of Mr Hatch, be administered with the antidote and will rest for one rotation. Mr Hatch will be afforded the next rotation for his rest period." Although they had all been expecting this statement, it was still nevertheless comforting to hear it in an official capacity. They were all relieved, and would, under normal circumstances, have shown more of a celebratory reaction, but the fatigue they all felt at this point was telling on their bodies and their emotions. The best that they could muster was a grateful nodding of the head. Daniels summed up the meeting.

"If anyone has anything to add or if there are any questions. I suggest that we secure the ship and prepare to go to sleep"

Everyone busied themselves with the tasks involved with preparing for their sleep period, and when all was ready, they each retired to their own quarters. In turn Anne Homer visited them to administer the antidote. The last visit on her list was the captain. By the time she entered his quarters; he was already in his sleepwear and tucked up into his bed. Anne administered the injection to her commander, bade him, fond dreams and left him to rest. Her final job was to administer the antidote to herself. She walked into the cockpit to bid Hatch goodnight then went to her quarters. She was in a shared room with Mary, who by this time was soundly asleep. Changing into her sleepwear she mused over the last six days. She climbed into her bed pulled the cover up and over herself, injected herself, placed the innoculator on the table beside her and within five minutes she was asleep.

Hatch knew that for the next rotation he would not sleep and would be alone. Unperturbed by this he shut down all non essential functions of the ship, dimmed the lights in the cockpit and settled down to occupy himself until it was time to awaken the rest.

15. Revulsion.

One entire rotation had passed when Hatch walked into Anne's quarters. Both she and Mary were sleeping soundly and it almost seemed a shame to wake them. He gently shook Anne, and she gradually came out of her natural sleep and stretched herself as she woke.
"Time to get up, come on, I do not come equipped with a snooze button, this is your one and only call."
With this he left the room to allow the two women a little privacy as they roused themselves for the rest of the mission. When she had completed her ablutions and was dressed she systematically checked on all of the crew to make sure they were awake, and that they were fit to continue, and to administer their next shot of the inhibitor. She then turned her attention to Hatch who had retired to his quarters and was awaiting his dose of the antidote.
It had been decided that due to their prolonged absence from the ship, J.D. and Watkins would be the crew members who would stay on board today to monitor the rest of the shore party. The assignments for the day were simple. Anne and Mary were to revisit Aaron and Beth, while Travis would team up with the Captain and visit the town centre. Their mission that day was to seek out Romans and to eavesdrop on them, allowing the computer to compile more of their language base.

This was the first time that Daniels had been ashore and his first experience of using the pods. Countless simulations in the pools back at the training camp had prepared him for this moment, or so he thought. The mechanics of operating the pod were, of course, exactly what he had trained for. But the experience of actually being in this place, at this time, on this planet was more than he had expected. He was enjoying the journey from the ship to the shore and made sure that he took full advantage of the trip and consequently was last to arrive. He anchored his pod and walked through the refreshing water onto the sandy beach and for the first time he had the chance to survey the scene before him with his own eyes. He was used to seeing it through a camera lens, but to see it with his own eyes, and to have all of his senses working; feeding him all of the information around him was truly breathtaking. It was a sensory feast. The rest of them waited and allowed him time to take in his surrounding. When he was ready he joined them. All four of them walked across the beach and exited into the overgrowth. Once there they parted company for the day. Anne and Mary started towards the house of Aaron and his family. Travis and Daniels started towards the town. For the duration of this day Daniels had instructed Travis to address him by his first name. He thought that it would be safer this way should they be overheard at any point, it would be one less embarrassing question they would not have to explain.

Jason and Travis had decided to try to find the tavern where J.D. had been on the first day. It was as good a starting point as any, and would allow them to retrace his steps through the town leading them up to the large building where the Romans were encountered. The Captain turned to Travis and asked him if he had bought any of the money with him. "Yes sir" he answered. Daniels stopped in his tracks and looked at Watkins. "Sorry Travis you can't call me sir today just treat me as you would J.D. or Matthew." "Yes sir, sorry sir" he replied and almost immediately cursed himself. Daniels shook his head, gave him a humorous shrug and they continued on their way.

As Mary and Anne rounded the outcrop to where Aaron's herd were usually grazing, they were surprised to find that they were not there. At this stage they were not suspicious that anything was wrong, they simply thought that he had changed his grazing pasture. They decided to go directly to the house uninvited. They were just about to knock on the flimsy door when it opened. Aaron and Beth were leaving. Aaron was carrying Luke and Beth stood behind them sobbing uncontrollably. The instant they saw her, their womanly instinct to support a fellow being in distress kicked in. immediately they placed an arm each around the shoulders of the distressed woman and asked what the problem was. She tried to explain the problem but every time she did, she would break down in floods of tears. On a couple of occasions the level of distress would cause her legs to buckle beneath her causing the two women supporting her to take all of her weight. Eventually they sat her on the rustic bench that sat along the front wall of the house. They gave her a drink and tried to calm her. Turning their attention to Aaron they could see that he too was distressed. He was, however, more capable of composing his emotions. Enough to tell the crew member what had caused so much distress. Beth's distress had caught the attention of everyone, who by now was listening intently to the conversation. Aaron explained that Beth's brother had fallen foul of the Romans and was due to be executed that very morning. They asked what his crime was and Aaron told them.

"For the last couple of months he has been publically vocal about the tyranny that the Romans bring. They had taken his livestock and ravaged his land leaving him with nothing. He had a right to speak his mind but the Romans do not allow any dissent. Late yesterday a group of their soldiers came and took him and today, he is due for execution. We have to go to be with him. We are his only family and we need to claim his body otherwise there will be no one to help him to his final resting place."

They were horrified that this was happening to their friends, although in reality they should not have been. It had been well documented within their own history that this sort of thing had been prevalent throughout the ages. Why should it be any different here? True, it part of this society that seemed a little distasteful, but they had become fond of these people which made it all the more difficult to accept. They asked what they could do. Aaron said there was nothing anyone could do and added that the Romans did not grant clemency, they were ruthless. Jason Daniels spoke. "Ladies, you should accompany them to the execution to offer support, it sounds like they need some friends right now. We will join you as soon as possible." The women agreed and said to the distraught couple that they would go with them. "There is no need, this is not your problem but thank your for your kind offer" Said Aaron. The women insisted that they would be there for them. Aaron and Beth gratefully accepted the offer and all four of them started in the direction of the town. They mused over the method of execution that would be used. As yet they had seen no outward signs of advanced weaponry. The only thing they had seen to date were cutting and stabbing weapons. The most popular guess from everyone was some form of beheading; it seemed to be the quickest and most compassionate form to take. Mary and Anne were, of course, not a party to the conversation to decide the method, but that was their guess also. It took almost an hour to travel to the town where the execution was to take place. Jason and Matthew were nowhere to be seen, so Mary requested the computer to activate the proximity alarm between Daniels and Emmanuel. The audible beeps began instantly in their ears and within a space of five minutes they had located each other. The instant Jason has seen them he instructed them not to reveal that they knew each other. The plan was for the two men to be in close proximity to the others without revealing who they were, this would enable them to observe without interruption and also to be close should they need assistance.

Aaron, Beth, Mary and Anne walked in the direction of the execution site. Mary and Anne had no idea where they were going, but Aaron explained that the place was set aside specifically for the purpose. This statement gave rise to fears that this was more than a regular occurrence. Mary asked Aaron what this town was called. He said that the Romans called it Tiberias but its true name was Kinneret and that it used to be the most beautiful city in the region. She then asked where they were headed. He answered that they were headed for the main building at the centre of town, the execution fields were behind the palace. He also added that they were situated there because the occupants, meaning the Romans, enjoyed the misery they inflicted upon others. As they approached, they could see the majesty of the palace. It was built in stark contrast to the rest of the buildings that surrounded it. Rising like a monument reaching for the sky, it featured impressive columns crowned with arches that supported the upper levels from where more columns reached skyward towards a sloping roof which was crowned with the most exquisite statues of what they guessed could be their deities or leaders. It was constructed with absolute symmetry in mind, obviously the work of master builders. The one thing that struck them was how secure it looked, not just the robustness of its construction, but it also looked like an impenetrable fortress. Each entrance was protected by a number of guards barring the entrance to all but the chosen ones who were granted access to this great edifice. Separately, all seven of them walked along the rough path, around the palace, to an area that stretched for a great distance. There seemed to be a large flattened area where spectators were already gathering. In front of this area the land dropped off into a small valley which had a depth of ten feet or so. On the other side to where they were, was a series of mounds. Rising from each mound was an upright post. They estimated that each post rose to a height that easily equalled two or three times the height of an average man. This was clearly not the arena for the type of execution they had envisaged. They were confused and bemused and were just about to ask what was happening here when their attention was drawn to a procession of people entering from their left on the other side of the rift. As the scene played out before them they found themselves being drawn into the theatre of what was happening. They came to realise that the crowd, who by this time had swelled to occupy almost every inch of free space that was available to them, were here for some form of macabre entertainment spectacle. Heading the procession was a column of soldiers, immaculately dressed in white and red uniforms dressed with leather belts which featured broader leather straps which hung down their legs. All of them wore helmets and armour, and carried a sword and a lance. Three people followed, each of them was dragging a smaller beam of wood. They were dressed in nothing but a loincloth, they were unshaven, and sported long bedraggled hair and none of them wore shoes. Behind them was another column of soldiers. The procession walked until the three central participants were about level with the upright beams. It was at this point that a solitary figure crossed in front of them. He wore an all white robe with a red sash. His head was crowned with a headpiece of golden laurel leaves. He stood and unrolled a scroll of parchment. He began to speak, and as he did, the entire crowd was reduced to an eerie silence which was only broken by the distraught wailings which came from the families and friends of the condemned.

"Today we have three executions by crucifixion. Firstly, we have Jacob of Galilee. He has been charged and found guilty with repeated theft, assault and crimes against the Roman Empire. Secondly we have his accomplice and partner in crime, Esau also of Galilee. He also has been charged and found guilty with repeated theft, assault, and crimes against the Roman Empire". It was now the turn of Beth's brother. "Finally, Thomas of Ganei. He has been charged with, and found guilty of resisting the authority of the Roman Empire, preaching ill against the Empire, and repeatedly soliciting support for his cause against the Roman Empire. Let the punishment be carried out without delay by the order of Caesar Augustus, Emperor of all of Rome and the known world. Velites commence with your duties."

At this point the crowd seemed split by their emotions. Some were cheering and whistling. Others seemed to be genuinely upset by what was about to happen. Thanks to the stage the computer was at extrapolating this new language, they had managed to understand most, if not all, of what had just been said, and now they waited in anticipation. They didn't have to wait long. The first man was ordered to place his beam on the floor and then lie face up with his arms along the length of the joist. When he was in position, two of the Roman soldiers tied his arm around the beam with lengths of rope. They repeated the procedure with each of the other two. When all three had been tied the crowd fell silent. Then the unimaginable happened. The two soldiers, who had tied the men to the beams, then placed their hands on the upper and lower arms of the condemned and applied their body weight. Two more soldiers approached carrying hammers and roughly made stakes. Anyone who could see the faces of the three men would instantly recognise the look of extreme terror, their eyes wide open and their chests rising and falling rapidly, anticipating the inevitable. They clenched their teeth and breathed so hard that saliva would shoot out and run in rivulets down the sides of their cheeks, tears ran from their eyes and mucus formed bubbles which burst from their nostrils. The two soldiers who attended each of the men then placed the points of the stakes on their arms above the wrists and with one mighty blow drove them through their flesh and into the wood. Simultaneously the men let out a blood curdling scream of intense pain. Once again the crowd were split, cheering and booing. The crew violently jolted in surprised terror as the hammers were bought down upon the stakes. Three more blows were rained down on the three men, which produced more painful screams. As each blow was delivered a part of the audience would cheer as the hammer drove the stake further into the wood. When they were securely attached to the beams more soldiers approached and hauled them up to the upright posts and secured them in place. As they did so the three men almost passed out from the excruciating pain that was searing through their bodies. When in place the ordeal was still not over. Their legs were then tied together. The pain continued as stakes were driven into, and through, the joints of their ankles securing them into their final place. During the entire procedure they screamed the most deadly, painful screams and the crowd cheered, booed and wept. Finally, the ropes that had taken the majority of the strain were cut bringing their entire bodyweight down upon their wounds. Two of them lost consciousness, and the third died instantly from the shock. Mary could not avert her gaze. She was on one knee with her arm around Beth's shoulder. Her mouth was agape with surprise and horror. Anne was vomiting violently, and the others just stared in disbelief. It was the most barbaric act they had ever witnessed and it sickened them to the core.

J.D. and Watkins could not believe what they had just witnessed on their view screens as the captain spoke to them. "Err…J.D., Matthew, did you get that?" For an instant neither of them spoke. Then J.D. cleared his throat and confirmed that they had a record of what had transpired he then excused himself and went to be sick.

They had been on their crosses for more than an hour; most of the crowd had dissipated leaving only a few of the more macabre spectators and the family and friends of the condemned men. The four friends sat, watched and waited for the merciful end to come. Thomas had been conscious for about fifteen minutes and was in pain. It was a pain the like of which he had never experienced before. Never in his darkest hour could he have imagined such horror. He could feel the entire weight of his body bearing down on him his breathing was laboured and he could see rivulets of blood dripping from the wounds on his arms. He wept with the unbearable pain he was experiencing and prayed for the end to come swiftly. Since he had awoken, he had seen his entire life played out for him in his mind. He asked questions of himself, questioned his morality, his ethics, his lifestyle. He wondered if he could have foreseen the outcome of his protestations against the Romans, would he have done anything different. After all who would have thought that just for speaking ones mind against acts that were blatantly wrong, that anyone would be so inhumane as to inflict this upon anyone? But here he was and this was clearly the end. He tried to move his body to a more comfortable position, but this was a mistake. His entire chest and lower abdomen seared with the most intense pain which caused him to cry out. It was a hopeless endeavour, there was no escape. By this time, Beth had stopped crying and now, she just sat, drained, not just physically, but emotionally also. She was a shell, just starring at her brother hanging helplessly before her. Her gaze never faltered, she was not going to waste a second of the last minutes, hours or days of his life. She too was reliving times gone by in her memory, asking the same questions as Thomas, but from a different perspective. Should she have been a better sister? Could she have prevented any of his anger towards these oppressors? All of the questions being asked were purely rhetorical and could not change the outcome at which they now found themselves. For the rest of the day they all sat watching for any sign that the end may be near. Occasionally Beth would occasionally, look around at the few people that were left and wonder why. What could they possibly get from being here? Slowly it would anger her, but she tried to control her emotions. As dusk fell, so did her spirits. They sunk to a level she did not know existed. She needed something to vent her anger upon. Behind her, there sat two strangers. They had been there all day, watching the spectacle. Although they had been together all day, neither Beth, Aaron, Mary or Anne had spoken much and as a consequence they were not too aware of each other. No one noticed as Beth rose to her feet without much attention, until she started running towards the two strangers who were not expecting her onslaught. She threw herself at them fists flailing, venting whatever anger she had. These actions were so far out of character for her she could hardly believe what she was doing. But she could not help herself, she needed an outlet. She pummelled Jason's chest as hard as she could, all the time shouting.

"Have you seen enough, had you fill? Or are you waiting for someone else to get hung up?"

The entire tirade lasted only seconds when the other

three reached Beth who by this time had been gently subdued by the captain and was being held secured against his chest. Aaron was just about to accost Jason when Travis did almost the same to him. Quickly Mary and Anne entered the affray and when they were both calm enough to get through, they had to explain that Jason and Travis was friends of theirs and had been watching over them all day to make sure that they were safe from the crowd. When Aaron and Beth had calmed down completely, they were released, upon which Aaron took his wife into his arms and they both collapsed to their knees and wept openly.

It had been a great emotional release for Beth who apologised to Jason and invited them to sit alongside the others as they waited. Fires had been lit on both sides of the ravine and save for the sound of burning wood the scene was silent. A lone figure approached the party and asked who represented Thomas of Ganei. Beth replied that she did and that the rest were her supporters. She was then invited to follow this representative and to bring her party with her. They were led around the ravine and taken to where the crosses stood. Only Beth and Aaron approached Thomas, who by this time was only minutes away from death. Thomas opened his eyes and looked down on Beth. His breathing was intensely laboured, and as he spoke, he did so with all of the energy he could muster.

"Aaron, Beth, my beautiful sister." He almost had to take a breath between every word. "Forgive me, I have been foolish but I need for you to know…know something. I may not have told you as much as I should have but I am proud of you, I have always been so very proud of you." He coughed and the pain caused his entire body to spasm. He did not cry out but the grimace on his face was louder than any cry could have been. Blood poured down his chin and ran down his chest. Beth hushed him but he needed to talk and with all of his remaining energy he continued. "I did not imagine that this would be my fate but here we are. It is almost time for me to go but know this. One day there will be someone who will do exactly as I have and speak against these barbarians. It is inevitable. When you find such a person, support them in any way that you safely can." His body, once more went into spasm. When he had composed himself he found the energy for one last sentence. "My darling Beth, I love you and always have done. Until we meet again…love each other and prosper. Goodbye my love good…" He never finished the last word. He shook violently for a second, and then his head fell forwards, rolled to one side and he exhaled one last time. He had died. Aaron placed his arm around his wife's shoulder, who, had lowered her head into the palms of her hands and had begun to sob. The others stood together cradling Luke and they comforted each other. They were left alone for ten minutes, then a medic went over to where Thomas hung and after examining him, pronounced him to be dead. They were given time to spend with their departed then they were joined by an official who said that they could collect the body at dawn the next day and that it was time for them to leave. None of them had any fight left and so, without question they made for the exit path where they had arrived earlier that day. As they were about to leave the arena Beth and Aaron looked back one last time and then left. As they walked away Jason saw someone wave in the direction of the soldiers and became curious. He lingered a little while longer. When they thought that the family of the deceased had left, the soldiers went to the body and without reverence removed the stakes that had held the feet which caused the body to fall, leaving all of the weight suspended by the two stakes which held the arms. Then they released the cross beam sending the body crashing to the ground where they used hammers to loosen and eventually free the rest of the stakes. Finally two soldiers stood at either end of the lifeless body and took the hands and feet of Thomas, who they then swung back and forth before releasing him. His body flew through the air where he landed on an open back truck. Jason had seen enough, he shook his head in sadness and joined the others. He was glad that, at least, Beth and Aaron had been spared this final indignity.

They did not return to the ship that night. They chose to accompany Aaron and Beth back to their home where they stayed to comfort them through the night.

The night was dark when they left to collect Thomas' remains. Only the men went. The women waited to receive him and prepare the necessary paraphernalia for the burial.

Dawn was breaking when the men arrived back at the place of execution. They had walked for over an hour pulling a small cart to transport the body back to the house where it would be interred. The gates to the arena were closed but cut into the wall outside the gates were a series of narrow shelves. And there lay the bodies of the three men who were executed on the previous day. A soldier stood guard over them and as they approached he ordered them to stop. Duly they did so and he asked their business there. Having established that they were the family of Thomas of Ganei, he released the body to their care. They approached the body and carefully lifted him onto the cart and started back. They pulled the cart slowly through the town and as they passed, people would bow their head in a mark of respect for the dead. This happened all of the way until they had cleared the populated area. The only people who showed no respect were the Romans. But then, this was only to be expected from this barbaric race. No one spoke during the rest of the journey; it took almost twice as long, pulling the extra weight but the burden was eased for Aaron by having the other two to share the load. As they arrived at the house they were met by the women who had been busy preparing. They had cleared the main room of the house and had hung coverings over the windows to darken the room. The three men gently lifted the body from the cart and took him to the waiting room. They laid him reverently on the table that had been placed centrally allowing access from all sides. Before they began to prepare Thomas, Beth and the others had prepared a small feast to celebrate his life. During the meal they chatted and the crew learned more about Thomas' life, and his relationship with his sister. The emotional air of yesterday had long gone and everyone had accepted that Thomas was dead, and that now was a time to reflect upon his life and to prepare him for his final journey. The daylight was beginning to fade when they turned their attention to the task at hand. Beth and Aaron had invited the rest of them to be present as she prepared the body. This was indeed an honour to be allowed to share in one of the most important rituals in their lives. The only person who would prepare the body would be Beth. The others were seated around the room. They were there for comfort, support and simply to observe.

She began by lighting several candles and placing them at his head and his feet. The glow from the candles washed the room in a soft orange glow and gave the entire scene an altogether more serene quality. The only garment he was wearing was the loin cloth which was now stained with the dry blood and the mud from the previous day. She removed the cloth which left the body naked and exposed. No embarrassment was felt or displayed by the assembled party this surpassed the flesh. On a table next to her were several bowls filled with the various items that she would need. Firstly she took his hand and proceeded to clean the blood from around his wounds. When she had done this they could plainly see the extent of the hole that was left. There was no further seepage of blood and the wound looked angry but clean. The other wounds were treated in the same way. Having cleaned the visible damage she turned her attention to his state of general cleanliness. This was the point where she needed assistance from Aaron. He handed Luke to Anne and went to help. He rolled the body onto its left hand side allowing her to wash the back. When she had finished he repeated the process and she washed the other side. When she had dried him she began to massage oil into the skin and laid a cloth underneath him. Aaron then rolled him back into place onto the shroud. Having completed his back she turned her attention to his front. She washed, cleaned, dried and oiled every part of his lifeless form until she was satisfied that everything was in order. Next, she went to the head of the table and repositioned the candles either side of Thomas, allowing her access to his head. Once again she tended to his cleanliness, before washing his hair and beard. Taking particular care in his appearance she trimmed his mousey blonde coloured hair until it fell at shoulder length and trimmed his beard. Ironically this was probably the cleanest he had been in ages. The cleansing process was over and Thomas had been covered in aromatic oils. The next stage was to wrap the body in the shroud. Starting at the feet, and working her way up, she pulled the cloth tightly around his legs tearing it as she went equally on opposing sides and tying the two ends together. This continued until the entire body had been covered leaving the head exposed. Aaron then brought more bandage like strips to the table. Between them they proceeded to place bandages underneath the body crisscrossing them along the entire length. With each new bandage they sprinkled a mixture of herbs into the folds of the fabric. When they had completed the wrapping procedure Aaron left Beth to complete the head. She placed a cloth over the face and then expertly bound his head. When the entire process was complete she went to the head of the table leaned down and tenderly placed a kiss on his forehead. At this everyone left the room. During the ritual neither she nor her husband recoiled at the body, it seemed, to all witnessing this tender procedure, that it was an honour to service their departed in such a manner. There was no sadness or anger, only a distinct air of love, and respect.

They walked in the darkness to an area about one hundred yards away from the house where they found several torches. Taking his oil lamp Aaron lit all of the torches. When they were all lighted, he picked up his shovel. He had been charged with digging the grave where Thomas was to rest. Jason placed his hand on the shovel and asked if it would be alright with them, if he and Matthew could have the honour of preparing the site. A tear formed in Beth's eye. She was touched by the generosity of these strangers. Her eyes met with her husbands and she gently nodded in his direction. Over the next two hours the three men took it in turn to dig a grave that was slightly longer than Thomas was tall, the same for the width and about the same in depth as the length. When the grave was finished Aaron and Watkins reached out their arms and pulled Jason from the hole. They then went to bring Thomas to his final resting place. Using three long lengths of the same cloth in which he had been bound all six of them lowered the body to the bottom of the grave and proceeded to cover Thomas with the same soil that had been removed. To finish the site large boulders were placed around the site as a memorial to remind them of him. They went back to the house leaving the torches burning in the darkness.

They stayed for refreshments and then they announced that it was time for them to take their leave. It was still dark, and concern was shown for their safety, but they insisted that it was indeed time for them to go, so, reluctantly Beth and Aaron thanked them for what they had done for their family and pledged to repay the favour in some way in the future. They said their goodbyes and vowed to return. As they walked away they could see the torches burning in the distance. The emotions of the last rotation had taken their toll on the crew; they were drained and looked forward to relaxing in familiar surroundings. The journey back to the beach was a quiet affair. Each of them was reflecting on events they had witnessed and the fortitude of their new friends.

16. Ghosts

Having been debriefed about the recent events, the captain had ordered six hours of rest and relaxation. Marius Hatch had slept throughout the whole episode and had awoken just as they were finishing their meeting. The captain stayed in the cockpit to bring him up to speed with their recent experiences. The rest of them retired to different parts of the ship. Although they had been granted a period of R & R, none of them could relax. There was no possibility of sleep, and besides which, they were mentally occupied with their work. Most of them busied themselves with checking equipment and preparing for the next time they would go ashore. Travis and Anne had been assigned the task of connecting the storage media that had been given them by the elders of the tribe. They had managed to free the disc drive from its sealed container of the orange stone and were surprised to find that it was in pristine condition, or so it seemed. The care with which it had been packed, had preserved it well. Had they have left it in the substance they felt sure that it would have survived indefinitely. It was of a format that no one was familiar with and back on the home world they had been searching for instructions to connect it to the main computer and hopefully extract any information that it may hold. They had direct contact with the technical engineers who had figured out a method that could possibly achieve their goal. It required the assistance of Anne and her micro surgery skills. They told her that she would be working on micro circuitry and that she should secure the drive on the workbench and ready her tools to do the job. Travis assisted her and when they were ready they contacted the engineers and started to try to achieve a connection. She placed the high powered magnifying glasses over her head and swung the lenses down over her eyes which activated the forward facing lights, which illuminated the circuitry she would be working on. The two problems that faced them were the electrical supply and the connection to their computers on board. The engineers had managed to trace the original specifications of the unit, so apart from making the link they could foresee no problems. It would be a simple case of hoping that time had not deteriorated the data. Travis handed her a connector cable that was compatible with the ships systems. She cut one of the ends off and stripped the cables. Following the instructions of the engineers, she traced each and every wire and attached and soldered the bare ends to the place indicated to her. When she had completed all of the instructions she removed her goggles and they both sat back and looked at what they had created. It was a strange contraption consisting of a board to which they had secured the drive. Wires led from the drive to a power supply and a network of wires, which had been soldered to the circuit board inside led to a compatible connector for the on board systems. The device was not attractive but hopefully, it was functional.

Carrying it carefully they took it to the cockpit. Travis cleared a place to set it down and then they waited until all of the crew were assembled. The engineers had uploaded a boot device to them and all they had to do was to switch it on and hope for the best. Eventually they had all finished what they were doing and joined the rest in the cockpit area. For Anne, it was not a moment too soon, she was itching to switch it on just to see if it would work. Daniels and Hatch were the last to take their seats. He then turned to Anne and said "OK, let's see what you've got." She connected it to one of the terminals in the main computer, connected the power supply and threw the switch. They all waited. At first nothing happened and they all thought that that was it. Anne turned to the others and shrugged her shoulders questioningly. J.D. motioned to her using his head in such a manner to indicate to her that she should use a little force to encourage it to react. She was still holding a screwdriver, so she turned it around in her hand and using it hammer style she tapped the outer casing of the drive. There was a painful scraping sound as the drive sprang to life. Before long, the scraping sound abated and was replaced by a gentle whirr. Hatch suggested that while it was functional they should download the content to the main computer in case it failed. The captain agreed and asked Travis to do so. The download took about ten minutes after which the contraption was switched off and placed into the storage of the ship. The archaic extensions of the files could not be opened by the computers and the engineers were called upon once more to upload converters to the main frame to allow them to view the content. This took even more time. It was frustrating for them all to have the files but not the means to view them. The final maddening cause for frustration was when they were told that now that they had the correct converters they must encode all of the information files to a format that the onboard computers could display. As it turned out this procedure would take some two hours to complete. They resumed their previous activities while they waited. Eventually the call was made and they all returned to the cockpit and took their seats. Anticipation was high as Travis opened the file he had, somewhat nostalgically named '106 the originals'. In the file he found three folders, one called 'Images' another was named 'Documents' and the third was named 'Video'. Onto one screen he opened the Images folder and started them running on a slideshow which would play in the background. He chose not to explore the documents folder for now and opted to open the Videos. In this folder there were literally hundreds of video reports, all meticulously dated. He arranged the files in date order and noticed that they all had prefixes, and a structure to the title. The structure was prefix, file number, date. There were four prefixes, All, MK, GP and BH. He selected the earliest file number and date of the 'All' series and pressed the play icon. Instantly the screen was filled with the images of three uniformed, clean shaven young men. The images were incredibly clear and the audio was crisp. They found themselves in the presence of legends.

"This is the first report from the crew of Alpha 106. My name is Malcolm Keogh, this person to my right is Gary Parr, and this is Balvinder Singh." They were filming this report from within their capsule. It was strikingly smaller than the cockpit where the crew was viewing from and bore no familiarity with the ships of today. It looked primitive and unworkable. "We have just landed on Epsilon Omega and have lost contact with home, but we hope to re-establish some sort of communication soon. We seem to have landed on a plain near to an inland body of water somewhere between thirty one and thirty three degrees inside the northern hemisphere. We have not ventured outside as yet so we have no idea how our ship is lying. The first order of business is to disguise ourselves to protect against discovery, if we have not been discovered already. Then we need to organise ourselves, we only have enough rations to last us for thirty rotations of this world. We need to check the body of water that lies near to us to see if it is drinkable if not then we must desalinate it to make it fit for consumption. We will make video journals periodically for as long as is possible and will carry out our orders to the best of our abilities. When we have secured the ship we will then test the outside atmosphere and hopefully it will support our vital needs. So, this has been the first report from 106. It has been short but for now there is nothing else to report. So this is Malcolm Keogh on behalf of the crew of Alpha 106 signing off." As he finished he could be seen leaning forward to turn off the camera.

This had been a first glimpse into their own history and it had a profound effect on them. To sit and watch images of people, fellow countrymen who had been dead for over two and a half thousand years was confusing to the sensibilities. It was hard to know how to feel about these three pioneers. They had watched the first report which was as fresh as the day it was recorded all of those years ago and it could have been yesterday. Effectively, they had been spoken to by historical figures. They were people who they had studied at school. They, of course had seen pictures of them, but now this was much more personal. The captain asked Travis to skip forward about one month.

"This is the weekly report for the crew of 106. We have finally finished the camouflage of our ship and now it is, we think, totally undetectable." This report was being filmed by Keogh, and the narrator was Parr. The camera was being hand held and was following Parr as he was making the report. "As you can see, we have built the sand and rocks from around the area up around the ship which forms part of the natural landscape." He pointed towards a small rock built archway that was set into the mound which now surrounded the craft. "You can see that we have left ourselves access into the ship via that doorway. Our task for the next few days is to create our settlement in front of that entrance giving us access to our equipment and at the same time disguising its existence to any prying eyes. Moses has been a great help to us and although communications are still a little impossible we seem to understand each other more and more each day."

They were confused as to who Moses was. They would have to backtrack through the reports to discover more about this stranger. "Balvinder is not around at the moment he has gone off on a hunting foray to boost our stocks. Not much more to report at the moment. Everyone is well and healthy; this planet seems to fit our needs perfectly. We will update you about our efforts to create our camp on our next report. This is Gary Parr on behalf of the crew of Alpha 106, end report."

Moses was a new character to the crew and they wondered how he became involved with the other three. For now the captain was content to take snapshots of the reports on a six monthly period. As they watched they witnessed the changes in them. The first to go was the uniforms which seemed to be discarded in favour of clothing that was more fitting for the environment and more inconspicuous to anyone that may stumble across them. It was interesting to watch as their skin became more rugged and their hair grew longer. All of them developed beards and moustaches and soon they were almost unrecognisable at the three fresh faced young men who had first landed there. As time went by the development of the settlement became more and more established. What started as a collection of three tents grew into a small community. New faces appeared on a regular basis as their group grew. Soon there were children in the group and it was clear that a small village was being created. While they were sampling the video library, Mary had been looking into the Document folder where she found a complete written account of the day to day happenings in and around the community. It was a journal of events that included births, deaths and new arrivals. Now that Mary was opening the entries around the date of the video that was being viewed, they could sometimes match faces that appeared with their exact circumstance.

They had been watching this society build for about four hours when the captain asked to see the last entry. Travis lined it up ready to play and waited for the captain. He gave Travis the sign and he pressed the play icon. On this occasion they were seated inside a tent, and were surrounded by others. This report would be made by all three of them.

"Hello friends." Began Balvinder, "This will be the last report from the crew of Alpha 106." This time they looked serene. They looked like true leaders of their people and it was almost sad that although they had never met, the crew felt as if they were saying goodbye to good friends and family. "You have watched us grow for the last twenty five years but now our equipment grows old and our storage is almost full. We have tried to fulfil our mission to the best of our ability, but now, we must continue onwards without your company. These people around us are our family. They are our wives, and our children. Together we will continue to grow and sustain our legacy. Our tribe now numbers one hundred and twenty seven and in the next few days it will be one hundred and twenty eight. So we continue to grow." Gary Parr was the next to address them. "We will secure these recordings as best we can and pass them down through the generations of our descendants. We hope that one day in the very distant future; someone will watch these recordings, they are our gift to you, a message to a world long lost to us. Our hope is that you learn much about our people and our way of life. We are proud to have been selected for this mission and none of us have any regrets. We have been given a unique opportunity to shape our own destiny, and for that we will be forever grateful." Finally Malcolm Keogh spoke. "We will continue on our path but know this about the crew of Alpha 106. We are proud men with proud families who will live the rest of their lives in peace and harmony. But above all else, we are men of God and will always hold true to what God means to us. We are and always will be servants of God and will always be at your service. Our beliefs will be passed on to our offspring, and they, in turn, onto theirs. Our hope is that one day when you return you will find our descendants and know that through us, they will be there to serve you. Do not grieve for us, celebrate our lives. Now it is time for us to take our leave. So, this has been the final report from the crew of Alpha 106. My name is Malcolm Keogh." "My name is Gary Parr." "And My name is Balvinder Hasar. May God be in your hearts now, and forever more. Goodbye dear friends. Alpha 106. out."

With this, the screen went blank and the crew sat staring. Tears ran down the faces of a few of them. Not tears of sadness, but tears of pride and fulfilment.

17. The final days.

Watkins and Hatch began to transfer all of the information they had collated back to the home world, including all of the information from the disc. With the amount of data they had collected, it was due to be a lengthy process. The entire crew was now in a melancholy mood as they prepared for the next shore visit. As they did so it was under a cloud of silence and deep reflection. The duties for the coming day had been given to everyone by Hatch who in this instance was also going ashore. It had been decided that on this journey they would take the cargo pod ashore to collect all of the equipment they had stored in the cave. The assignments for the day were much the same as usual. Mary and Anne along with Travis were to visit Aaron and Beth to see if there was anything they could do after their tribulations. This was a task that they all were cherishing. J.D., Matthew and Hatch were scheduled to revisit the town to try to complete the Roman language database. The captain alone would stay on board the ship to finalise the data transfer. In light of the barbaric traits that had been displayed by the Romans, Daniels had decided to issue non lethal weapons to the shore party. Each of them was issued a tazer gun with strict orders not to use them unless it was absolutely unavoidable. None of them even considered the possibility but it was the duty of the captain to try to foresee any and every eventuality.

By the time they left the ship daylight had broken. For Daniels, who was monitoring the departure on the screens, it was a surreal sight to see six people floating away from the ship heading upwards and towards the shore. The first order of business upon arriving on shore was to load the cargo pod with all of the equipment. They all set to the task and although there was not much to load, arranging the three cycles into the pod turned out to be more of a puzzle than at first thought. In all it took about thirty minutes to successfully get everything in so that the top would form a watertight seal. With the packing complete they sent the pod on its way back to the ship and then made their way to their own destinations.

By the time the three men had arrived at the town it was bustling with life. J.D. recognised the flow of people heading towards the centre of town and surmised that, yet again, it must have been market day. Their mission for the day was to complete the Roman language banks and they expected that there would be Romans in the market place, making it an ideal spot to allow the computers to sample more of the speech patterns. On the outskirts of the marketplace they found a tavern with a sheltered side which afforded a little respite from the intense heat of the sun. Where they sat was within earshot of a garrison of the soldiers who were observing the bustle of the buyers as they haggled for the best deals. The soldiers were talking amongst themselves which gave an ideal sampling situation for the crew. They had drunk two drinks each in the space of an hour and a half and had witnessed one change of the guards. One of the guards had remained during the change, and had been there since they had arrived. Watkins noticed him paying attention to them and alerted the others to the unwanted interest. They decided to leave the tavern and find a less conspicuous place to make their observations from. They paid the innkeeper for their drinks and as inconspicuously as possible they walked around the market in an attempt to mingle with the crowds and disappear from the soldiers view. They had not counted on the detective skills of this tenacious individual. Something about them had attracted his attention, he didn't know what it was about them, but to him, they seemed out of place. There was something about them that didn't quite fit in. He decided to follow them. He and one other soldier tailed them through the market area and out through the town. They kept a safe distance to avoid detection but surreptitiously kept them in sight. The three men had no idea that they were being monitored. As a result of this they felt relaxed and unsuspecting as they walked through the town. The two soldiers had decided to question their targets as soon as they could find a quiet back alley where they could inflict their own kind of interrogation without being disturbed. For them this was going to be private entertainment. On many occasions they had done this before for fun. But this time they were curious as to the purpose of the strangers. They had reached the end of the town and decided to take advantage of the pleasant day and explore their surrounding further. The decision had been made to walk through the outskirts of the town and to make their way back to the market in the hopes that there had been another change of the guards so that they may find another place to observe the Romans from. As they turned around the back of one of the outermost buildings, none of them saw what was coming. The soldiers quickened their pace and caught up with the three strangers. Without warning or forethought the solider who was the instigator rushed up behind the men and bought his lance down. As he did so, the blade pierced deep through the calf of Watkins bringing him screaming to his knees. The force of the fall snapped the head of the lance off its shaft and the tip through the front of his leg. The pain was so intense he thought that he may lose consciousness. A scuffle ensued but the Romans were too strong for the crew who were quickly subdued and were ordered to their knees facing a nearby wall. The soldier who had accompanied the first, detained the two and guarded them against the wall as the other went over to Watkins who was by this time grasping at his injured calf. Blood ran between his fingers and, for a while, collected in a pool on the sandy floor before it seeped below the surface. Tears ran down his face as he tried to control the searing pain in his leg. His face was contorted and his eyes screwed tightly against the violent destruction that had been inflicted upon him. As the soldier approached he found himself scooting himself backwards in an effort to escape his attacker. The soldier, feeling no threat stood over him and started to question who they were and what they were doing here. The computer heard the question and tried to provide a response. The reply was at best patchy, but it had an unexpected effect. When he listened to what Watkins had to say he quietly reached for the spearhead that was bloodied and protruding from Watkins calf. He gently gripped it then with one cruel movement twisted the blade inside the wound which caused Matthew to let out another agonising yell as the pain in his leg intensified to such a degree it became even more unbearable. This was pain like no other he had felt in his entire life, and he was not sure weather he could cope for much longer. The twisting of the blade had released more blood and now the crimson red patch beneath him had started to collect in a pool. He brought his face close to Matthews and quietly said in his own language that he knew that there was something strange about him and his companions. No one in this town spoke their language, it was against the law to learn, teach or even speak it. So how did these three develop such a command of a forbidden tongue? Watkins' bottom lip quivered from the pain, he had no idea how to answer this man. No idea how to stop the pain. Desperately trying to find a way to reply, had created a pause that had become too long for the soldier and to further press his point he slowly twisted the spearhead some more. Once again Matthew yelled. Both JD and Hatch knew they had to assist their ailing colleague. They were both aware of the tazers hanging at their sides beneath their robes and knew that they had to use them. The attention of the second guard was firmly taken with the scene that was being played out. The two captives glanced at each other and with a quick nod they made their move. In one fluid movement J.D. swung his entire body with all of the strength he could muster against the guard. The force sent him careering to the ground. J.D. then fumbled his way into his tunic and drew his gun. Simultaneously Hatch did the same and as the first guard rushed toward him he discharged the tazer into his body at exactly the same time as J.D. did the same to the other one. The two Romans instantaneously lost all control over their muscle functions and fell to the ground. The pained, confused look on their face told a story. They were aware of what was happening to them but unaware of what it was. They lay contorted on the floor twitching for a few minutes then they started to recover. J.D and Hatch had little time to act, they had to ignore the pain that Watkins was suffering and secure the guards. They started to tear strips from their robes and from the garments of the guards to fashion ropes with which to tie them. Once they had been bound and gagged they then turned their attention to their fallen companion. His wound was severe and they could not remove the weapon without causing further damage. They dressed around the obstruction as best as they could and found a small cart which they would use to transport him back to the ship. It was not in their nature to kill these assailants but how could they leave them. They would be free of their bindings, or someone would release them, soon and they in turn would raise the alarm. Then they would be hunted until capture, interrogated and then crucified. It was a fate that none of them relished. Between them and the ship they had decided to bind them even further and to leave them outside of the village tied to a tree. Then using a small explosive device they would attract attention to their location allowing them to be found and released. There was of course no guarantee that this plan would work, and that the guards may never be found and would perish. But, it was the only plan they had and it was imperative that they got Watkins back to the ship. They helped Matthew onto the cart and made their way out of the town. When they thought that they were at a safe distance away they retied the legs of their captives and tied them to a tree. They then set the charge on a timer giving themselves three hours to make their escape. When they were sure that the soldiers were secure they began their journey. Watkins had lost a lot of blood and was feeling lightheaded. Before long he lost consciousness they knew that time was running out.

Anne, Mary and Travis had spent the morning with Aaron and Beth. It was like visiting long term friends. The morning had been pleasant and they had visited the grave of Thomas to pay their respects. They were just sitting down to take a meal when the commotion started. They had heard the entire episode through their ear pieces and instinctively knew that they had to return to the ship. They made their excuses to their hosts, and quickly made their way back to the beach. Upon their arrival, Mary and Travis returned to the ship to prepare for Watkins arrival. Anne stayed ashore to administer triage and primary care for the patient.

While she waited the cargo pod had been dispatched to ferry them back. The pod had been stocked with medical supplies that Anne would need to treat him in transit. It was about half an hour before they appeared in the distance. As soon as Anne had seen them she picked up the stretcher and ran across the sands to meet them. It would have been to strenuous to pull the cart through the soft sand, so it had been pre arranged that from the line of vegetation they would stretcher him back to the pod. As she met them she threw the stretcher on the ground for them to pick up and unpack. She immediately went to attend her patient. Firstly he received a shot of a morphine type drug to ease his pain. He would not feel the effect of this until he regained consciousness, if he ever did. Once she had done this she quickly inspected the damage and decided that she could not remove the spearhead here it would have to wait. By the time she had applied a tourniquet to his upper leg the stretcher was ready. Carefully, so as not to aggravate the injury any further, they lifted him from the cart and laid him on the ground. With the stretcher underneath him, they then carried him to the waiting pod. Both Anne and Matthew travelled in the cargo pod so that she could begin to tend him on the way. Within seconds they were in transit. The loading bay of the shuttle had been transformed into a hospital bay; this was a function of the ship they had hoped not to have to use. It was a state of the art medical unit complete with equipment to meet the needs of almost any emergency and now it was being pressed into service to save the life of one of their fellow crewmen. The pods arrived and as soon as they were cleared, Matthew was taken from the pod and rushed into the waiting medical unit. The first thing she had to do was to stabilise him before she could tend his wound. The best way for her to gain control over his body was to place him into a drug induced coma. When she had achieved this she was able to slow his metabolism down giving her more time to work on him. Thanks to the machinery, he was now stable, not out of danger, but stable. The crew that was going to work on him then donned their surgical garments and masks. The entire area was then bathed in the purple iridescent glow which signified that the entire are was being sterilised against infection. The glow lasted for thirty seconds. When the room returned to its normal light the procedure was complete and the room had been sealed. They then scrubbed their hands and began to repair his wound. The machines were now in control of his life. His respiration, blood circulation and vital signs were all being controlled externally and everything was as it should be, stable. Now that they were content that he was at least safe for the moment they began. Anne was in charge of the proceedings and asked Hatch to monitor his life signs, Matthew was asked to deal with anaesthesia and Mary to assist in the operation. They had all been trained for this eventuality but had never, with the exception of Anne, needed to put their training into practice. So essentially, this would be their first time. Although Anne was a little concerned about this, it was the best she had to work with and was content that they would do their jobs. She began by inspecting the spearhead. It was a flat bladed instrument forged from iron; the blade was about twenty centimetres long and showed signs of rust. It passed straight through his leg. The exit point was visible by about three centimetres, and the entry was larger than the weapon due to the twisting of it. The blood had congealed, not to the point of forming a scab. It was a dark red gelatinous mass that needed to be cleared so that she could gain better access. As she sprayed it with a saline jet, it dissolved revealing the true extent of the surface damage. It was quite gruesome. The wound was still oozing blood from the damaged capillaries, veins and arteries and she knew that if she released the tourniquet it would allow for more blood loss. She decided to apply a second surgical tourniquet below the knee joint to lessen the volume of blood that could escape. Having done that, she turned her attention to the removal of the spear. There was no easy way to extract it and so she just took a firm grip of it and pulled it out. As she did a slurping sound could be heard as the rough iron was pulled through the muscle fibre of his calf. What was left was a conical wound that was filling with the rest of the blood supply that was available from below the tourniquet. The wound was cleaned out using the saline jet and Anne examined the wound to see what the actual damage was. There was much tearing of the inner muscle but she felt confident that using microsurgery she could repair the damage with every chance of a full recovery for Travis. She primarily examined the inside of the wound with her index finger. She was checking for any debris that may have been left. When she was sure that most of it had been removed she inserted a probe that would make a finer check for foreign bodies that may cause complications in the future. The probe located one rogue flake of rust that had embedded itself deep inside the muscle, it had to be removed. Carefully she began to search for it using a pair of hook tipped forceps, the two tips of which carried a camera and a light. Watching the screen she delved around in the damaged flesh to find the flake. Once she had extracted it she set about the task of repairing the tissues. This would be work of the finest, most intricate nature and would take six hours to complete. She had sewn and repaired every layer of damaged tissue, reconnected every severed nerve, and sutured every disconnected vein and artery and now, it was time to check her handiwork. Above the tourniquet that was below the knee she injected a solution containing a radio isotope which she would track through the capillary systems that she had just repaired. Mary brought over the scanning device and placed it over his lower leg. She connected to the computers, and they watched as Anne released the two tourniquets to let the blood flow back into the damaged leg. What they were particularly looking for was leaks in Anne's workmanship. As they watched the isotopes highlighted the blood flow as it began to circulate. All seemed well. She had done all that she could from a surgery aspect. Her work would now be one of nurse, administering as much aftercare as she could for her patient. Antibiotics were administered and Travis was brought out of his coma. The operation seemed to be a success and he was moved to his own quarters to recuperate. Between them they cleared the operating theatre and stowed all of the equipment back into its rightful places.

As he opened his eyes he was aware of Anne holding his wrist, checking his pulse. She smiled at him and said "Welcome back." He smiled at her and asked the only question that was on his mind. "Have I still got two legs?" Anne smiled at him and said that she had managed to save his leg and everything was going to be alright." He sunk his head back into his pillow and he sighed a deep sigh of relief. He could not feel his injured leg and thought that this may be the result of some form of pain killer Anne had given to him. He prayed that it was not some form of paralysis, only time would tell. His leg had been encased in a tube of diagnostic wizardry which kept a check on every aspect of his healing. Any anomalies would show on Anne's control panel alerting her to the problem. It fitted tightly around his leg, and was not cumbersome at all. In fact, it would allow him unrestricted mobility while he was on the ship. She left him alone to continue with his recovery.

The captain had relieved Travis of his duties and had reassigned them throughout the rest of the crew for the last two days on this planet. He was concerned about the soldiers that had been left tied to the tree. They had been there for about nine hours and he wondered if they had been discovered. Fearing that they had not, he was about to send J.D.

and Watkins to discover their fate. He called them all to an emergency meeting and without discussion he said," J.D., Watkins, I want you in full fatigues, take what you need and get to those two men. What ever this race may be, I will not be responsible for their deaths. We need to know that they are alright. Be ready to go in five minutes. The rest of you will monitor this operation." Watkins tried to address the captain but he was cut off mid sentence. "I am sorry mister Watkins this is not open for discussion, get ready I want you to go in five" Watkins and the rest of them had realised that this was a different captain speaking. Daniels had recognised the fact that he had let himself become to complacent with this mission and had let his guard down and as a result he had an injured man. He needed to rectify his error the best way he knew how. This time he had ordered them to arm themselves; he could not take the risk of injuring any more of his crew. But by the same token he could not leave people to die as a consequence of his orders, regardless of whom, or what they may be. The two man reconnaissance team were dressed in full camouflage attire, this was a serious mission. They were armed with full combat weaponry and were ready to depart.

It was night when they arrived at the shoreline and, stealthily, they raised their pods above the surface of the water by only a few inches to enable them to survey the beach. They scanned the beach using their night vision goggles and their heat signature detector devices. There was nothing to indicate the presence of anyone except themselves. They proceeded to bring the pods into the shallows and like shadows in the night they moored them and continued into the night. Their entire field of vision could be seen only in green and black, due to the goggles they wore. This was the same for the crew. The night was so dark that it would have been impossible to make anything out without them. Using flood lighting or torches was not an option, this was a covert mission. They travelled through the trees without sound, heading for their target. When they arrived they checked out the area to see if there was anyone around. Satisfied that they were alone, they approached the two heat signals that were being displayed on their wrist monitors. It was evident that the explosive device they had left had become defective and had not deployed. They had to disarm it and place it back into one of their backpacks. The two Romans thought they were experiencing an apparition. They had never seen anyone quite so menacing, they sat with terror in their wide open eyes. This was something that was beyond their sphere of understanding, worse than any nightmare their minds could conjure. For one of them the terror was so bad it caused him to urinate. To facilitate an easier communication link their ear pieces were connected to speakers which were connected to the webbing straps that hung on their shoulders. Using the Roman language base the captain inputted the first question which was relayed through the speakers. "We are going to remove your gags, do you promise not to shout out?" They were by this time completely terrorised and would have agreed to anything, they nodded their heads rapidly and violently in agreement. As they reached to remove the gags, the two soldiers were still unsure and shielded their heads away from the two strange figures. The instant their mouths were free one of them began to call for help. Watkins firmly placed his hand over his mouth and held him firm. Placing one finger to his own mouth he shushed him. Even more terror appeared in his eyes, and realising the error of his ways he once more rapidly nodded to signify his compliance. When they were calmer the captain sent another message for them in their native tongue. "Are you harmed in any way?" The voice was not of this earth, they were in the presence of some beings or gods even, and who were inquiring as to their well being. They were afraid and confused. One of them, with his voice trembling, said that they were unhurt and asked what was happening. The captain explained that they had made a mistake by ensnaring them in such a manner and that his men were here to release them. Shortly they would be released but any sudden movements would result in them being restrained once again. He asked if they understood and also asked for their cooperation. Eagerly they agreed to all of his terms. Watkins took up position about ten yards away from the tree and trained his gun on the group while JD untied them one at a time. Upon being released they rubbed the areas where their bindings had been tightest to encourage circulation to return. Realising that any attempt to subdue these men would be futile, and so, they meekly complied with the wishes of their captors or indeed their liberators, dependant on your viewpoint. Now that they had been freed Watkins stood on guard waiting for any slight move on their behalf, but there was none. He was, however, alert and ready to act. J.D. reached into his backpack and removed four containers. He gave two to each of the men who looked confused. The speakers at his shoulders simply said "Eat, drink." The men looked at the containers mystified. Realising that they had no clue as to what was expected of them J.D. took the containers and unscrewed the tops and handed them back. He then motioned that they should drink the contents. Cautiously at first, they took a sip from each of the foil bottles and discovered to their amazement that one contained water and the other a liquid, the like of which they had never tasted before. To them it was one of the best tastes they had ever experienced. In fact it was standard field rations. When they had finished it was time for J.D. and Watkins to safeguard themselves and the crew from further discovery by this race. The gamble was that when their story was retold it would be met with ridicule, but at least these men would be free and safe. J.D. reached once more into his backpack and produced two hypodermic pumps that were filled with an anaesthetic prepared by Anne from her medical supplies. She reckoned that the effects of this shot should render them unconscious for about three hours. He went up to one of the soldiers and deftly injected him. Almost immediately he fell to the ground. Before the other had realised what was happening he too had succumbed to being injected and was also in a state of sleep. J.D. checked their state and signalled to Watkins that all was safe. He checked his gun and went to assist. They lifted the men from the crumpled position in which they lay and placed them comfortably at the base of the tree, collected the empty packaging from the rations they had given to them, and then proceeded to return to the ship.

The daylight had arrived when the two soldiers began to regain consciousness. They were sheltered from the intense heat in the shade of the tree. It took a while for the effects of the drug to wear off and to leave them fully cognoscente. For an instant they looked around them half expecting that the two strangers would still be there. Realising that they were long gone they headed back to their garrison wondering how they were going to explain their absence to their superiors.

This was the last day on Epsilon Omega and although the highs and lows of the mission had left them with conflicting feelings about this place, the general consensus was, that given time and a little more on the evolutionary scale, it had the potential to be a world not unlike their own. Although Daniels had made the town a no go area he knew that they would like the chance to bid farewell to Aaron and Beth, so he consented to them making one last visit to their house. Hatch and Daniels would stay behind, as would Travis, he was confined to the ship due to his injury. But the other four would make one last journey ashore.

The four pods arrived on shore and all four of them would exercise great caution while leaving the water. They moored the pods and started toward the house. None of them said it, but they were relishing this last visit. Walking along this pristine beach and sampling the clean, fresh, warm air. They thought that they would never experience such a perfect place again in their lifetimes. The topic of conversation on the journey was Travis' injury, the crucifixion, and the family they were about to visit. The congenial banter had speeded up the journey somewhat and before they knew it they were amongst the flock of goats that Aaron kept. He waved and greeted them from the other side of the flock, and began to make his way through the animals to meet them. He invited them to his home and between them they herded the flock back to the safety of the holding field next to his house. Once secured they all went to see Beth and Luke. Before entering the house they all went to the site of Thomas' grave to pay their respects. As they stood there talking Beth felt that there was more to their visit than they had said. She felt that this was not just a social encounter, This seemed, somehow, planned. She could not shrug this feeling and wanted to know what was different about this call. They retired to the house where they were treated to food and drink by their hosts. Mary was the one to broach the subject.

"Beth, Aaron. This will be our last visit to you. Tonight we must leave for our home. We wanted this last chance to see you and to thank you for all that you have done for us."

Beth knew that there was something afoot. But she didn't think that their new friendships would be so fleeting and this news took her a little by surprise.

She found herself feeling a little cheated that she would not be able to nurture her new found circle of friends. Beth looked at them and asked where they were from. They knew that this question would arise at sometime during this day and had concocted a story to use when explaining their destination. Mary seemed to have become the spokesperson for the moment and she explained that they were members of a nomadic tribe who had been searching for new lands to travel. Aaron asked if these were the lands that would be suitable for their tribe. Mary replied that these lands would be ideal except for the presence of the Roman occupiers. They would have to search wider to find a place that was safe for their peoples. It was not a satisfactory reason for not staying, but it was plausible and for now it had placated Aaron and Beth. It was a lie and Mary felt uneasy about deceiving her friends but she could not tell them the truth, they would not, nor, could not understand what was being told to them even if she did. The conversation about their impending departure was the topic of conversation for most of the morning. Gradually, different subjects were discussed and the day became more of a social event. Four hours into the visit the captain apologised but said that it was time for them to return and ready the ship for take off that night. They told their hosts that it was time for them to depart and for the next half an hour they helped tidy the utensils that had been used and said their goodbyes to Aaron, Beth and Luke. Before finally leaving they said that they had a parting gift for the family and presented them with the coins that they had manufactured for their stay. Beth almost lost the rigidity of her body when her legs buckled slightly, she had never seen so much money and to them it would certainly be an answer all of their dreams. But she knew that they could not accept such a generous offer and politely refused the gift. Fortunately for them, refusal was not an option. The crew explained that where they were going this currency was worthless and would just be thrown away. It took a little convincing that this was a genuine gift from the crew and eventually they accepted the gift. As they walked away from the house for the last time Aaron shouted after them. "If you ever need us for anything, know that we will be here ready to help you in any way".

The crew turned and waved goodbye to the people they had, over a short space of time, come to know well and had shared so much with.

Within an hour they were back on the beach placing their feet into their pods. They all took one last look around. Not to see if they were being observed, but to enjoy for one last time the surroundings of this place. Then with heavy hearts they returned to the ship.

It took the crew a few hours to prepare the craft for departure and when it was ready they had a few hours to kill before take off. With nothing else left to do they rested.

18. Disaster.

Everything was readied for their departure back to the home world and final checks were underway. They had about twenty minutes to wait before they finally left. Local time meant that most, if not all of the inhabitants would be asleep and this would allow them to make their departure with minimum observation. The crew were all seated at their respective stations completing their final checks, when they heard the mission control on the ship wide system.

"Hello 1472 this is mission control ready to take your final instructions for departure. All is looking good and everything reads green for take off. We have calculated your flight path and trajectory to place you on course for God and have already fed the coordinates into your main frame. We will of course talk you through procedure as we go. We estimate that your journey home will take approximately four days. Stand by for launch instructions. Launch will take place in ten minutes from my mark…mark."

Each of them was calm and collected and totally in control of their stations. But inside, the excitement of returning home was a source of great excitement. Everyone was busying themselves awaiting the instruction to secure themselves for take off. There was about five minutes left and it was time for final preparations to commence. The familiar pre flight cacophony of shouted commands and status confirmations began from the crew. "Fuel level show constant..." "Flaps and ailerons functioning..." "Hull secured for take off..." "Ready to break moorings sir on your command"

This was one of the pieces of information Daniels had been waiting for. They had left one small camera stationed outside the craft to enable them to see the shuttle from an outside perspective. Daniels could clearly see the ship on his screen and was ready to give the order. "Mister Hatch, blow the moorings please." Without hesitation, Marius flipped open the red protective casing that had hidden the detonation button from accidental activation, and pressed the red button beneath. The explosive charges detonated simultaneously. An almost inaudible dull thud was heard as the charges went off. From the outside camera the screen showed that all four charges had successfully freed the ship. As Daniels watched he could see a dim flash from the base of each mooring cable followed by a cloud of bubbles that rose to the surface. Some of the bubbles had to find their way around the body of the shuttle as they tried to escape upwards. The ship was now free from its moorings and free to manoeuvre into position for their departure. The shockwaves from the detonations had sent an unseen reaction through the sub aqueous mountain that rose up from the shuttles position. The effect of this disturbance had dislodged a boulder that had been precariously teetering on an upper ledge. It was now balancing hazardously over their position. Watkins had been monitoring the surrounding area and had found nothing untoward with their topography that would impede their departure. The captain instructed Mary to get them into position for take off. There was now only two minutes left and all was ready. The only thing they were waiting for was the final countdown from mission control and they would be on their way home. "Alpha 1472, this is control. Everything is showing green for launch. Countdown commencing. Take off in 30…29…28…"

At the instant the countdown had begun, high above them the boulder started to shift. The sheer weight of the rock had crushed a smaller one beneath it that had held it in its precarious position. As the smaller rock disintegrated under the weight, the larger one, which was the size of a small family car, careered towards them.

" 9…8…7…6…" The impact was strangely subtle yet violent. The rock had hit them on the wing closest to the rise. It was totally unexpected but was severe enough to throw Mary from her seat, where she was securing her safety harness for take off, over the centre console and onto the floor at Anne Homer's feet. The entire craft lurched upward in a fulcrum motion before it thudded back down to land firmly on its undercarriage jolting everyone. The debris from the landslide had destroyed the camera that had been monitoring the ship from the outside, so there was no visual available to the captain. The interior of the cabin was flashing red rhythmically to the sound of the alarms that were sounding. It was a piercing loud claxon sound that had started instantly the rock had hit them.

"Someone Turn those bloody alarms off." Daniels shouted. They all knew that this was the worst case scenario playing out in reality. The seriousness of this situation could not be ascertained from inside the ship. Daniels ordered J.D. to take one of the pods out to see what the damage was. He quickly suggested that it would be quicker if he swam. The captain agreed and J.D. ran into the departure bay and got into a swim suit and exited through the smaller escape chamber. The scene was chaotic as they tried to make sense of what had just happened to them. Mission control was further confusing the proceedings trying to collate information from their readings to see if there was anything that could be done from home. "Stand by control; we will brief you as soon as we can."

J.D. had reached the site of the impact and what he encountered horrified him. He spoke to the captain. "Sir, I can see what the problem is and things are not looking too good. Switch your monitor to my camera and see for yourself." Daniels changed the view screen to reflect what could be seen by DeVie. The scene outside filled the monitor and everyone starred in disbelief. They all left their posts and gathered around the screen. No one spoke they just starred. Mary was clutching her abdomen where she had been injured during the impact. She began to cry. Nothing more than a sob at first but as she realised the gravity of the situation her sob turned into a cry, the more she thought about their present position the cry turned into a panicked howl and finally she was screaming uncontrollably. Anne grabbed hold of her shoulders and slapped her firmly across the face. This was the jolt Mary needed to snap her back from panic. She was then helped back into a seat where she sat and whimpered. All was quiet and the captain mentally explored the options. The first thing he did was to cut communications between them and mission control. He could see that they were not going to be able to leave. The rock had damaged the port side wing. He could see from J.D.'s camera, that the damage incurred had left the craft incapable of flight. He thought that it was not beyond repair but by the time they had effected any restoration, the home world would be too far out of orbit for them to have any chance of catching it up. The immediate options available to them were simple. Stay or go. Things were moving at a pace and some serious life altering decisions had to be made within a short space of time. He ordered J.D. back to the cockpit but told him to remain in contact. He turned to the others and laid out the options to them. They could not think straight under the pressure of the situation, and the lack of time to decide. So any decision made would be taken on a majority vote and on impulse. They would consider the consequences later. Firstly he pointed out the obvious to them and that was that the damage meant that they could not fly. He said that although he thought that they could repair the damage there was no way they could catch their planet and they would be lost in space and eventually they would perish. He, however, was not ready to die, they were here on a planet that was perfect for their needs, and they could start a new more simple life here. In essence, there was only one vote on the table. Live or die. One by one he asked the question of them all. J.D. re-entered the cockpit and immediately said that he wanted to vote live. Hatch, Homer, Wheatley and Watkins also opted to live. When the question was asked of Mary she said that for her it was irrelevant, she was dead already. The captain had already made up his mind to live, so the vote was in. The captain now had to react quickly, because he and the rest were aware of the intentions of the home world to destroy the ship with all occupants. Knowing this he reminded everyone of their plans, and then he began to put into action measures to counteract the inevitable.

"Hatch, Watkins I need you to find a way to disarm the core explosive. We cannot let them activate it. Get on it now! Travis, download anything you can find from home, whatever you can find. Fill our databases with as much as you can get. I don't care what it is just get it. J.D., encrypt all signals that we are sending and receiving. Hide them somehow I don't care how just buy us enough time to save our asses. Come on people lets go!" He turned his attention to Mary. It was obvious that she had taken this situation harder than anyone else. He knelt before here and took her hands. His voice was full of compassion as he spoke. "Mary, we are all going to lose our loved ones, so we all know how you feel and believe me if there was another option, I would take it. None of us want to stay here for ever but, if this is what it is then I would rather be here than dead. At least our families will know that we are safe. So Mary, I need you now. We all have to do this to survive." He paused for a while to give her time to think. "Mary, can I count on you?" she considered it for an instant and came to the conclusion that this was a shared plight and her friends and colleagues needed her, so she said, through her tears, that he could count on her and asked what it was he wanted her to do. He asked her to work with J.D. on hiding the signals from the ship. She stopped crying and joined J.D. who put his arm on her shoulder, squeezed it in a supportive way then turned his attention back to his console. They all knew that from this point onwards they only had each other to rely upon and suddenly it had become a life or death struggle. Now that the hastily hatched plan had been put into motion Daniels ordered the communication with mission control to be re-established. "Alpha 1472 to command are you receiving us over." They waited for the reply. When it came, the attitude of the voice sounded different. "Err…please hold Alpha, control of this mission is being transferred to Alpha Prime." While they were waiting for the connection to be made Marius motioned to the captain. He motioned back that he should cut communication. When he had, Marius said that they had secured the codes for auto destruct and had changed them so mission control could no longer activate the device. They reconnected the communication just as Alpha Prime was coming online. They now had the upper hand in all ensuing conversations and felt more secure in their own future. But they were not going to tip their hand. The captain had decided to keep secret the fact that they had control of the detonation codes.

Alpha 1472

"Alpha this is Prime are you reading me, over." They acknowledged the call and he continued. "Jason this is Lyle here. I've got Tom and Peter with me. I want you to put this conversation on the speakers. This concerns all of you. OK, well we have had our people look at the footage from outside and I have to tell you that it doesn't look good. We estimate that for you to effect repairs on the ship will take two to three weeks. So in this instance this is not an option. We have a change of brief for you." Everyone was expecting them to drop the bombshell at this point. "Our historians have begun to revue the data that you sent to us and it has become apparent that our history and that of Epsilon Omega share many similarities thanks mainly to the original members of 106. We feel that their research and documentation of their mission will prove to be invaluable to us here at home. Now listen up everyone. Before you embarked on this mission there was a command placed in your captains higher orders that was only to be activated in the event of highly unusual circumstances. We never expected to have to use this option; it was a last resort instruction. But here we are. We have arrived at that point that no one ever expected or could have foreseen. The order was to initiate a self destruct sequence on board the ship to prevent contamination of the indigenous population. But, the events over the course of this mission, leads us to believe that our descendants could benefit from your presence there just as we will from the presence of 106. And so, it has been decided to rescind this order. What we are proposing is that you continue with your mission and with the mission of 106" Although they were already secure in the knowledge that they could not commit the ship to self destruct, it was comforting to know that their fellow men had compassion for their plight and would assist them until it became impossible for them to do so any longer. With this they relaxed their inwardly hostile feelings for their superiors. "Major Hooton, Peter wants to talk to you for a while now." "Hello everyone, we are shocked that this mission has come to this. It's no good beating about the bush at a time like this; we haven't got the luxury of time, so I will cut to the chase. Now that we are sure that there is no likelihood of getting you out of there, we are arranging for all of your family to come to the centre here. We will arrange private time for you to say your goodbyes, and give you as much time together as is possible. When they arrive we will let you know." Harrison came back on line. "So here is your new mission brief. From this point onward you will be our representatives on Epsilon Omega your orders are simple. Observe and record everything you can for posterity if you carry out your orders half as good as 106 did then when we return there should be a lot of data for us to collect. For now, try to come to terms with your position. Travis we imagine that for the foreseeable future you will have your work cut out, so to help you we are downloading the entire psychology department library files. For now this is Alpha Prime signing off"

At this the communication went dead. They all looked at each other. No one spoke, they simply left their posts and tried to find a private place to contemplate their fate. Jason sat at the controls of the stricken ship and starred out into the deep blue of the ocean that held them captive. Under normal circumstances he would have enjoyed the peace and tranquillity. But he felt nothing, no emotions, no thoughts…nothing. He just starred blankly at the sea. The computers were busy accepting as much information from God as quickly as they could. Hatch just watched as the lights flashed before his eyes. He couldn't help but wish that he was a computer at the moment, simply doing what they did without feelings. He had always thought that all he needed was his intellect, but for the first time in his life he truly felt alone. It was an alien emotion for him and he did not know how he was going to come to terms with this new situation he found himself in. The ship was inharmoniously silent everyone was on their own reflecting.

The silence came to an abrupt end as Mary cried out in pain. They were all shocked to their senses and given the present circumstances, and Mary's demeanour all of them expected the worst. They ran to her assistance. Anne was the first to get to her and she found her doubled up crouching on the floor grasping her stomach. The accident earlier had caused more damage than they had thought. She and Watkins gently lifted her onto her bunk as she called out in pain. J.D. went to fetch Anne's med kit as she began a preliminary examination. The pain Mary was feeling was intense enough to bring a fresh flood of tears to her eyes. John returned and Anne administered a shot of pain killer into Mary's arm. Within minutes the pain had become more bearable. When she could be comfortabley moved she was escorted to the medical bay. Anne began a thorough examination to determine the cause of the pain. She started by taking her temperature and her blood pressure. Then she hooked her up to equipment to check her circulation and her oxygen levels. Finally she scanned her stomach. When she had all of the information at her disposal she turned to Mary and gave her the prognosis. The accident had caused minor bruising to her hip and arm. The pain she was feeling in her stomach was due to nothing more than an intense cramp, probably brought on by the stress of the situation. She then told her that her baby was fine. This started Mary crying again, Anne place her arm tenderly around her shoulder and sat on the bed next to her.

"David will never see his child. We had such plans. Everything would have been perfect, but now, it's all gone. All ruined." She broke down and wept. Anne held her tightly and asked "Do you know what you are having?" Mary said that she and David had decided that it should be a surprise, they didn't want to know. But now all of that had changed she would like David to know before it was too late. Anne flipped on the screen to the scanning device she had used during her examination and replayed the results. As they watched, Anne paused the playback, and pointed to the screen. Mary starred in disbelief. There it was her unborn baby. It was a boy.

Jason called his crew to the cockpit for one final meeting. He had made an important decision that affected all of them. When they were assembled he started to address them.

"What I am about to say, I would like to say without interruption so if you could wait until I have finished to ask any questions I would be grateful. This has been an eventful mission, with an unexpected end. But we now have an even bigger mission to accomplish. We are going to need each other for much longer than any of us thought. What the future will bring is unknown, but I would like to think that whatever it throws at us we would be there for each other. Whatever our lives were in the past is now irrelevant. I know that I will miss my wife and my sons but I have a choice and I would not like them to think that I had given up. I intend to go on and make the most of the situation. I would like to think that all of you feel the same and assuming that you do, I want you to know that we need each other now. Travis, all of us are going to need guidance to come to terms with what has happened, we will all be looking to you for that, and when you need help, because there will be times when you will need someone, we will all be there for you. Marius you are the most logical thinking person I have ever met, your intelligence and problem solving skills are going to be invaluable to us all. Matthew, your knowledge of weather systems will help us to understand our environment and assist with growing food to feed us all. JD, your understanding of the soil and the terrain is going to help us to survive in this alien environment. Anne we need you to service our medical needs. And Mary, you already possess one of the most important elements of our survival here. You and your baby are the hope for our future. So, you see we all have a role to play, we are all as important as each other and we need each other to survive. From this point on there will be no order of command. For us there will be no rank no superiority, we should start as we mean to go on, as equals. Therefore I am no longer your captain; I am nothing more than your friend. From now onwards please call me Jason for that is who I am"

The stark truth of their situation had just hit them, and individually they realised that from now on the people in this room were all that they could rely on for their safety, their sanity and their future.

Anne was the first. She stood up and approached Jason and placed her arms around him. J.D. followed suit, then Mary. One by one they all joined in the embrace and for a few minutes there, they all stood, huddled into one group. Each of them with their eyes closed soaking in the support of the others. For the first time since they had been stranded they had found solace in each other, and they were glad of the unity they all shared.

19. The Roundup.

Harrison was more abrupt than normal. He was on a personal mission to get all of the relatives of 1472 to the command centre as soon as possible. He knew that this would be the last chance for them to say goodbye. He had dispatched units to the homes of relatives and he had spared none of the resources at his disposal. Those that were close, he had sent fast response units to with top level clearance and military escorts to get them through any traffic with minimum fuss. The ones who were further afield would be transported using helicopters and fast response personnel. Luckily none of the relatives were abroad, all were easily within transportable distances, but time was of the essence.

David sat at his desk and looked out of the window, this was going to be the last day he would sit here for a while. He had taken a vacation from work to spend with his wife when she returned. He was oblivious to the situation that was unfolding on Epsilon Omega. He had planned a romantic vacation for her, some quality time before the birth of their first baby. His mind was not on his work, he was preoccupied with the arrangements for the trip. He had already packed suitcases and left them in the hallway of the house. He knew that if she got comfortable at home then their trip would be delayed. He looked at the photograph of her that he had on his desk and smiled. The intercom on his desk spoke, it was his secretary. "Sir, there are some gentlemen here to see you." Before she had finished the sentence they burst through his door. He demanded to know the meaning of this intrusion. They confirmed that he was David Emmanuel and escorted him to the waiting car. This was like something off the television. He demanded to know what was happening. All that they would tell him is that they were from the space centre and it was to do with his wife. He was suitably panic stricken, and he complied with their instructions without hesitation. The journey was high speed, it was faster than he had ever travelled before, apart from flying, and he found it quite nauseating. Before long the speeding car pulled into a small supermarket car park that had been cleared of all cars. Standing in the middle was a helicopter; its rotors were running at full speed ready for take off. He was rushed into his seat and almost before they had fastened his safety belt they were in the air and on their way to the space centre. All around the city, approaching from different directions, by road and by air, they came. Sirens were blaring and lights flashing. Eventually they converged onto a field within the centre from where they were all rushed to a conference room where they waited for Harrison. He estimated that he was standing in a room of about a hundred or so people. Most of them looked confused some were upset. The reality was that there was only about twenty relatives present the rest were company personnel trained in various skills associated with trauma and shock. When they were all assembled Lyle Harrison entered the room. They all braced themselves for what he had to say.

"Ladies and gentlemen, my name is Over Commander Lyle Harrison and I am in command of mission Alpha 1472. We are undergoing an unprecedented situation on the planet where your families are. During the take off procedure their space ship was damaged. They are all safe, but," He braced himself before he continued with his next sentence. "There is no possibility of their return"

At this, the entire room exploded with the sound of terror, panic, despair and people shouting questions, demanding answers. In an instant, David's world collapsed. He fell to his knees unable to grasp the fact that he would never see her again. Although everything around him was a scene of panic and turmoil, his world had stopped. He could hear nothing, he was aware, but he had gone into a complete state of shock. He found himself being escorted, half carried, by two men towards a private room where they sat him down with a councillor who tried to prepare him to speak with his wife. He heard every word that she said but none of it made any sense. The only thing he could think about was her, his wife and the more he thought about her the further he slipped into himself. The councillor could see that she was making no headway and called for a medic to administer him with a sedative. Gradually, as the drug took effect, he became more lucid, more able to talk to her. She explained the situation fully and told him that very soon he could talk to his wife. The gravity of the situation began to dawn on him. Then, slowly at first he began to weep. Not for himself and not for her but for them both. Soon he was openly crying. He cried for about an hour, non stop. His face was puffed and his eyes were red. He could not let her see him like this; he had to be strong for her. He asked his councillor if there was somewhere he could use to tidy himself for the meeting. She said that there was and took him to a shower room where she left him to clean up. Outside the door she posted a guard…just in case. He took about half an hour in the shower room. All the time he tried to prepare himself. What would he say? How will he react when he sees her? No matter how many times he asked himself the questions, the answers evaded him. All that he knew was that right now she needed him, and he was not going to let her down. He left the shower room and was met by the guard, who escorted him back to the room where his councillor was waiting for him. She was a pleasant young lady who seemed full of compassion for him. He knew that she had been trained for this type of event and that she was just doing her job, but, it was comforting to have her there, someone to talk to in this dark hour. He was somewhat calmer now the initial shock had subsided, and they were able to strike up a superfluous conversation. "Are you married" he asked her she said that she was and he nodded. It was a strained conversation but he needed to talk. "How long?" he asked. Three years she replied. They talked along the same lines until it was time for him to go to the communications room where he would see his wife's face for the last time. As they walked along the corridor it felt like he was the condemned man taking his last walk to the execution chamber. Maybe that would have been easier. They paused at the door and he gathered himself, mustering all of his composure…he hoped that it would be enough. He turned to his councillor who held him by his arms; she leaned towards him and kissed him gently on the cheek. "I will be here when you have finished" she said to him. He nodded and closed his eyes for a moment not wanting to speak. She knew that this was more than a thank you. She let her arms drop and he went through the door. He sat down in the darkness opposite a TV screen and waited for her face to appear. It was an anxious time, and although he didn't want to be there. There was no other place in the world he wanted to be more. Not knowing what he was going to say, he waited for the connection to be made. The few moments that he had waited had seemed an eternity. And then…her face appeared.

20. Fond farewells.

The only difference between Alpha 106 and themselves was that, 106 never intended to make the return journey. Whereas they, had been forced, by circumstance, into staying. The crew of 106 had no family to bid farewell to, but if they did at least they would have had the chance to hold their loved ones one last time. This situation had precluded them from this tender luxury. Everyone was finding this particular aspect difficult to come to terms with. Now that everyone was equals Travis took the initiative to try to help his fellow travellers. He asked them all to join him in the cockpit.
"Right, I have sent the signals to Alpha Prime for the location of our individual terminals. I hope you don't mind but I have tried to give all of us privacy for these calls so here is where I have put you all. Captain, sorry…Jason, you and Marius will be in your own quarters Anne you will be in your quarters and Mary you will be in here. J.D. you will be in your room I will go the departure area and Matthew; I have put you in the multipurpose section. I have made sure that we are all comfortable and private during this time. Now, this is going to be probably one of the emotional moments of our lives and although, strictly speaking, I am no longer your psychologist, I would like to think that when this is all over you would

think that you can turn to me if you need to. I will be there for you." His voice became calm and steady as he continued. "We know from experience that situations like this have a profoundly strange effect on our bodies. During your time with your loved ones you will experience a multitude of emotions. Sorrow, longing, fear, distress, unhappiness, misery and grief. But there will also be times when you will experience the opposite, love, happy memories you have together that you will share with each other. All of these emotions are important. But if you concentrate on the positive emotions together they will help you to cope much easier. After you have finished, you will all be drained. And this is when all of your pent up feelings will rise to the surface. Anger, pain, sorrow. You will want to vent all of this aggression out on anything or anyone who upsets you. And this is when we need to be strong for each other. We will all need to help each other to grieve and to move on."

Jason stood up from his seat and went over to Travis. He hugged him and thanked him for his advice and compassion before retiring to his room to wait for his family. One by one they all did the same then found their respective places within the ship to wait.

Mary had been left in the cockpit and she was alone with her thoughts. She felt strangely calm and serene. She knew that this would pass as soon as the connection was made. She took the time to compose herself. Trying to keep all of her emotions in check, she was determined that she was going to be strong and not break down. The wait was agonisingly long. The anticipation of seeing her husband was almost too much to bear. And then…his face appeared.

For both of them the initial sight of each other bought about an intense rush of emotions. Together their hands instinctively reached out for each other and they touched each others faces on the screens. A tear emerged from the corner of Mary's eye, it quickly rolled down over her cheek and came to rest at the corner of her mouth, he could see it glistening, illuminated by the light of the monitor. She felt her top lip tighten and her bottom one quiver slightly as she tried desperately not to cry. His lips were tightly clenched as he tried to smile at her beautiful face, summoning all that he could find to retain his composure. Neither of them spoke. For now they were just content to be in each others company. Mary was the first to break the silence. Her head tilted slightly to one side and she took a deep breath in through her nose, it was not a smooth continuous intake, it was laboured and it happened in stages. She let out her breath and as she did so she spoke his name in a whisper. "David." She closed her eyes and slowly shook her head. She took a deep breath and looked at him. "Oh David…what are we going to do." She could feel the heaviness in her eyes, as she waited for him to speak. He just sat there starring into her face. He started to shake his head, almost imperceptibly at first and then more pronounced. And then his face seemed to collapse as he began to weep. He held his forehead in his hand and his shoulders jerked up and down in perfect rhythm with his sobs. She just sat and watched him with pity and compassion. Her only instinct at that moment was to take him in her arms and comfort him. But this was not to be. He was trying desperately to fight every instinct he had to cry. He needed to compose himself…for her. Eventually he managed to bring his emotions into check and reached for a tissue to dry his tears. Having regained a modicum of stability he spoke to her for the first time. "Mary…Oh Mary, why us? Why not someone else? We were supposed to be together forever." As he spoke he could hear himself speaking and crying at the same time. Mary reached for the screen and placed her index finger over the image of his lips and shushed him "I know" she said "I know, but we are here now, together, lets not waste a second." He said nothing, just nodded in agreement. "That first day you walked into the centre I knew that we would be together. Do you remember you asked me my name and I asked who wanted to know? Then you said that if I played my cards right you may be the man who was taking me out that night. You were so sure of yourself back then." He smiled and nodded. "I knew too, when you insisted on a really pricy restaurant." For a brief while all of the pain and hurt was forgotten and they sat intently starring into each others eyes and reminiscing about their past. Recalling all of the times they had spent together, the places they had seen and people they had known. There had even been times when they laughed together and at times it felt like the most natural conversation they had ever had. The weightiness of the situation had, for a while, been lost to them. They were totally engaged in being together for this one last time. There were no awkward pauses, when there was nothing to say they just studied the image in front of them, lovingly examining every contour of the others appearance. Occasionally she would stroke his hair on the screen or he would run his fingers down the side of her face. They continued in this manner until they had discussed their lives together up until now. Then David asked about the accident. The instant the question was asked, the mood changed. It went from one of loving attention to one of a defensive, unwillingness to discuss the very thing that would keep them apart. She found it hard to explain the accident to him. It was like reliving recent history. It was surreal and unbelievable, cruel and unjustified. It was a freak accident that no one could have predicted or avoided. He asked her who was to blame; He felt that he needed to use someone or something to vent his inner anger towards. She assured him that no one was to blame; it was just one of those things that could not have been prevented. He could tell from her reaction and the look in her eyes that it was what it was, an accident, pure and simple. She then described the accident she suffered when the impact occurred, and the fact that the medic had to give her an examination. Then she spoke about their baby. When she did she could immediately see the hurt in his face. "David, I am so sorry." From the unfortunate way in which the sentence was constructed he had instantly jumped to the conclusion that she had lost the baby. Thankfully he had misconstrued what was being said to him and she was quick to rectify the mistake. "No...no don't panic there is nothing wrong everything is still fine. There is one thing that I have to tell you though. When I was being examined, I had to find out the sex. Under the circumstances I think you should know." He did not know how to feel. Of course he was relieved that they were both OK, but, he felt cheated and despondent that he would never see his child grow. He would never know the joy of holding his own baby. In the blink of an eye he had already imagined what it would have been like to be a dad. And in the same blink reality had cruelly snatched it from him. His emotions took over once more and he could feel himself starting to cry once again. He looked at her, hardly able to control his facial quiverings, trying desperately to hold it all together. She looked back at him fully understanding the turmoil he was going through. She spoke quietly and lovingly "I am going to send you a copy of the scan that was taken earlier so you can see for yourself" Reaching over to the console she located the image and sent it to his computer. A separate smaller screen appeared on his monitor displaying the image for him to see. He leaned forward and touched the screen tenderly. Then he broke down into a deep sob. His whole body began to spasm as he fell into a state of complete distress. "Jeremy...oh...Jeremy my boy." She left him for a while with his grief then she tried to pull him back to reality. "David...David, listen to me. David, I need to ask you something." Having regained his attention she put her proposal to him. "I know we have discussed a name for our baby, and we agreed that if it were a boy we would call him Jeremy. But we also said that if it was a girl we would call her Susan. Do you remember?" David agreed that he did, but he didn't understand her point. "Well, I've been thinking that I would like to name him for both of us." Through his tears she could see that he was a little confused. They had agreed upon his name and felt a little wounded that she wanted to change the only legacy he could give his son. "What do you think about this for a name? If we take both names and amalgamate them into one then we can both be remembered through him." She had his full attention, and he asked what she was suggesting. "I would like to call him…Jesus David Emmanuel." As soon as she had said the name there was silence while he considered the proposal. He could see the logic of what she was saying, and indeed he liked the name. He looked at her and smiled that smile. It was the smile that she was so familiar with when she had won. Although this was not an argument or a competition, for her it was so comforting to see it on his face once more. "Jesus David Emmanuel, I love it." Their faces had hid nothing, every emotion they had felt, had been displayed over the last four hours. Now, they both shared the same emotion. It was the realisation of the reality that was now theirs, a reality which they could not escape. They would both have given anything not to have been in this position. But here they were and they were both aware that very soon they would be saying goodbye to each other for the last time. They were calm and content in each others company when the door behind David quietly opened. The head of his councillor peered around the edge of the door and in a quiet almost apologetic tone she said that their time was nearly at an end. David thanked her and she left silently closing the door behind her. "Oh well," he said to Mary, "it seems that our time is up." As he said it he wished that this moment would last forever. He knew in his heart that she felt the same. She touched the screen as if to caress his face "David, I have always loved you and until the day I die I will always love you. I promise that I will take care of our baby, and I promise that he will know who you are and never forget you. Be safe my darling and think of me often and all that we could have shared." He swallowed hard, he too touched the screen, "Mary you have always been my world. You know, I thought that our lives would have lasted forever. I never thought that fate would do this to us. Mary I love you with all of my heart, I always have, and I always will. I know we will be together again someday. Maybe not in this life, but somehow we will be together." The door opened again to signify that it was time. He looked at his wife, touched the screen as if to dry her tears. He could not have known, but at the same time she was doing the same. They lovingly looked at each other and together almost under their breath the said to each other "Goodbye my darling...I love you." Their screens slowly faded to black. They both lowered their heads and wept.

All around the ship similar family meetings had been taking place. Mary and David's conversation was not exclusive. This crew now shared the common bonds of emotional pain and anguish. They all understood what each other was feeling at this moment in time. All of them were drained and although they wanted to be alone with their grief, the absurdity was, that they also needed the comfort of their fellow suffers. When they were sure that Mary had finished speaking to her husband, they all congregated in the cockpit. No one spoke, they sat together deep within their own thoughts, but they were together, and in this surreal moment the support that they feeling from each other was indescribably calming. Travis had been the first to end his call and had realised that they all needed something to give them closure in this dark hour. He knew that their planet would be out of range within the next few hours and that they would be stranded here to start their new lives. He had decided to use the time he had before everyone else had finished to prepare for what he hoped would help everyone. He opened the cargo pod and into it he loaded a large monitor and some other equipment that he needed. He then accessed the main computer from the departure bay and set up some minor adjustments to enable him to achieve his plan. When he was prepared he contacted Alpha Prime and briefed them on what he wanted to do. They, in turn, agreed without hesitation and assisted him in achieving what he had set out to do. By the time he had prepared everything they had all completed their conferences and were sitting together. He was the last to enter and took a seat with the rest. Recognising the fact that they needed this time he said nothing, just sat with the rest. By keeping himself busy he had had more time to deal with his emotions and, for now, was quite calm and in control of himself. He knew that at some time in the future he would need the support of the others. But for now, he believed that they needed him more. As they sat Travis kept an eye on the clock that he could see above the control panels near the front window of the ship. He knew how long it took to get to shore and was trying to time his plan with the position of their planet. He wanted to help them but didn't want to prolong the situation and aggravate an already volatile situation. When he thought that the time was right he spoke. As he spoke his words cut into the silence and everyone looked at him with sadness in their eyes. There was no anger, no discord just silent suffering.

"I have been talking to Prime and between us we have something to show you." They all looked confused. Jason was most bewildered. He wondered why Travis should be talking to Prime without permission. Then he realised that they were all equal and he now had as much right as anyone. Travis continued. "We all need to go ashore. I have prepared all of the pods, so if you follow me" as he finished he started for the departure bay. They all looked at each other and shrugged in confusion. They all realised that they had to do something to break the cycle of depression, so, without protestation they followed him to the pods.

Within half an hour they were all standing on the beach in the warm evening air. It was good to be standing there away from the ship. They were still confused but they went along with what Travis had planned. He activated the proximity alarm on his wrist controller and when he was sure that they were alone he set to work. He raised the cargo pod out of the water and began to unpack its contents. Firstly he set a stand on the sand onto which he placed the large monitor. He then connected the monitor wirelessly to the ships computer. They all stood in front of the screen and shortly the image of their collective families stood before them. This was one last chance to say goodbye. Lyle Harrison addressed them. His voice was not that of a military man, it was softer less authoritative he looked at his crew and said. "Very soon we will be out of range and this will be the last time that we will meet. I want you to know that if there could have been any other conclusion to this we would have sacrificed anything to get you back. We have taken recordings of your conversations with your families and have downloaded them to your personal files so that you will have them forever. We are all so proud of you and I know that you will be sadly missed. I know that for you it is little consolation. But you will go down in our history and be spoken of for many generations to come." He then handed the screen over to the individual families. Each family in turn said their last goodbyes to their loved ones. The last to speak was David. He looked at Mary and with tears rolling down his face he said "I love you Mary. Be safe and raise Jesus well…I love you, goodbye" She looked at him longingly and said "My sweet, precious David I will always love you, and I promise to take care of our baby…I love you, goodbye". When they had all had their last chance to say their farewells, Lyle Harrison spoke again. "Goodbye Alpha 1472. Live long and prosperous lives. God blesses you and hopes that one day we shall all meet again. Remember you are, and always will be people of God, but now you need to be there for each other. Farewell friends…Farewell" Mothers, fathers, sons and daughters, husbands and wives all waved to each other and blew kisses and as they made their final farewells, the reception started to fade and within minutes the only thing that could be seen on the screen was static. They all looked to the skies as they gathered together in one huddle and stared into space. God was gone, and they were alone.

They stood watching the skies for about an hour before they decided to return to the ship. Having repacked the cargo pod they all stood on their own pods and made their way back. On their return they secured all of the equipment and one by one they embraced Travis and thanked him for his gift to them. Anne Homer reached into her med kit and took out her hypo spray. She said that it was time for them to take the antidote to the sleep inhibitor that had kept them awake for so long. She suggested that they all retired to their quarters where she would visit them. They knew it was time and that they needed the rest. Without any argument they all retired and one by one Anne injected them.

The last person she visited was Jason. She stood over him and before she gave him his shot she said "Captain." He looked at her and said that his name was Jason. She screwed her face a little and started to speak again. "Captain, we are going to be alright aren't we?" He looked at her, then reached out and took her hand and said "I don't know what the future holds for us, but, I am sure of one thing. We all need each other now and if we help each other get through this then...yes we will be alright." She sighed and nodded. His words had comforted her. She gave him his injection and said "Goodnight Jason, sleep well." As she went to her room she took one last look around her and she wondered what the future held for them all. She closed the door climbed into bed and injected herself. Before long they were all asleep and the ship was silent.

21. The power of the press.

The journey home was more sedate than his arrival. There was no urgency, no sirens and no flashing lights. In the car with him were two men from the agency and his councillor. No one spoke during the journey, but the atmosphere was not strained, it was calm and reflective. As they pulled into his drive he could see that both his car and Mary's had been brought back in his absence. One of the men stepped out of the car and opened the door for him. As he was getting out his councillor handed him her business card and said that if he needed her day or night for whatever reason, he should call. He looked at the card and read her name 'Angela Bernstein'. As he did so he suddenly realised that up until this point he had no idea what her name was. He apologised to her saying that he was normally not so insensitive and that it had been a long day. She waived this remark and reassured him that if he needed her she would be there for him. David thanked everyone and started up the drive toward his front door. He stood on the doorstep until they had driven away then he reached into his coat pocket to search for his keys. As he offered the key to the lock he found that his hand was trembling. He tried, unsuccessfully, several times to open the door and each time, the key scraped past the keyhole. In aggravation he threw the keys on the floor and collapsed onto the doorstep. He sat with his back to the door and in his frustration he banged his head violently against the hard wood. After a while he reached for his keys, stood up and tried again. This time he was successful. The door swung open and he stood there for a while just looking inside, unsure whether to enter or not. Eventually he decided that he had no where else to go, so he went in and closed the door behind him. The house felt empty, it used to be their home and was full of life and love, but now it was nothing more than a shell. He slipped off his coat and let it fall to the floor, where he abandoned it. As he walked across the room he could see reminders of her everywhere. Everything she was, was here in this room, in this house, and it was all that he had left of her. He went to the drinks cabinet and took a bottle of spirits, it didn't matter what it was, it could have been anything, just so long as it had the effect of numbing his feelings, he didn't care. He held the glass in front of him and poured himself a drink which he downed in one. He thought for a second and then filled the glass. Before long the bottle was nearly empty and he was very drunk. He tried to stand up and stumbled over landing on all fours. The glass rolled away from him spilling the remnants of his drink. He looked at it and decided to leave it where it lay. Then he made his way to bed. Getting there was not the easiest of journeys and he found himself crawling up the stairs. When he finally managed to get himself onto the bed he lay there in the dark. He could smell her scent on the pillow next to him and he wished she was there to hold him. The room span around him and normally he would be violently sick. But on this occasion he just lay there motionless. Before long he was asleep.

He was awoken the next morning by raised voices outside his front door. He lay there for a while listening, then he decided that he should see what was going on. He raised his head off the pillow and experienced the pain of a major hangover. He gathered himself against the pain and went downstairs. He was still fully dressed in the same clothes that he had worn since early the previous day. He could smell himself, but he didn't care. He went to investigate the disturbance, on his way he kicked his jacket out of the way and opened the front door. He was met by the two men who had driven him home the previous night, who were holding his friends at bay. It was Alan and Amanda. They asked him if he knew these people. He said that he did. They apologised to them and let them pass. He wondered why the men were here and asked them. They explained that since the previous night the news of Alpha 1472 had broken on the news networks and that they had been assigned to look after his security. They added that all of the other relative's houses were being stormed by news teams and that they were expecting the same for him very soon. As they spoke the first outside broadcast vehicle could be seen approaching drawing up the road. They suggested that he went back inside and close the door; they would take care of the news teams. He did as he was advised and left them outside. As soon as the door was closed Amanda flung her arms around him tightly. He didn't want the attention at the moment, but they were his friends and he was glad of their company. Alan also hugged him for a while and then went to the kitchen to make some strong black coffee. Up until this point no one had spoken. They were all aware of the situation and what had happened, and although they were there for him the awkwardness of the situation meant that they did not know how to start a conversation. Alan had made coffee and they sat around the breakfast bar sipping their hot drinks. David broke the silence. He looked down into his coffee cup and said, "I've lost her. She's gone and I don't know what I'm going to do." As soon as he had said it the horrors of the previous day came flooding back to him and he began to cry. This was the catalyst they needed. As soon as he had broken down they felt freer to comfort him. Amanda put her arm around him and shared his grief. After they had both cried for a while David composed himself and said that it would be easier if she had died, at least he could grieve properly but as it was he knew that she was out there somewhere feeling the same way that he did and he could do nothing to help her, and that was what made it all the more unbearable. He spoke about ending it all and taking his own life but Alan and Amanda said that that they knew that Mary wouldn't want that. It was a morning of highs and lows and they talked steadily for hours. Eventually Alan managed to talk him into taking a shower. He knew that he would feel better but he couldn't be bothered he was just not in the mood to do anything. By the same token he needed a break from his friends and so he agreed.

He stood in the shower and let the warm water cascade over his tired body. As he showered his thoughts turned back to Mary and he cried once more, the water from the shower mingled with his tears and washed them away. He had been there for about ten minutes when he suddenly decided that this had to end and so he steeled himself against his grief and made the conscious decision to pull himself together. He quickly finished his shower, went to the sink and shaved his face, cleaned his teeth and went to get dressed. Laid neatly on the chair next to the wardrobe, was a pile of Mary's clothes. He had seen them but had decided that if he ignored their existence, for now, they would not affect him. This ploy worked and he went downstairs to join his friends, clean and fresh. They were on their third cup of coffee when the front door bell rang. Instinctively he went to answer it. As he opened the door he was met with a myriad of flashing cameras, people thrusting microphones at his face, and a million shouted questions. It took him by surprise and he was visibly shocked. The guards held the tide of reporters at bay while the councillor entered the house, ushered him back indoors and closed the door behind them. "Where the hell did they come from and what are they doing at my house?" he demanded. She greeted him and said that they were all looking for a story it was the same at all of the houses of the relatives, and that the agency was trying to find a solution to the invasion. He introduced her to Alan and Amanda and offered her a coffee. For a while they talked about how he felt today and how he saw his future. Then she turned her attention back to the hoards of reporters. It was suggested that he was re-housed in one of the agencies safe houses until the furore had settled and he was more able to cope with the inevitable attention that would come his way. David refused to be hounded out of his house and was adamant that he would stay where he was. No one thought that this was a good idea but, Alan suggested that he should go and stay with them for as long as it took. The press weren't looking to speak to them, and as far as they knew they had no idea where they lived. On the face of it, it seemed to be an ideal short term solution. Angela said that she would arrange for him to leave the house incognito the next day. For now he would have to sit tight and let security worry about the press. She would return when she had arranged everything. Her top priority was to find a lookalike to stand in for him here so that they could fool the press long enough for them to make their escape. She bid him farewell and left the house through the barrage of reporters to begin her subterfuge.

He had sat and talked all day with Alan and Amanda and he really did appreciate their company. But now he was feeling claustrophobic and needed to get some fresh air. He wanted to be out in the cool evening, but how? They were watching him like a hawk and the press that were encamped on his front lawn would be on him like vultures if he dared to venture outside. He wandered around the house looking for an escape. He noticed through one of the windows a light shining from his neighbour's house. Suddenly he had an idea. He went into the lounge and picked up one of the cordless telephones and went into the conservatory. He quickly checked to see if he had been seen and if anyone was watching him now. When he was satisfied that he had not been discovered he called to his neighbour. He spoke in a whisper. "Peter" he said. Peter was having difficulty hearing him and asked who was calling. "Peter, its David Emmanuel." The instant he had realised who was calling he became genuinely apologetic. "Oh David I am so sorry to hear about your problems," David listened to him for a while and then fearing he would be discovered he asked him for a favour. What he wanted was to borrow his car for a while so that he could escape the attention and have a little time to himself. Without hesitation he agreed to help his friend and asked how he was going to get it to him. David said that he should leave that to him and that he was to wait by his car with the keys, he would be there soon. He put the phone down and took it back to the lounge. To cover his escape, he went back into the kitchen and sat for a while with his friends. He told them that he was feeling a little weary and thought that he may go to bed soon. He said that they were welcome to stay and use their usual room but felt that he needed a little rest. They agreed that he could do with some sleep but thought that it was a little early for them to retire and if it was alright with him they would watch the television for a while. He said that that would be OK, bade them goodnight and went upstairs. He could hear the TV from his room, he waited a while and when he was sure that they were settled he began to creep back down the stairs. As he reached the bottom he could see both of their backs as they sat watching the news reports of 1472. He silently crept past them, into the kitchen and quietly opened the door that led to the utility room. Bracing the door against his hand he held down the handle and closed the door. He held it shut for a second and then slowly released the handle without a sound. He sidled up to the window and carefully peered outside to see if there were any reporters around. At least security had done its job. There were none. He opened a cupboard and took out a small rucksack that he had prepared. He then left using the door, trying desperately not to make a noise. He was outside but not in the clear. The back of the house was lush with large shrubs and bushes which provided excellent cover for him to reach the fence that ran along the back of the property. He took one last look around, reached his hands onto the top of the fence, hauled himself over and disappeared into the night bound for his neighbour's house. When he arrived Peter was standing by his car, he handed David the keys. David thanked him profusely and climbed into the driver's seat. He wound the window down and as he drove away he said that he would not forget this and thanked him once again. Cautiously he drove out of the drive and from his position he could see the hoards of reporters waiting to snatch an interview with him...but not this night. He turned the car in the opposite direction and drove away.

22. The final goodbye.

They had slept soundly for almost a whole rotation when they began to wake up. It was strange waking up naturally and not all at the same time. One by one they would wander into the cockpit area of the ship and greet everyone. The last to arrive was J.D. he looked dishevelled and completely drained but he insisted that he felt better for the sleep. This was the first day of the rest of their lives, and they had to have a plan to move forward with. For now it had been agreed that they would use the ship as a base from which to start. They realised that eventually they would have to leave the ship and truly begin to integrate into this society. The computers would play an integral part in their assimilation. The language libraries were almost fully complete and until they could speak the language unaided they would rely upon this quite extensively. The discussion continued and would continue for quite some time while they decided the best way to move forwards. They were, of course, all peers now and to speed the process for everyone to accept that the chain of command had now disappeared. The former captain had relinquished all upper level computer commands. Everyone now had the same access to all parts of the ship and to all levels of the computer command sequences. They were all free to come and go as they pleased, free from command orders. The one thing that they all agreed upon wholeheartedly was that under no circumstances should any technology from their society be allowed to be discovered by anyone on this planet. If anything should be discovered it could jeopardise their position here. The general consensus was that if any tech was to be taken ashore it should be with the consent of at least three of their number. They knew that to formulate a working model for their integration and survival would take several meetings over the next few days. So, they decided that at this time every day they would meet to discuss further advancements to their plan, and also report on their days activities. This first meeting was quite short. They needed time to interact with each other and become used to their new status on the ship. They also needed time to reflect on their position in this strange, new society. Most of all they needed was to find their own space. They had all decided that it would be necessary for them to create their own sleeping space and to facilitate this some alterations would have to be made. This job fell to Marius. Travis and Jason remained in the cockpit to discuss possibilities. Anne had decided to try to get some more rest and had decided to read in her bunk. J.D. and Matthew began to explore their options for food when their rations had been exhausted. Mary was at a loose end. She asked everyone if she minded if she went ashore for a while, and far from objecting they all said that they could all do what they wanted now. Anne asked if Mary would like some company but she declined saying that if it was OK with her she would like some time to be alone. Everyone said that if she needed them she only had to say and they would be there as soon as they could.

It felt strange leaving the ship by her own decision. But at the same time it also felt quite empowering. The computers had been fully voice automated and she gave her order, "Computer, release pod 1." As she spoke her pod was sealed and the compartment was flooded for her departure. When she saw the green light indicating that this part of the process was complete, she spoke to the computer again. "Computer, open bay 1" The computer complied and she drifted out into the open ocean.

David had been driving for an hour and the further away from his house he drove the calmer he became. He had no idea where he was going, he just drove. Before long he found himself on the outskirts of the neighbouring town. It was late evening and the town seemed quiet. He decided that this would be a good place to stop for a while. He pulled into the car park of a local bar, got out of the car, closed the door and locked it. The bar was small and empty; accept the barman who was polishing glasses. He walked up to the bar and sat on one of the stools and ordered a triple with ice. He remarked to the barman that it was quiet tonight to which he replied. "Company policy." David was confused and asked what he meant. "The bosses in their infinite wisdom have a policy here of no TV screens. It's a place to come for a quiet drink and seeing as everyone wants to see about the space

shit…" David was quite glad about company policy and sat drinking his drink. When he had finished he called the barman over and asked for the same again. He poured his drink and set it down in front of him. "So how come you ain't watching the news." He asked. David looked at him and said that he had had enough of it for one day. The barman nodded and said that he was glad of the company on such a quiet evening. The phone in the bar rang and the barman answered it. From the conversation David guessed that it must have been his boss.
"Quiet, only one guy, OK, thanks, Goodnight"
David caught his attention and said that he gathered that he was getting an early night. He lifted his glass and downed the last of his drink. When he paid for what he had drunk he left the barman with a very large tip. He looked at what he had left and protested that there was no need to leave such a large amount. David looked at him and smiled.
"Listen, I have, for the first time in the last forty eight hours, been able to relax for a while, and you have just done your job and left me alone. You see my wife is one of the people left on that planet and I needed this time to think. So thank you, treat yourself to something nice and enjoy the rest of your night off. See you around." With this he left the bar, got back into the car and continued his aimless journey.

Mary had arrived at the beach and had moored her pod. She didn't know why she had come here but she was grateful for the fresh air. The recycled air of the ship was fine but it was no substitute for the real thing. She was dressed in local costume. It had been decided that this should be the way they dressed from now on. The water felt good on her feet. It was chilly but not unbearably so. She could feel the soft sand give way under her toes as she walked along. The proximity device on her wrist told her that she was alone, and normally she would have felt exposed and vulnerable. Tonight, she felt peaceful and safe. She could not explain to herself why she should feel this way. The night air was warm and comfortable and as she walked along the sea front she could hear the waves lapping into the sand. Up ahead she could see the outcrop which hid the cave they had used to store their equipment and she had decided that this was her destination. She could hear and was aware of everyone's conversations on board the ship. She heard Jason ask if everything was alright with her and remind her that if she needed them to call. She thanked him and then instructed the computer to mute all communications coming from the ship. They could still hear her but now she could hear nothing except the natural rhythm of the sea and the occasional breeze as it brushed against her ear. Before she knew it she had arrived at the outcrop where she stopped and just stood in the shallows. The night sky was spectacular. The deepest shade of blue she had ever seen. The thousands of stars twinkled against the velvet backdrop and she knew that somewhere out there was her David. There was a smooth surface at the front of the rock face that was inclined at an angle. She sat on the edge and lowered herself back until she was lying down gazing up at the sky.

David had driven as far as he wanted to for now and found himself in the car park of a lake. He got out of the car, grabbed his rucksack, locked the car and began to walk to the lakeside. There was a chill to the air but the night was clear and the moonlight created by the network was strong enough to light his way. As he approached he came across a grassy hilled area. Without thinking he stepped onto the grass and sat down. All was quiet. He could hear nothing at all. He opened his back pack and removed an unopened bottle of whiskey. Holding it between his legs he looked at it for a while, then, he opened it, discarded the top and took a long hard swig from the bottle. He lay back on the grass and gazed at the sky. He knew that out there somewhere was his wife. The more he thought about her, the more he drank. After a while he reached into his bag once more and pulled out a revolver. He lay back on the grass, bottle in one hand, the gun resting on his chest.

Mary lay on the rock looking at the sky trying to imagine what David was going through. She hoped that he would be able to cope.

The tears began to run down their faces and as they lay there in the still night air, they both realised how much it hurts to love someone with every fibre of your body. The intense, emotional pain of longing. They lay there for what seemed to be an eternity. Mary caressed her unborn baby and David held his gun more securely. These were the most unbearable emotions they had felt since the accident and neither of them knew how to cope without each other. Mary once again caressed her stomach as David raised the gun to his head and held the barrel against his temple. They looked at the sky and imagined that they were together for one last time, and at the same time they both said "I love you…goodbye" and with this, they finally realised that they were both truly alone. For them, it felt like the end.

Alpha 1472

Acknowledgments

Hollie Bourne
Brian Young
Editing

Made in the USA
Monee, IL
14 June 2022

97897555R10167